THE HUNTRESS OF WOODMYST

The Huntress of Woodmyst

THE WOODMYST CHRONICLES BOOK V

Robert E Kreig

WHITEKEEP BOOKS

For Evie, the huntress

THE FROZEN WASTE

THE CORE LANDS

BLACKROCK HAVEN

WINTERMARSH
IRONFIELDS
ERIMOOR

WHITEKEEP

BLACKSHORE

THE CANYONS OF TERRETH

REDLOCH

MALLOWHILL

STRONGHOLDT

LIGHTHOUSE

THE
SEA
OF
SOLACE

MELAMWED

THE PILLARS OF MOHAA

HAVENCREST

KALISARD

CLEARFOX

OAKBEACH

BROODNESS

NEWHOLT

WINTERSPRING

MEADOWMOOR

WOODMYST

OSTFORD

DELLMOOR

OLDCASTLE

GRASSBEACH

BELBURN

PRYHOLT

LUNKHUL
FOREST

GREYROSE

DWEAGAN

BARROWFIELD

THE SEA OF LUNKHUL

REDEDGE

LINPORT

N

BUTTEREDGE

BYVIEW

W   E

ROSSPORT

FREYMOOR

S

BELMORE

THE WESTERN SEA

THE EASTERN SEA

Prologue

A shadow silently watched from its place high above the dusty gorge. The dark night sky secured its hiding place as it observed and listened to the inhabitants that encircled the many campfires below. Its attention drawn to the largest encirclement of reptilian beings, the place where the eldest sat, imparting knowledge and teachings to the youngest of their kind.

The canvas awnings stretched over the entrances to meagre mud-brick huts, flapped softly in the gentle breeze. They had burrowed many caves into the canyon walls, their openings formed and hewn to resemble places of hospitality, trade and dwelling.

Scrawny dogs kicked dust up around their feet as they snapped and growled, fighting over the scraps discarded by the large reptilian folk gathered by the fires.

"Fish and quedia would go down well right about now," one of the elderly creatures hissed as he dangled the leg of a broiled rabbit between his leathery fingers. He wore a collar of iron claws that hung from his shoulders and over his chest, resting on a black bearskin cloak.

"Why do you torment us?" an adolescent female spat, moving her head to the side with a snarl. "We can only catch rabbit, rat and raven. Perhaps a deer or steed if we have the favour of Q'sharh. What talk is this of fish and giant fowl?"

"I was leading to a tale of old," the elder replied angrily. "Some of our young haven't heard of the lands we came from."

"Tale of old," a young adult male chided, before spitting into the fire. "Why tell such tales of grander days?"

"It is good to remember, Greil," the older one suggested. "It is good to know our history and where we have been."

Greil eyeballed the elder angrily before moving his green eye across the faces of the other old ones sitting closer to the fire, edging nearer and nearer with each passing year. One day, he supposed, they would sit upon the flames if they lasted that long.

"Is it good to teach our children of how miserable our forefathers were?" he asked.

"Miserable?" the elder replied.

"They brought our people out here to die after they sent us running from our homeland."

"We survived," the old one argued. "We found a new way to live and be satisfied."

"Satisfied?" Greil raised his head, disgusted by the word. "Is that why we lost so many of our brothers when the White Witch called us to her side?"

"She was not the answer to any of our concerns," the elder told him. "We should not have got involved."

"No," the younger replied. "We should not have listened to her false promises. We should have united and taken the land back on our own."

The elder got to his feet, his long tail coiling behind him.

"We have no right to that land," he bellowed. "Not any longer. They took it. It is theirs. We belong here, now. For twelve generations, we have been here, and we have survived."

"We were warriors." Greil raised himself upright. He stood taller and broader than the other. "Our brothers knew this."

"And now they are dead," the elder barked.

"Listen to Kayl'sro Marrok, child," another elder remarked, holding up his hands to calm the fire burning in the younger one's chest. "We are content. We have families. We have homes."

"Our food is limited," the young female told them, siding with the younger male. "The cold is coming and our stores are lower this year than ever before. They have fish, and fowl aplenty."

"And you would do what?" the second elder asked. "Ask for some of their hard-earned provisions?"

"No," Greil told them. "I will take it all for our people."

The younger males and females grunted and hissed their approval for such action. Some rose to their feet, nodding and patting Greil on the shoulder in support.

"You fools." Marrok shook his head. "They will kill you just as they killed your brothers."

"Men are weak," the younger male growled. "Their flesh is soft and easy to break. We will take back our land and kill those who stand in our way."

Growls and hisses echoed along the walls of the canyons as more and more rallied behind Greil.

"Then you will need to start with me," Marrok roared, pulling his curved sword from its sheath.

"And me," said another elder, joining his leader.

Within moments, they had drawn lines as two opposing forces faced one another over the flickering light of the fire.

"We have the numbers," Greil told the old ones. His sword glinted in the firelight. "We have our strength."

"I have the Iron Claws of Agrodia." Marrok touched the collar around his neck.

"Not for long," the younger slurred as he stepped over the hearth, swinging his blade high above his head.

Marrok swung his sword upwards, blocking the younger Agrodien's blow with a loud clang. But strength was on Greil's side, knocking the elder off his feet and sending him tumbling to the dust.

Greil turned his blade downward and struck forward, intending to pike Marrok through the back. The elder rolled to his side and regained his footing in one quick move.

"I'll take the claws," Greil told the other. "I will be the Kayl'sro."

"You have not earned the right." Marrok swung his blade towards the younger. Greil blocked it effortlessly, again and again.

The sound of clashing blades and snapping jaws erupted around the two Agrodien as the others siding with each of them joined the fight.

The younglings scurried to the edges of the canyon, hugging the rocky walls in fear as blood spilt and cries of pain filled the gorge.

Greil seized his moment, tripping the elder with his tail before plunging his sword deep into Marrok's chest, spilling dark blood onto the ground.

The elder tried to stand again, his legs shaking beneath his weight.

"Now," the young one snarled, "I have earned the right."

"No." Marrok dropped to his knees. His tail drooped into the dust. "You do our kind a great dishonour today, Greil."

"Kayl'sro Greil," the younger corrected him, retrieving the blade from the elder's chest.

As the sound of clashing iron subsided, Greil hoisted the bearskin from the shoulders of the elder and draped it over himself. He then carefully lifted the Iron Claws of Agrodia over the head of Marrok and placed the collar on his neck.

"You bring shame," Marrok hissed. "You are no Kayl'sro."

Greil lifted his sword and licked the dark blood sticking to the blade with his long, forked tongue.

"The old ways are dead," he growled. "As are you."

With a quick swipe with his sword, Greil sent Marrok's head to the dirt where it rolled towards the hearth. His body twitched, and his tail shuddered as dark blood seeped from his reptilian body.

The young female moved her gaze to Greil, staring at him hungrily.

"Hail Kayl'sro Greil," she hissed. "Hail Kayl'sro Greil."

"Hail Kayl'sro Greil," another joined her, then another.

Greil raised his stained sword above his head triumphantly.

"Hail Kayl'sro Greil," the Agrodien chanted. Their voices echoed along the walls of the canyon. "Hail Kayl'sro Greil."

The shadow chose that moment to retreat. It moved to the lip of the gorge and swiftly floated away into the darkness. The Agrodien voices grew like thunder, reaching into the night sky and shaking the ground like tremors.

One

A chill breeze swept over her in the early morning hour.

Shivering slightly, Alice pulled her grey cloak about her chest tightly as she knelt by the foot of the oak tree, waiting for the sun to lift its head above the mountains far to the east. Her breath escaped in tiny puffs of vapour as she gave thought to her father.

She ran her hands over the rough skin that covered the surface roots of the great tree. It was the closest she could get to him, uncertain where exactly his ashes rested.

"I miss you, Papa," she whispered as a tear rolled down her cheek.

Her eyes lifted towards the thick branches that spread widely in all directions. The leaves had changed from a lush green to a muddle of yellow and orange. Many of them had already fallen, covering the grass that filled the expanse that once was the Great Hall of Woodmyst.

"I wish you were here to teach me," she said. "I don't think I belong here."

A gentle wind swept over the ground, lifting fallen leaves and causing them to rustle softly around her. It didn't bring comfort with it. Instead, coldness swept over her, giving a bitter taste of the winter to come.

Alice moved her hands to the hilts of her two swords, resting in the sheaths strapped to her back. She gripped her fingers around the new leather strapping she had applied only the night before. It creaked slightly in her grasp as she rose to her feet.

She turned her face towards the sun, into the breeze, sending her long, dark hair over her shoulders. Closing her eyes, she felt the welcoming warmth of the first light caress her skin as she pulled her cloak around her.

"I think the snow is coming early this year, Papa." She peered towards the broad trunk of the oak. "The last of the grove trees were felled just yesterday for firewood. With the rate people require timber around here, I fear the forest will soon be cleared all the way to the ruins of Oldcastle before long."

Her hand touched the rough surface of the tree. She stroked it, as if it could feel her in the same way an animal would the touch of its keeper.

"Don't worry..." She smiled sadly. "I won't let them touch this one. She's sacred."

As her hand retreated to the cover of her cloak, she made her way across the grass to a stone path that hedged the oak tree in a large circle. Her boots clicked against the hard surface as she followed the path where it broke away from the ring, heading towards a gate set into an iron fence.

She looked over the dark barrier that bordered the grounds where the Great Hall had stood many years ago. They set the gate into pillars made of hewn stone that stood as high as she did.

A significant amount of effort had gone into beautifying the area.

But it wasn't just the ruins of the Great Hall that had undergone such construction. Masons had repaired the roads of Woodmyst, setting them with stone surfaces to ease travel for the ever-increasing population of Woodmyst.

With many of the cities destroyed, people had little elsewhere to turn but to Woodmyst and her allies. The village grew into a city and continued to expand.

Alice pulled the gate shut behind her as she stepped onto the street and glanced at the stone buildings across the way that lined the well-paved road.

The path before her was straight, intersecting to run in three directions.

One wide path would take her directly south, crossing a new bridge into more of the community. The crossing that stretched over the river was wide, purposely built to allow carriages to pass by one another as they moved from the northern bank to the south, and back again.

To her right, the road would take her to the Western Gate. New guard towers had stood there, linked by a new wall of iron and stone. Two towers stood on either side of the monstrous gate that opened onto the road to the west, manned by archers at all times.

They built another seven towers at intervals along the wall. The last of these sat neatly on the corner where the wall bordering the northern edge of the community started its journey to the east. Atop the monolithic walls was a broad wall walk with thick merlons and narrow embrasures along the outer edge.

Even from the gate to the ruins of the Great Hall, she could just make out the men moving along the wall, relaying messages to the personnel in the towers.

Turning east, Alice made her way along the stone road, listening to her footfalls echoing off the surrounding buildings that neatly lined the street.

The village had grown immensely over the past five years. Sophisticated men with sophisticated ways had helped to redesign and build Woodmyst into what it had become.

A developing city.

It didn't take long for the council to realise that people would come for refuge. And come, they did.

She didn't like it. She felt uncomfortable and threatened. The sounds and appearance of her environment were no longer natural.

Breathing even felt different here, compared to walking in the woodlands.

"It's not the same, is it?" an old man leaning on a staff called to her gently from the corner just ahead of her. "This old village of ours isn't what it used to be."

"What are you doing out of bed so early, Richard?" she asked, moving towards him. "And how are you able to read my thoughts?"

"You are easy to read, my child." He smiled. "You are your father's daughter. He preferred the simple things of life, too. I don't know what he would think of his home if he were to see it now."

She wrapped her arms around the old man.

"You should be inside keeping warm."

"I was just out for my morning walk," he told her. "What were you doing?"

"Talking to my father," she answered, supporting his frame as they slowly made their way along the road.

"What did he tell you?"

"Nothing," she replied, giving him a puzzled glance.

They walked a little way in silence. Richard looked across the river to the houses on the southern bank.

"It's as if we have come full circle," he said solemnly.

"What do you mean?"

"Hmm?" He moved his gaze to the girl. "We used to occupy both sides of the river once. We used to have a great big wall around it all too. Though this one is much, much bigger. Or at least it will be once the north-eastern section is complete."

"From what David told me, the old wall didn't reach the hill like this one," Alice said.

"No, it did not." Richard nodded. "It wasn't anything like this. But we didn't have this many people in our village back then. We have so many now."

He stopped moving and put his weight onto his staff, relieving the girl of her burden. His eyes moved along the straight road that stretched on ahead of him as he pursed his lips.

"What is it?" she asked, concerned with his sudden change of demeanour.

"So many have come," he said. "So many have lost their homes and families and have come here to start again. More will still come when they find their way to us. When they hear of us.

"I don't know if we can handle this. We're not a coastal town that can open a port to trade ships. We can't spread outwards forever like they can in Newholt, Belburn, or Dweagan.

"We're surrounded by mountains to the north, the south and the east. And we have miles and miles of forest to our west.

"We have moved our farms to the southern end of the valley," he continued. "But if more come for refuge, where will we extend to? I have many fears for you and your generation, young Alice. Many fears."

"You talk as if you plan to leave us," she said, moving her eyes over the lines on his face.

"I'm not planning it." He chuckled softly. "It's just the way of Gwendra and Grolle."

"There are no gods." She lowered her brows.

Richard laughed out loud before exploding into a coughing fit. She moved her arms around him tighter and rubbed his back.

"You are your father's daughter," he managed.

"I should get you back to Becka," Alice told him. "And I don't think you should take any more morning walks. At least not in these colder times."

He nodded and started on his way, leaning on her again.

"Your swords?" he said as his arm reached around her shoulders, brushing against the hilts.

"I forged them from my father's sword," she told him.

"You melted it down?" He sounded upset.

"One thing that I remember about my papa was that he was a practical man," she explained. "My mother gave the sword to me after Catherine refused to take it.

"It was too bulky for me, so I asked the blacksmiths to teach me how to forge. When they believed I had learnt all that I could, I melted it down and made two smaller swords and a hunting knife."

"You forged your own weapons?" the old man questioned. "Why am I only hearing of this now?"

"I didn't think it was such a marvel," she replied. "It was a useful skill to learn, and I needed a weapon I could handle easily."

Richard chuckled again, shaking his head as they rounded a corner and headed north along another road.

"*You* are the marvel, young girl." He smiled. "I'm sure Tomas would be very proud of you."

***

"Put him in his chair by the fire," Becka instructed the girl. She pointed into the room with one hand as she gripped a shawl that was wrapped about her tightly with the other.

Alice helped the old man through the foyer and into a cosy room with a few cushioned seats and a small fireplace embedded in the far wall. Flames crackled in the hearth, filling the house with a welcoming warmth.

"Put *him* in the chair by the fire!" Richard snorted. "You speak about me as if I'm not even here."

"You won't be for long if you keep going out in the cold like that," his wife snapped back to him, placing her hands on her hips. "I swear you'll be the death of me, Richard Dering."

"I love you too, dear." He smiled as Alice lowered him into the seat.

"Do you want a blanket?" the girl asked.

"Thank you, no," he replied as he took her hand in his. "Stay and have some tea."

"I don't know if I should," she replied, moving her eyes to Becka. "I left home while it was still dark. They probably aren't even aware that I left."

"Then they won't even miss you," Richard told her.

"They will if they find her bed empty." Becka moved through a door to the side of the room and into the kitchen. "Still, you are staying for tea. I insist."

Alice didn't want to stay for tea. She would rather race home to appear just long enough to be seen before taking off again to spend the day in the woods.

But to turn down an invitation to tea was regarded as a great, personal offence.

Alice unbuckled the leather bonds across her sternum that held the sheaths fastened to her back in place. Slipping the shoulder straps off her arms, she carefully lowered the contraption to the floor, placing it beside the fireplace.

"Take a seat." Richard gestured to a seat across from his that faced towards the hearth.

"That's Becka's chair," she replied, feeling slightly uncomfortable taking the prime position by the fire.

"It's all right," Becka called. "I can sit anywhere."

Alice reluctantly lowered herself onto the cushions. Her body felt rigid and unable to relax.

"Did you make that?" The old man nodded towards the sheathes and strapping.

She nodded.

"A blacksmith and a tanner." He raised his eyebrows. "There's more to you than you let on, Alice. What else don't I know about you?"

She frowned and shrugged.

"Do you like horses?"

Creases formed on her forehead as she gave Richard a quizzical look.

"Do you like to ride them?" he continued. "Do you visit the stables? Do you have a horse of your own?"

"I have a horse," she replied. "A chestnut stallion. He's three years old and as big as I think he'll ever get."

"And you ride him often?"

"As often as I can." She continued to look at him questionably.

"Where do you take him?"

"Into the woods," she answered. "Sometimes I go up to the quarry and watch the men cut stone. Sometimes I go to the caves."

"You go to watch the men, do you?" Richard smiled. "You do that often?"

"I find the craft fascinating." Alice moved in her seat, feeling less comfortable than she already did. "There's a great amount of skill involved."

"And a lot of shirtless men."

"Leave the girl alone," Becka commanded from the kitchen.

"I'm just teasing," Richard chuckled.

"Why do you want to know about what I do with my horse?"

The old man peered into the flames. His eyes glinted a little as she watched him. She wasn't sure whether it was from the light or from water welling.

"Your father was a horseman," he replied. "As a boy, he would sneak into the stables and spend long hours with the beasts. That was during the time of the Night Demons.

"There was one horse that he seemed to have an unspoken bond with. A brown mare. He was hers and she was his for many years."

"I don't remember him having a mare," the girl said, keeping her eyes on the old man.

"She died when your father helped to liberate Blackrock Haven." He stroked his long, white beard. "My, she was a splendid horse."

There was so much about her father that she didn't know. Others had told her bits and pieces, but there were so many blank spaces.

She only remembered his big hands holding her tenderly and gentle kisses on her forehead. Then there was the image she saw in her darkest dreams. The one where he faced the White Witch on the field. The one where he was pierced by steel and smeared in blood. The one that caused her to wake in a cold sweat.

"Tell me about him," she urged. "What kind of man was he? What was he like as a boy?"

Becka entered the room, carrying a tray with three cups and a teapot. She placed the tray on a small table to the side of Alice's chair, poured a cup, and handed it to the girl.

"Remind me." Richard peered at her. "How old are you now?"

"I'm almost thirteen," she answered. "Why?"

Becka handed him a steaming cup.

"Thank you, my love," he said, and smiled.

She leant down and kissed the top of his head.

He sipped it slowly and settled in his seat, stretching his legs towards the hearth.

"Five years ago," he started, "or thereabout, your father was the chief of Woodmyst. He loved his people, especially his family. During his life, he always placed others and their needs before himself and his own. I can honestly say that there are few men like that in this world."

As he spoke, Becka dragged a wooden chair from the kitchen table and placed it between the other two before sitting down on it. She nursed her tea, peering into the flames as her husband talked on.

"I had noticed it after the attack of the Night Demons," he continued. "Something special. I had hoped he would lead our people. It seemed a natural path for him to follow.

"When the Sovereign's men attacked your mother's village, it wasn't much of a surprise that your father would be so willing to go after them. He didn't even know those people, but he was willing to go and help total strangers.

"That's the kind of boy your father was and that was the kind of man he grew to be."

Richard lifted his cup and sipped again. He took a deep breath and turned to face the girl.

"After your father died, my heart was broken. I loved him like a son. Becka will tell you I aged almost overnight. He kept me young and full of joy. Now my legs can barely move.

"Don't misunderstand me," Richard waved his hand a little. "David is a wonderful chief. But he isn't your father. Your father differed from most men. It's hard to explain what I mean."

He stopped talking and looked at Alice for a long time.

"I can see a great deal of him in you," he said finally. Becka nodded, silently agreeing with her husband. "I miss him."

Alice felt a tear roll over her cheek.

She missed him, too.

Two

"Where have you been?" Catherine asked as Alice came in through the door, her auburn hair trailing over her shoulder in a long plait. "We looked everywhere."

All eyes turned and rested upon her as she unbuckled the straps over her shoulders before lowering her swords to the floor.

"You can't have looked too hard," she replied. "I didn't go far."

"You weren't in your bed when I woke." Her sister approached her, moving from the kitchen and past the dining table where several people sat.

"I was with Papa," Alice answered as she placed her cloak upon the coat stand by the door.

The three adult women seated around the table, two with auburn hair, the other fair, seemed to pay particular attention to the girl's words.

"You went to the oak tree?" asked one of the auburn women, pushing her chair backwards with her legs as she rose to her feet.

"Yes, Mama." Alice approached her mother with her arms stretched out. The two embraced.

"I worried you might have run off again," her mother stated.

"Not before breakfast." Alice smiled as her mother kissed her forehead.

"Let the girl be, Emily," the other auburn woman said with a smile.

"Sit down." Emily gently placed her hand on the girl's back and guided her towards the table. "I'll get you something to eat."

Catherine returned to her place. She lowered herself into a seat beside a young man who was shovelling a load of bacon, dangling precariously on an iron fork, into his mouth with a loud slurp.

"Slowly, Takmel," she instructed him, lifting a napkin to wipe the oil from his chin. "You'll choke."

He replied by leaning towards her to place his greasy lips against her cheek.

"Takmel," she chided playfully, smiling as she applied the napkin to her skin.

"So," Alice said as she sat in her place across from them. "What are you two going to be doing today? Will you go for a walk to that clearing by the river where you like to suck face with each other? Or are you going to climb the mountain behind the quarry where you can see the entire valley, and suck face with each other?"

"Alice," a fair-haired woman with a little girl sitting on her lap said, and chuckled.

Catherine's and Takmel's eyes became daggers, staring widely at Alice as her mother placed a plate of bacon and eggs and a mug of tea before her.

"What?" she said, lifting a knife and fork from the table.

"How did you see...?" Takmel started, as Catherine looked at her mother.

"We didn't, Mama," she said defensively. "I mean, we did. But it's not like..."

"Ah, young love," sighed the other auburn-haired woman sitting at the table. "Do you remember what that was like, Emily?"

"My beautiful daughters remind me of my one and only true love every day, dear sister," she replied, sitting in the chair at the head of the table. She moved her sad eyes over the faces of the little girl on the fair woman's lap and a small boy seated beside the other adult. "All of our children remind me of him."

Alice noticed tears welling in the adults' eyes as her mother reached across the table to take the hand of the other auburn-haired woman.

"I miss him too." The blonde woman kissed her daughter on the forehead.

Alice shovelled a fork-load of eggs into her mouth.

"What was he like?" she mumbled through a mouthful of food.

"Swallow first," instructed the woman seated by the little boy.

She did as she was told.

"Sorry, Aunt Joanne." Alice frowned. "What was he like?"

"We shouldn't talk of such things at the table," Catherine interjected.

"Why not?" the younger girl asked, stuffing a portion of bacon through her lips.

"It's not right to speak of the dead."

"Says who?" the fair-haired woman questioned.

"Aunt Lucy?" Catherine furrowed her brow. Aunt Lucy, although not related by blood, was indeed a part of the family. She had married Tomas Warde, Catherine's and Alice's father, when the girls were very young. Whilst the fair-haired woman could be construed as the girls' stepmother, it felt more comfortable to refer to her as *aunt*. This seemed fitting, considering Tomas had also wedded Joanne, Emily's younger sister. The girls, Emily's daughters, already called their mother's sister Aunt Joanne. It just seemed natural, if not polite, to do likewise for Lucy.

"Who told you it's not right to speak of the dead?" Lucy asked the older girl.

"I just thought that was the way it is," she replied. "It seems inappropriate. Especially at the table."

"I can't speak for your mother or your Aunt Joanne." Lucy leant onto the table with an elbow, pointing to her chest. "But your father is still alive in here. And he always will be. I look at you and see more of your mother. Antony there has his eyes, but he's yet to discover who he is. Holly here lucked out and took after me. She's still so pretty though." She kissed her daughter on the forehead again. The little girl scrunched her nose in disgust as she took a bite from a slice of buttered toast.

"Your sister there…" Lucy looked over at Alice, who was chewing loudly. "Well, she is everything that I remember about your father. Untameable, wild, more at home under an open sky than in the confines of a house. But also, very caring by nature. Always putting others before himself.

"You want to know what your father was like?" she asked Alice. "Look to yourself. You're just like him."

Alice noticed the other women at the table nodding in agreement.

She stretched her arm over and took a piece of buttered toast from the top of a stack sitting on a plate in the centre of the table.

"That's what Richard told me," Alice told them before tearing a large portion of toast off with her teeth.

"You went to see Richard?" Joanne queried as she attempted to use a napkin to wipe the mess from around Antony's mouth. The small boy protested, turning his head in every other direction as he moaned.

"No," he blurted as his mother cleaned his face.

"He found me," the girl replied with a mouthful of food.

"Alice." Her aunt gave a disapproving glare. "Swallow."

"Sorry." She forced the morsel of toast down her throat. "He found me outside the ruins."

"Why was he there?" Emily asked, sitting back in her chair as she nursed a mug of steaming tea.

"I don't know." Alice stabbed at some bacon and lifted it to her lips. "Morning walk, I think."

"I would think Becka was none too pleased," Takmel put in.

The girl shook her head as she shoved a load of eggs into her mouth.

"Slow down, Alice," Catherine instructed. "You'll choke."

"Hungry," she mumbled through the food. Her eyes immediately flickered towards Joanne, ready to receive a correction for her bad manners. Her aunt was too engaged in cleaning Antony's face.

"Did you talk to Becka?" Emily asked.

Alice nodded, grunting in the affirmative as she noisily chewed on some crunchy bacon rind.

Lucy watched the girl in awe. Her smile slowly grew wider as she chuckled to herself.

"What's so funny?" Joanne asked.

"She's exactly like him," she answered. "Look at her."

Alice stopped eating, a portion of meat sticking from the corner of her mouth as she gazed wide-eyed around the table at all faces staring right at her.

A sharp whistle from outside the front door broke the silence.

Alice jumped to her feet, lifting her hot mug of tea to drain it dry in four large swallows.

"Time to go," she said, moving away from the table and towards the front door.

"You just got here," Catherine said, standing up.

"That's Akasati," her sister replied, wrapping her cloak about her. "I've got archery training today."

"You can at least say goodbye properly," Emily told her, placing her mug of tea on the table.

"Sorry, Mama." Alice crossed the room and kissed her mother on the cheek. Emily took her daughter's face in her hands and kissed her forehead. "Bye, Mama."

"Bye, my princess." She smiled. "I want you back by sunset."

"I'll try," the girl answered as she moved around the table to her aunt. She kissed Joanne on the forehead before doing the same to Antony.

"No," he grunted, tilting his head away from her.

Alice then rounded the table to Lucy and Holly, followed by Catherine, pecking her lips upon each of them.

"Where's mine?" Takmel jested.

Alice poked her tongue out in reply before crossing back to the door, where she retrieved her swords from the floor.

"Bye," she called as she opened the door, stepping back into the cool autumn air.

***

They stood upon a large patch of turf behind the armoury, a large building to the north of the new assembly hall. A stone wall encompassed the square ground, adding an extra element of security to the compound where the community's weapons stores were located.

At the northern edge of the grassy yard, posted against the wall, were some straw men. Alice recalled stories of straw men attacking her village when she was younger. But these did not move or pose any threat. They were her targets.

"This is too easy, Akasati," she complained, hoisting a fully laden quiver over her shoulder. "I could hit all of them from the river bank."

"I have no doubt about that," the woman standing beside her agreed. "But this is a test of speed. I would like to see you hit all the straw men by the time I count to three."

Alice moved her eyes along the expanse of the wall. There were twenty targets.

"All of them?"

"Yes." The Erilian smiled. "Are you ready?"

"I'll try," the girl replied, raising the bow in her left hand and taking an arrow from the quiver on her back.

"One..." Akasati started.

Alice wasn't quite ready.

Her heart skipped a beat as she quickly loaded the bolt and took aim. She pulled the bowstring and let the arrow fly. As it streaked through the air, she loaded the second arrow and fired at the next target. Then the next.

"Two..." the Erilian called.

Shit! Alice reached for the next arrow. *She's counting too quickly.*

Her chest felt too tight and her legs stiffened. She got another five arrows free before Akasati called the last number.

"You hit eight," she told the girl. "You need to be faster."

"You need to count slower," Alice argued, realising that her words were useless as she spoke them. An enemy would not wait for her to reload her bow.

"I counted slowly enough." Akasati started towards the first target. "Let's retrieve your arrows and try again."

The girl nodded and followed her instructor across the grass.

The sun slowly climbed high into the autumn sky. Alice continued to run the drill with Akasati by her side. With each attempt, her arrow counts increased.

"Seventeen," Alice blurted excitedly. "I hit seventeen that time."

"It is not twenty." The Erilian frowned. "Three of the enemy are still alive."

"But I'm improving," the girl said. "I want to try again."

Akasati peered back towards the armoury and held her gaze.

"You have drawn an audience," the woman whispered.

Alice turned to see thirty soldiers by the structure. Standing amongst them was a large bald man with a long, plaited beard.

"David!" The girl ran towards the man, a broad smile stretching across her face. The soldiers moved out of her way, allowing her access to the giant. She wrapped her arms around his waist and squeezed him as tightly as she could. "Did you see? I hit seventeen that time."

"I saw." He placed a broad hand on her back, his face expressionless. "Most impressive, little one."

"I can do better," she said, pulling away to look him in the eyes. "I'll show you."

She ran back to her position on the shooting line, passing Akasati, who was making her way towards the tall man.

"Chief Gyfford." She smiled, moving to his side.

"Miss Ulauwen." He bowed his head slightly. "How fares our little warrior?"

The girl closed her eyes and took a deep breath.

"One..." she whispered to herself.

Alice started firing her arrows.

"She is better than anyone I have ever encountered or fought beside."

"But she cannot reach all twenty targets?"

"Two..."

"No one should be able to reach twenty," Akasati told him.

"By the gods," one soldier gasped. "That was fast."

"Nineteen," the girl cried joyfully. "Did you see? Nineteen."

David grinned politely and nodded. A look of concern grew in his eyes.

Alice scrambled to collect her arrows.

"No one should be able to reach ten," the Erilian said. "Nothing about this is natural, David. I took her to run the Kyhur Circuit three days ago. Most of the men in training can complete it in an hour. She was quicker. I watched her clear the Rakmha trench."

"What steed was she upon?" he asked. "I'd like to see the beast that could do such a thing."

"She was on foot."

David turned to the woman, the colour seeming to drain from his face.

"On foot?" He lowered his brows. "She cleared the Rakmha trench and completed the Kyhur Circuit in under an hour on foot?"

"She did." Akasati nodded.

"Is she a threat?"

Akasati looked at him, furrowing her brow.

David's face was stern, serious.

"She is her father's daughter," she answered. "Her heart is for her people. But even she knows she is different. We should not push her away. We should embrace this."

"You think she will make an outstanding leader," the chief said. "As do I. But people fear her already and an outstanding leader shouldn't inspire others through fear."

"They feared the Seven once." Akasati turned to watch the girl moving along the wall, plucking her arrows from a strawman's chests. "They feared the crew of the *Adelandria*. They fear a great many things that they do not understand. Perhaps when they get to know her, they will change their minds."

"She was born here," he said. "She is one of them and still their fears have increased. She spends more time in the wild than she does with her people."

"You can't send her away, David," the woman pleaded. Tears welled in her eyes.

"I don't think I'll need to," he replied. "I have a feeling that she will leave us before it comes to that."

"She's too valuable," the Erilian touched his arm. "You can't let her go. We need her."

"I don't doubt that," the chief agreed. "But I don't think it will be our decision."

Alice took her place on the shooting line again.

"One…"

"Her mother told me she has started to flower," David said as the girl started firing arrows again. "Emily said that her sister, Joanne, could always do strange things, but it was when she reached the age of womanhood that her abilities became truly apparent."

Alice focused, reloading and firing her bow. Arrow after arrow stuck into each straw man in rapid succession.

"Two…"

TWACK!

TWACK!

TWACK!

"I fear Alice may begin using powers we didn't believe she possessed," he continued. "I don't think she has abilities like the Seven. But, as you said, she fights like no other. She is a master of all weapons and no man can spar with her and stand afterwards."

Akasati sensed where David was leading the conversation. She understood the girl differed from any of the other children her own age. Alice had taken to the art of warfare like a fish would take to water. The Erilian shook her head, her eyes fixed upon the giant.

"She's the daughter of Tomas Warde," Akasati argued. "She belongs here. She's just a little girl."

"Twenty," Alice called excitedly, thrusting her bow into the air triumphantly. "Did you see? Twenty. I hit all twenty."

"Very good," David called out to her with a smile before lowering his voice and turning his back to the girl, his face close to the Erilian's.

"She is potentially dangerous. I need to be certain that she poses no threat to the people of Woodmyst."

"Why do you hate her, David?" Akasati asked quietly.

He looked over his shoulder at the girl, watching her momentarily as she walked across the range to the targets to retrieve her arrows. After letting out a long breath, he turned and walked away, leaving Akasati's question unanswered.

Three

He touched the iron claws resting upon his chest as his eyes scanned the expanse before him. A strong, cool wind swept in from the east, picking up dust and loose litter that rested upon the desert floor.

Turning, he peered down from the ridge that he and a small few had climbed, back to his people who waited on the plateau for his instructions. There were males, females, and younglings huddling together, draping themselves with animal skins for protection against the grit being carried through the air.

They had trekked most of the night, stopping briefly to allow the little ones to regain their strength before setting off again. The exodus was relentless, but it had a purpose that he will see fulfilled.

Already, there were murmurings among the travellers. He heard some females complaining that he was being too ruthless and that they should have simply remained in the Canyons of Terikith.

They whispered about how their lives were sufficient where they were. They mumbled about how they had everything they needed and that it was enough.

They were wrong.

The lands to the south were theirs by right.

He moved his eyes back to the southern horizon, where great stone spires jutted from the ground like twisted, broken teeth.

"The Pillars of Mohaa," said one male by his side. "We should go wide to the west or east to avoid this place, Kayl'sro."

"They have horses, Yuri," Greil replied. "Lots of horses. We could ride into our homelands instead of wasting energy using our own legs."

"They have dragons." Yuri lowered his head submissively, knowing it took little to offend his leader.

"Are you afraid?"

"Of dragons?" the other queried. "Yes. But I am afraid of being set on fire even more. Some say that death is not instant. You feel the flames lick at your flesh before release comes."

Greil kept his gaze upon the spires. The dust sweeping across the expanse made it difficult to gauge the distance from their current position to the land of the dragon keepers.

"It could take the best part of the day to reach the Pillars of Mohaa," the leader told the others. "We should get underway now."

"We will be exposed, Kayl'sro," another male put in. "There is no cover on the plain before us."

"Gharnef is right," Yuri agreed. "If the wind ceases, they will certainly see us coming."

"Am I to be surrounded by cowards for all of my life?" Greil snarled. His tail coiled in anger. "We will cross the plain. We will kill the Haigok. We will butcher their flying lizards, eat their children and take their steeds."

With that, the Kayl'sro moved towards the west. The few gathered with him, looking to one another briefly, exchanging looks of concern as their leader marched away.

"Gather the others," Yuri told them. "We're moving on."

Within moments, a little over three hundred Agrodien trudged over the ridge and into the dusty plain. Large bundles and packs weighed upon the adults as they carried their belongings on their backs.

The children, old enough to toddle, gripped their mothers' tails or held onto the hands of their older siblings. The ones still too young to use their legs strapped to the chests of their parents, shielded from the harsh wind by the cloaks and garments of their caregivers.

The Kayl'sro didn't look back to see how his people fared. Forward and onward, he marched. The land of the men would belong to the Agrodien again.

Forward and onward.

Forward and onward.

Four

Mallets, hammers and chisels struck the rock face with consistent repetition. The sound of iron splitting stone rang out across the vale as the masons continued their arduous task.

Teams of bullocks pulled long wagons through the pit, pausing at the base of lever-controlled cranes. The operators lowered the ropes, threaded through the tackles and pulleys, so that the ground crews could fix the straps to large pallets laden with stone blocks or tiles.

The great metal arms creaked and moaned as they took the weight of the load. The crane operators turned wheels to recoil the ropes, hoisting the cargo into the air. Members of the ground crews would lift long poles, pushing and holding the base of the heavy pallet to prevent it from swinging as the crane rotated the load into position above the wagons waiting below.

"All right," a tall man signalled to one crane operator to lower the cargo, waving in a downward motion with his hand.

Closer and closer the pallet drew to the wagon.

"Slowly," the man called as he moved around to the rear of the trailer, limping slightly as he crouched to see the closing gap between cargo and cart.

The pallet touched down with a soft thud. All heard a loud creak as the wagon strained under the weight of the stone blocks.

"She's down," the man signalled for the operator to stop. Men from the ground crew clambered onto the vehicle and started releasing the straps that attached the cargo to the crane.

"All done," he called to the crane operator, who lifted the metal arm into the sky, recoiling the ropes as he turned his attention to another crate being loaded in his zone.

"Take her out," the man called to the bullock driver. "Bring in the next one."

Another, much younger man moved to his side, passing a canteen to him.

"She's back again, Baldwyn," he said, pointing with his chin to the top of a ridge that overlooked the quarry.

Baldwyn took the vessel, looking to where the other was gesturing. He could see her, mounted upon her chestnut stallion, watching them.

"She's never come down here," the man said. "Not once. She just sits up there and watches. What do you think she wants?"

Baldwyn drank from the canteen and wiped his brow.

"By the gods, I miss the ocean," he said.

"Baldwyn?" The other looked at him quizzically.

"Perhaps she doesn't like the idea of us cutting into this mountain," he replied. "She is a child of these lands, after all. Maybe she believes she is custodian of it."

"The quarry has been here longer than her," the man argued. "Longer than Richard, even."

"Ay." Baldwyn limped towards the awaiting pallet. It was almost ready for loading. It needed a few more blocks, however, before he called the crane would. "The pit has been here for hundreds of years. Hasn't been used for hundreds of years either. Most of it was overgrown when we first came up here to reopen it.

"The last time they took stone from here was to build the walls that encircled the old village. And I'm convinced that it must be good stone because the walls stood for hundreds of years. Damn things only fell thanks to bloody dragons."

"I've heard the story," the other informed him.

"Well, you can hear it again," Baldwyn answered. "And again, if you get the chance. We should never forget such things. This is our home now and we should know what we can about it. Our children need to know this story. And their children.

"Never forget. People died here. A whole civilisation was almost destroyed here. They spared only the children.

"Her father," he continued. "One of the greatest men that I ever had the honour to know, was one of them. That's her history. That's her legacy.

"If she was to ride down here and command me to stop cutting stone, I would. This was her land before it became mine."

"The council wants this," the other interjected. "She is just a child."

"I respect her father more than any man on that council," Baldwyn said, frowning. "I will stand by her side before any of them."

The younger man turned and looked back at the ridge.

She was gone.

"The girl is strange," he blurted.

"You fear her?"

"Most of us do," he acknowledged.

"Then you are all fools." Baldwyn moved around the pallet as several men carted the last few blocks of stone on barrows towards them. "You and the council alike."

***

The stallion bounded along a narrow track that followed the edge of a steep precipice. Alice let the reins hang loosely in her hands as she allowed the steed to navigate the path of his own accord.

She peered over the valley to her left, absorbing the warm colours of the autumn leaves still clinging to the surrounding trees. An assortment of reds, yellows and earthy browns stretched on for as far as she could see. Patches of green pierced the canopy here and there were pine trees stretched their pointed heads towards the sky.

Slowing to a trot, the stallion turned to the right, climbing to the top of an embankment, pausing upon the ridge. This was a regular stop for the girl and her horse. He took a moment to munch on the sweet grass that grew in a small clearing while she scanned the area for game.

A few birds chirped nearby. She heard them fluttering their feathers as they hopped playfully from branch to branch.

But it was the scent that drew her attention.

Carefully, she reached for her bow with one hand as she let the reins rest against the stallion's neck.

He sensed her motions and lifted his head in anticipation, snorting with excitement.

"Shhh," she ordered him.

The breeze struck her face slightly from her left side. She moved her eyes towards it, searching for the source of the aroma.

It was strong and sweet. The smell of fur and blood.

Through the tiny gaps between the trees in a thicket, she saw movement. A dark pelt with tan flanks glided to the right.

A buck.

It was moving fast, possibly reacting to the hissing rebuke she had given her stallion.

She kicked him softly with her heels, urging him forward.

He responded by lunging down the embankment towards the fleeing deer.

With her hands free of the reins, she reached with her right hand to the quiver strapped to her saddle. In one swift motion, she loaded the arrow and used her legs to steer her charger to the right.

The stallion turned, racing on a course to intercept the buck as it attempted to dodge thick shrubbery and leap over fallen logs.

Alice angled her body as her steed made the necessary adjustments to its path to keep up with the fleeing deer.

Pulling back on the bowstring, she prepared to fire.

Suddenly, the stag bounded to the left, altering its direction away from the predator.

"Bugger," she spat as the stallion shifted its weight to chase after the game.

The trees were thicker here. The ground was steeper.

The deer was tearing down the embankment, lifting leaf litter and dust in its wake.

The stallion pushed himself harder, increasing his speed on the downward slope. His hooves thundered as they pounded against the ground with ferocity. His nostrils flared as he took in exuberant amounts of air. His heart pounded so loudly in his chest that Alice could hear it.

He wasn't about to give up.

Within moments, they were gaining on the buck.

She took aim again.

The angle was wrong.

Her target was directly in front of her.

Its head was low as it fled as fast as it could.

A headshot would guarantee a quick death. An arrow in the rump might allow the animal to escape, only to die slowly and painfully far away from here.

She pulled back on the bowstring again and looked for an opportunity.

Loose leaf litter and clumps of turf flew into the air as tree trunks and shrubbery streaked by in a blur.

She stiffened her jaw, parting her lips slightly, and allowed a quick blast of air to shoot past her teeth.

The piercing whistle broke through the air, causing the stag to lift its head to glance over its shoulder.

SNAP!

The arrow shot through the air and pierced the creature through the eye and deep into the skull.

It toppled over and over, collapsing to the ground, eventually coming to rest a few yards away.

The stallion slowed instantly, bringing itself to a complete stop by the side of the fallen stag.

Alice lifted her leg over the neck of her steed and dropped to the forest floor. She reattached her bow to the saddle straps before stroking her stallion's nose.

"You did well," she told him. "You always do."

He nuzzled her and gave a soft nicker in reply.

She turned from him and approached the carcass.

"Now comes the hard part," she said, plucking the arrow free from the stag's head. "Do I skin it here or do we take it back to the cavern?"

The stallion turned his head to look at her. He tapped the ground anxiously with his front hoof.

"You're right," she said, nodding. "We'll take it back to the cavern."

Five

Chief Gyfford leant against the chest high fence of the training yard. He was watching a stableman attempting to break in a sandy-coloured colt.

It kicked and bucked, squealing loudly as it tried to pull free of the rope attached to its bridle. The stableman had looped the cord around a post jutting from the centre of the yard, keeping it taut with his gloved hand as he moved with the colt.

The young horse maintained his distance from the human, keeping as close to the fence as it could. With David watching from the side, the horse tried to stay to the far end of the enclosed ground, away from the two men.

Eventually, the colt stood still. Its ears twisted and twitched nervously as it moved its eyes this way and that, always returning to the two men nearby.

Its nostrils flared.

Its breath was rapid.

The stableman gripped the rope in both hands and pulled with all his might. The cord scraped loudly against the post as he tugged the steed closer to the centre of the yard.

It was quick to react, protesting by digging its front hooves into the ground.

The stableman drew the beast in a few inches only before it started stamping and leaping about. Twisting to the left and right with its head kicking wildly with its legs, the horse tried desperately to break free.

Holding tightly to his end of the rope, using his weight to keep the advantage, the horseman placed his boots against the base of the post and leant away. A small canvas bag dangling from a hook low on the post swayed as the horse pulled with its head.

The colt wasn't going anywhere.

The steed settled down and stomped the ground angrily with its front hooves.

It snorted grumpily and shook its head, shaking its long fringe away from its eyes.

The stableman seized the opportunity and pulled the rope again. Catching the colt off guard, the man took three backwards steps, drawing the steed a couple of feet closer to the centre post.

It raised itself onto its hind legs and kicked at the air with its front hooves.

The stableman moved back to the post, keeping the rope as rigid as he could. He placed his boots against the beam again and readied himself for another outburst from the colt.

David almost laughed as he watched the beast fling its back half in every direction as it kept its front half stationary, except for its head, which twisted just as violently.

It took even less time to realise that the fight was useless.

Within moments, it stood face to face with the stableman again. It snorted and stomped the ground.

The man pulled the cord again, drawing the beast closer.

It struggled, bucking for a moment before coming to a complete stop.

The fight was all but over.

With another hefty tug on the rope, he brought in the horse to a few feet from the post.

It tried to stand its ground, but exhaustion overcame it.

The stableman tied the cord off before approaching the colt cautiously.

He reached into the canvas bag and took a handful of grain.

"Shhh," he told the steed as it stomped upon the ground, flaring its nostrils.

David stood to his full height, watching with anticipation.

The stableman opened his hand and showed the beast the grain, keeping his other hand on the rope where the horse could see it.

"It's okay, little one," he said. "I won't hurt you. Look what I've got."

The colt grunted, moving its eye from the man's face to the hand on the rope and back.

"You can trust me," the stableman said softly. "I'm your friend."

Flickering back and forth, the steed's eye looked at the hand on the rope before moving to the hand with the grain. It looked back to the man's face, then to the hand on the rope again.

"Come on, little one," he said again as he placed the open handful of grain before the animal's mouth.

It sniffed at the morsel, keeping its eye on the stableman's face.

The temptation of food was too overpowering.

With delicate bites, it took the grain from the man's hand.

The stableman slowly lifted his other hand and stroked the beast's muzzle. It nickered softly, allowing the human to touch it.

The fight was over.

Chief Gyfford smiled and nodded as he looked past the yard to the long building that housed the cavalry's five-hundred horses along with the steeds belonging to many others in the developing city of Woodmyst. There were almost one thousand steeds and two hundred pens for the bullocks used for lugging cargo from the farms, quarry, and timber yards.

Behind the stables stood the north-east guard tower of the city. Great timber scaffolding with cranes positioned on top surrounded the stronghold and stretched towards the west and south. The wall was still being constructed here.

The site reminded him of his childhood when he returned from the caverns to see his home ablaze after the attack of the Night Demons. The walls were rubble then, and the neatly piled stone blocks by the base of the scaffolding were reminiscent of the debris that once surrounded his home.

He glanced back to the stableman and the sandy colt, who seemed to be getting along well. The man reached into the canvas bag for another handful of grain as the steed nuzzled against him.

David turned away and started towards the centre of the township. He could see the high peaked roof of the new assembly hall in the distance. Even from this far away and on such a strange angle, he could read the clock that faced towards the bulk of the city.

Set into the façade of the structure, it was a gift from the Queen of Newholt. She had it constructed and transported from across the sea, all the way from Dendadia in the east. They needed teams of draft horses to cart its monstrous iron and timber frame over the mountains, and teams of men to install the instrument, setting the levers, springs and gears in place.

David couldn't recall seeing anything so intricate, delicate, and technical in his life. His son, Arthur, lapped up every minute as they set the clock in place, finding the spectacle fascinating. He asked so many questions of the specialists that accompanied the timepiece on its journey. How often should the gears be greased? How long before the springs needed to be wound again? How should it be cleaned? How did it work?

While his son was engaged in the clock's functionality, David was taken by the appearance. Adorned with steel numbers and hands that sparkled in the sunlight, the face made of a dark maple stood out above the rooftops of all buildings surrounding it.

If there was one thing to be said of Amicia Elynbrigge, Queen of Newholt, it was that she had impeccable taste.

David looked at the hands of the clock. It was almost the eleventh hour of the day.

It was almost time for the council to meet.

"Good morning, Chief," he heard someone call. He turned his head to see a man leading a cow along the muddy road.

"Good morning," David replied with a smile as he pondered how long it would take the masons to cover the streets in this part of the community with their nice paving.

Several other people greeted him as he made his way along the straight streets. No longer did Woodmyst have the twisting, bending roads he remembered from his youth.

He recalled a very old memory of racing along the edge of the old wall, laughing as he fled past rickety fences that housed small yards and cottages. He remembered the sound of chickens squawking as he spooked them by thumping his hands on the top of their coops, sending a flurry of feathers in every direction as the birds seemingly accused each other of the intrusion.

Chuckling to himself, David continued to walk towards the assembly hall, monitoring the clock and the minute hand that slowly crept towards the top.

A few more greetings and a couple of turns around a corner or two, and he found himself at the steps of the assembly hall.

He strode up the stairs in haste and entered the open doors of the hall. Giant oak panels hung upon iron hinges on either side of him. A guard stood beside each door, peering down the stairs to the people moving upon the street below them.

"Chief Gyfford," they said, standing stiffly to attention and bringing their spears to an upright position.

"Relax, lads," he said, passing by them.

Rows of seats filled the hall, flanking a wide passage through the centre. His boots clomped loudly on the stone floor as he made his way along the aisle.

Upon a platform at the front of the room were four long tables set into a square for the council meeting. Several already gathered and engaged in discussion.

"Putting the construction on hold is unacceptable," said one man seated to the far right of the table. "We need the wall completed as soon as possible."

"Winter is approaching," replied a woman with her back to the chief. "The snow will come with it and construction cannot be completed then. The wall will not be built in time."

"We should double our efforts," the man argued.

"The men are not immune to exhaustion, Henry," David announced as he drew near to the five steps leading up to the platform. "Gilda is right. We will need to face facts. It is getting colder by the day. We cannot expect our men to work in the frost and snow. Besides, from what I understand, laying stone in winter is not advisable. Something about possible weaknesses in the setting.

"I don't know exactly." He waved his hands as he made his way around the table and sat down in a seat that faced towards the assembly hall's doors. "It's all technical and like a foreign language. But I trust the advice of the masons regarding this, and my son assures me they are correct in what they say."

We should concern ourselves more with housing and paving the streets," said a burly man seated to David's left.

"There you go." Chief Gyfford pointed to the man. "Chief Harling has hit the nail on the head. We finish the houses and pave the roads. I just came from the stables. And did you know the roads aren't complete over there yet? I mean, it's one thing to step into horse shit. But to top it off with mud and filth that sticks to your boots! The walls can wait."

"And what if we're attacked again?" another man offered. "We have towers, yes. But walls would give us a greater advantage."

"Come on, Andris." A bearded man to one side of the table shook his head. "Walls mean nothing. They're just something for some enemies to climb over. Others will use certain beasts to turn them to ash."

"The Night Demons said they would not return," the other replied.

"And you believe them?" The bearded man raised his eyebrows. "They're the enemy."

"They gave their word," said Andris

"I was here, boy." The man stood to his feet. His chair scraped loudly against the floor. "I remember the sounds of horns blowing and the smell of burning flesh. I remember the cries of the great lizards as they tore through the sky. I remember it all."

"Simon, please..." A woman by his side reached over and took his hand. He responded with a nod. Pulling his chair back in place, he resumed his position.

"I apologise for my outburst," he said sheepishly.

"No need to apologise," David told him. "I was there, too."

"I should apologise," Andris agreed. "I wasn't there. I only have the stories I've been told."

"You've seen your own terrors, son," Richard told him as he laced his fingers through those of Becka sitting by his side. "From what I have heard, the Sovereign instilled a few things that will give you night terrors of your own."

"That she did." Andris nodded.

"Which brings me to another issue we should concern ourselves with," Henry announced.

"The honourable member of Oldcastle has a proposition," grunted another man seated to the left.

"Are we still doing that?" asked another, much older man by his side.

"Doing what?" questioned Simon.

"Calling each other by the names of where we came from?"

"If they are," said the man to Henry's left, "then that makes me an honourable member of *Adelandria* and you the honourable member of Dellmoor."

"I don't want that," said the other. "I'd prefer Ruttger, if you please. I don't really want to remember Dellmoor at all."

"I'm with him," said the other. "The *Adelandria* is at the bottom of the sea. Call me Jeremy."

"Have you been drinking?" David asked him.

"Not since breakfast," he replied.

"I don't have a proposition," Henry piped in. "I simply would like to discuss the situation arising with one particular individual."

"I sense lots of big words coming." Jeremy pointed across the tables to the other.

"I'll keep it simple then, shall I?"

"Please do."

David moved his eyes around the table, pausing momentarily upon each of the Seven. He was never quite certain if allowing them to be a part of the council was the right decision.

His eyes stopped on Joanne, seated across from him. She must have detected his change in mood, as her attention fixed upon him.

"I'm talking about Alice Warde," Henry stated. "She's dangerous."

"She's my niece," Joanne growled. "And you are ignorant, Mister Cunningham."

"I don't mean to offend." He held his hands up.

"You have," she replied.

David noticed the other six members of the coven leering towards the man from Oldcastle. Joanne's anger had triggered a response in all of them.

"Ladies?" David tried to gain their attention.

"I'm merely trying to bring an awareness to how people feel towards her," he said calmly.

"They are afraid of her. She spends more time out in the wild than she does with people. She can beat down our armed soldiers with no weapons of her own. She is stronger and faster than any man in this city."

"So, because she is different," Gilda said, standing slowly, "and a girl, you wish to do what with her?"

"Perhaps burn her at the stake," another woman suggested, also rising to her feet.

"Maybe cut her head off with a silver blade," mentioned another, lifting herself from her seat.

"She could be drawn and quartered if we can find horses strong enough."

There were five of them standing, their angry eyes fixed upon Henry Cunningham as he sank into his seat.

"I think he would prefer to hang her in the market square," a blonde woman said.

"Isabel," muttered a man seated by her side.

"Sorry, John," she said, touching his shoulder. "But where would you be if everyone treated people who were different how he wants to treat little Alice? Not with me, that's for certain."

John nodded.

"Hold on," Henry blurted. "Wait. I said nothing about execution."

"Exile then?" said the last of the Seven.

"It isn't as if she wants to be a part of us anyhow," he argued. "She's rarely here."

"She's a little girl," Joanne hollered. "She's my family. My husband's and my sister's daughter. How dare you suggest such a thing."

"I'm not the only one thinking it."

"The only one here," Jeremy barked. "We all love that girl."

"Not the only one here," Henry cried.

"Who?" Andris asked. "Who else at this table feels this way?"

His eyes betrayed the others as he flashed a glance towards Harling and Gyfford.

"No," Simon huffed. "No bloody way. David, she's like a daughter to you."

Chief Gyfford furrowed his brow.

"The people fear her," he whispered. "I am ashamed to say it, but so do I. She's unpredictable and capable of things that no one should be able to do."

"So are we, David," Gilda put in.

"I've seen your power," he replied. "And while it struck terror within me, I knew you were in control. I knew I was safe. I don't get that feeling when I see her in action.

"She can beat all the men under Andris' charge in unarmed spars. She has learnt how to forge and fashion weapons much finer than anything our soldiers carry. She's quicker, faster and stronger than anyone that I've seen.

"Akasati told me this morning that she had Alice run the Kyhur Circuit on foot," he continued. "She was able to leap over the Rakmha Trench and complete the circuit in less than an hour. Our best horsemen can't do that, and no horse that I know can leap that trench.

"This morning, I saw her hit twenty targets with twenty arrows faster than it took me to climb those stairs. An impossible feat for the best archer."

"So?" Joanne shook her head. "She's good with weaponry."

"It's not just that," he told her. "She's started her cycle."

"I don't see how that applies to this discussion," Simon protested. "Nor do I think it to be appropriate at a council meeting."

"It is," David assured him. "It wasn't until these seven women reached that time of their lives that their powers came to full fruition. We know what they're capable of. But I have to wonder what it is, what secret thing hides within Alice.

"Her weapons skills and fighting abilities are beyond outstanding, yes," he said. "The way she interacts with animals is beyond comprehendible. I remember her playing with a wild dog on the field by the forest when she was still learning to walk. Do you remember?"

"Yes," Joanne replied, resuming her seat, her chin quivering slightly.

"That dog came out of the forest," he continued. "It wasn't one of ours. There she was, tugging on its ears and rubbing its lips, and it was happy to let her do so. But no sooner than when she toddled away from it, little Randel Fargus ran up to pet it. The damn thing nearly ripped his arm off.

"I've never forgotten that. I've had sleepless nights thinking about it. Why did it let her touch it but almost maul a boy to death?

"There is something different about her." David frowned. "She has abilities beyond the physical. We didn't notice because we're too amazed by what you seven lasses could do.

"I believe she has the potential to be dangerous." He looked around the table. They were all listening intently. "I don't know if exile is the answer, but I took a ride out to the caverns about a week ago. Did you know she has built a house out there?"

Joanne shook her head, tears streaming down her cheeks.

"She used timber that she collected and cut herself. I let her use the equipment. Arthur helped her with the measurements, but I had no idea what the two of them were doing. I just thought they were building a child's fort or something.

"Just inside one of the smaller caverns, near to a stream, she made a level floor and walls to separate two bedrooms from the living area. Similar to the one that Tomas and I built for you and Lucy.

"She must have taken one of the iron stoves from the yard behind the wood mill. You remember the ones that we used in the old huts that we knocked down a couple of years ago? I was intending to clean them all up and reuse them. But the people in Dweagan and Newholt kept sending new ones that their forgers made for us.

"She stuck a series of pipes from the stove out to the mouth of the cavern. After that, she used mud bricks and stone to seal it all in, leaving spaces for windows and a door. There's even a neat little veranda with an awning along the front. Very sturdy. Quite safe."

"What's your point, David?" asked Simon. "You're rambling."

"I think she's planning to leave us, anyway." He looked Joanne squarely in the eye. "I don't think she will need to be coerced. I think she may already realise that she is different and is setting herself up for a life away from us."

"We never made her feel a part of us," Andris put in.

"Some of us did," Jeremy grumbled. "At least we tried. The rest of you didn't try hard enough."

"We should try to make her feel more included," Ruttger suggested. "Give her a position on the council or as a military leader."

"She's still a child," Joanne disputed.

"Perhaps we should just let her go if she wants to do so," Henry put in.

"You're a heartless man, Cunningham," Simon spat.

"If she leaves," Jeremy warned, "then so do I and mine. I owe her father, not this city. My allegiance will be to her."

"And what about the others of her family?" Chief Harling asked. "Will you leave them for one?"

"I can speak for the rest of her family," Joanne countered. "And I can confidently say that we will leave any city, town or stable house that won't accept one of us. We will stick together as a family. It would be what Tomas would expect us to do."

David felt his heart tighten as he lowered his head, wondering if his dearest friend frowned upon him from beyond the here and now.

Six

With the stallion relieved of its riding gear and roaming freely on the grass nearby, Alice sat upon the porch of her hut with the stag's carcass at her feet. She had removed the straps from her shoulders and placed the sheathed swords on a long bench that stretched along the length of the porch, nestled against the wall of the cottage.

She surmised Arthur must have paid a visit in her absence, as a new door hung in place, the key still resting in the lock. Someone had also filled her two portals with timber window frames and clear glass panels.

The first thing she did, after lowering the stag from the stallion's back and removing the saddle and bridle, was go inside to test the new frames. They slid up and down with ease.

She would need to thank Arthur somehow.

Perhaps a leg from the stag?

She scrunched her nose up at the thought.

He deserves more than that.

Alice pushed herself forwards, so that she sat on the edge of the veranda. Her feet touched the ground nicely. Not too low and not too high.

With a dagger in her hand, she pulled one of the buck's rear legs towards her, stretching it to the side. Carefully, she plunged the blade into the flesh of the crotch, popping through skin and soft tissue.

Blood slowly seeped from the wound as she started carving along the line where muscles separated. She moved the blade past the knee, cutting through the pelt with a few sawing motions. Gradually, the knife made its way to the hip of the beast.

There, she stopped.

Retracting the knife, she returned to where she had made her initial cut and started slicing in the opposite direction, towards the rump. As she did so, she hoisted the leg up higher with her other hand, causing a sickening crunch to emit from the flesh.

The hip joint opened and slid out of place as she continued cutting sinew and soft tissue.

Eventually, the leg came free.

She used her dagger to cut a tiny slit through the leg where the tendon at the ankle met the bone. She then lifted herself to her feet, taking the leg with her, strode across the veranda a short distance to a support beam where she hung the piece from a nail jutting from the timber.

Droplets of blood fell to the floorboards, leaving a dark stain.

She looked at it momentarily and wondered how she should clean it.

The hairs on her neck suddenly pricked up.

Alice turned to the stallion, who was standing motionless on the grass. Its ears were pointed forward as it stared silently towards the tree-line at the end of the clearing.

She sensed it, too.

It was upwind from them.

The scent of fell breath was strong, pungent.

A predator approached.

She surmised it smelled the stag's blood and came in search of an easy meal.

With a soft whistle, she summoned the stallion to her.

It complied, walking precariously as it kept its eyes and ears fixed on the tree-line.

The smell grew stronger.

She stepped down from the porch, her bloodstained dagger in her hand as she approached the stallion.

"Behind me," she whispered. The steed moved away, allowing Alice to stand on the ground between itself and whatever was approaching.

A twig snapped directly ahead of her. Her eyes moved to the place from which the sound had come.

The teeth were what she noticed first.

Long, jagged and sharp, forged together in a wide grin as it crept out of the shadows and into the light.

It was as big as the stallion and dark like the night.

Lowering its box-shaped head, raising the hackles upon its shoulders, it emitted a deep, guttural growl.

Slowly, it stepped towards her, one paw after another. Its whip-like tail swished from left to right and back again as it moved its black eyes from the steed to the carcass lying on the ground.

Eventually, its gaze met the angry stare of the girl.

It cocked its head, measuring the human as it edged forward.

Alice took a step forward, towards the beast.

It stopped moving, seemingly confused by the bravery displayed by the little girl.

For a moment, it stared at her feet, growling loudly.

Its stare flickered to the carcass and the stallion again before it inched forward.

The girl lowered her head and stared into the creature's eyes, locking her glare with its own.

It crept forwards, moving to a distance just shy of striking distance.

The stallion backed away, moving farther and farther from the danger.

Alice held her ground, continuing to bore into the creature's eyes with her stare.

Growling on each exhale, slurping its saliva back with every inhale, the creature tried to hold its ground. Eventually, it fell silent and its lips uncurled and covered its sharp teeth.

Slowly, the creature looked away to the ground, flicking its gaze back to Alice momentarily as it lowered its head to the ground submissively.

The girl held her ground, maintaining her eye contact with the beast as it slid onto its side to bare its belly to her.

She backed up slowly, returning to the stag. Keeping her eyes on the creature, she cut into the remaining rear leg of the buck, removing it with a little more haste than she had with the first.

The dark beast remained on its side, watching her.

Tossing the leg onto the veranda, she grabbed the stag by the antlers and dragged it towards the beast.

It turned onto its belly and backed away from her slightly, its eyes moving from the girl to the buck.

Alice dropped the carcass onto the ground and backed away from the creature, keeping her eyes on it all the while.

It waited until she was back by the hut before closing its mouth around the stag's neck. With one bite, it removed the head. Sickening, cracking, and crunching sounds followed as the creature feasted.

Alice summoned the stallion back to the hut. She immediately started preparing her steed for riding. Within moments, she loaded the saddle with her equipment and set the bridle in place.

She tethered the two stag legs to either side of the back of her saddle before draping her cloak over her and lifting her swords into place.

"Time to go," she said to her steed as the two of them watched the dark beast greedily feed in the middle of the clearing.

She took the key from the door and placed it in her saddlebag before hoisting herself onto her horse. A moment later, she and the stallion started away slowly so as to not spook the feeding creature.

It peered up at her momentarily, cocking its head curiously from side to side. Its muzzle touched the wet meat at its feet, watching the girl ride away before returning to the feast.

Seven

Takmel shrugged violently, setting the laden basket on his back a little higher to ease the pain between his shoulder blades. He continued to the next stalk and started peeling the foliage away from the corn jutting from the side.

With a hefty snap, he broke the ear free and dropped it over his shoulder, into the large woven basket on his back. Reaching high, he found another ripe piece ready for the taking. Pretty soon, he picked the stalk clean.

He removed his straw hat and wiped his brow with the back of his forearm. Beads of sweat trickled down his face as he moved onward.

"Are you hot, Takmel?" called a voice from the next furrow.

He turned to see Catherine wheeling a barrow before her as she stripped the stalks free of their fruit.

"It's autumn," he replied. "The leaves are falling and I'm sweating like a pig."

"You need water." She lifted her canteen from her shoulders and tossed it to him. He caught it with one hand and popped the cork before taking three big gulps.

"Thank you," he said, replacing the cap.

"Drink it all," she told him. "I'll refill it once we reach the end of the line."

"What if you need it before then?" he asked, eyeing the distance to the river. They still had at least fifty yards to go.

"I'll be fine," she assured him with a smile.

He shook his head and grinned.

"You are too good to me," Takmel said. "I could kiss you right now."

"Not here." She glanced around nervously. "Someone could be watching."

"I seriously doubt it," he chuckled. "And besides, most of the talkers are saying we are already husband and wife."

"Well, we don't need to fuel their fire with public displays of affection," Catherine argued playfully. "Not yet, anyway."

"Stop your teasing and take your canteen back, temptress." He tossed the vessel through the stalks.

She caught it with both hands and strung it back over her shoulder.

"Maji," called a deep voice. The sound reminded Catherine of distant thunder.

"Who is it?" she called.

She started peering to the left and right, ducking and leaning to see through the gaps in the tall stems around her.

A dark shadow moved by her, weaving between the crops to her side before it burst onto her furrow.

It was a massive cloud of darkness, moving with a will of its own.

"Maji," the voice called again, radiating from deep inside the misty form.

"What is it, Takmel?" she called, raising her hands in a defensive gesture.

"Please don't attack me, Mistress," it said. "I mean no harm. I simply come to speak to the Maji."

"Vonavo?" questioned Takmel, remembering the giant being that his mother once imprisoned in armour. "Is that you?"

"Yes, Maji," it replied, snaking between the corn stems to move into his line of sight.

"I didn't think I would see you ever again," the boy said, eyeing the churning darkness curiously.

"Nor did I," Vonavo answered. "But I bring news, Maji."

"Please..." he held up his hand. "Don't call me that. My name is Takmel. Takmel Hamond. I took my father's name."

"I know this story," the cloud softly rumbled. "Mulbir, one of my kind, has been watching the progress of Woodmyst closely. I see that you have found life and love here. I have heard that you are growing into the man you intend to be."

Takmel felt his cheeks turning warm as he moved his eyes to Catherine, still in the furrow next to his. She watched the black smoke demon cautiously.

"She is Catherine," he told his old friend.

"I know," it replied. "The daughter of Tomas Warde, the slayer of the White Mistress."

"Yes." Takmel lowered his eyes as he recalled when his mother died on the battlefield. He suddenly realised that he stood not too far from where it happened.

"I'm sorry, Takmel Hamond," Vonavo said. "I fear that I have opened an old wound."

"The wound never closed," the boy replied. "It just became more bearable with time."

"I bring news," the mist told him. "Invaders are coming from The Core. They once dwelt in these lands almost a thousand years ago. Now they wish to reclaim it."

"The lizard people?" Takmel gasped.

"What?" Catherine asked, tuning into the conversation. "What are you saying?"

"They call themselves Agrodien," the cloud rumbled. "I witnessed a change in leadership occur. The young slaughtered the old ones. Many others died. The young, more fanatical, are now in charge."

"How many, Vonavo?" asked the boy.

"A little over one hundred and twenty warriors," the smoke demon answered. "Three hundred in total."

"We have more warriors," Catherine stated. "We will be fine."

"Your overconfidence is foolishness, young Mistress," Vonavo thundered. "The Agrodien race is a strong and driven force to be reckoned with."

"I am no mistress," she corrected the being. "Why do you refer to me as such?"

"You have great power within you," it said. "Much like Takmel Hamond. Great power resides in both of you."

"How long until they reach us?" asked Takmel, avoiding the discussion about power and abilities. He wasn't ready to talk about such things.

"They are on foot," Vonavo said. "They could be here within three days. Maybe less."

"We should inform Chief Gyfford," Catherine told Takmel.

He nodded, agreeing silently.

"Will you come with us, Vonavo?" he asked. "Your presence may bring extra validation to the news."

"I cannot, Takmel Hamond," it answered. "My place is in The Core and I must return there."

"Perhaps we'll see one another again?"

"Perhaps," thundered the smoke demon. With that, Vonavo whisped away into the thick corn crop and out of view.

"Now what?" Catherine asked, peering into the cornfield after the being.

"We should find the chief," Takmel answered.

"We should take this load to the carts at the end of the furrows first. I'm not leaving this barrow here for the crows to pick at."

***

"And how many, did he say?" David stood outside the timber yards; his hands clasped behind his broad back as he peered towards the forest in deep thought.

The clatter of hammers knocking on wood and saws slicing through timber resonated from within the strange-looking building behind him. The structure was nothing more than a large roof that met at a sharp apex, hoisted high upon wide beams.

"About three hundred in all," Takmel answered. "One-hundred-and-twenty warriors among them."

"And you trust this Vonavo character?"

"He practically raised me from an infant to the time that I arrived here," the boy assured the chief.

"If these Agrodien are who I think they are," Chief Gyfford said, "then they were once in league with your mother."

"It would seem so."

"Did you know of this back then?"

"No." Takmel shook his head.

"Are you sure?" The chief turned to face him.

The boy stared at the man quizzically.

"David," Catherine chided. "Are you accusing Takmel of something?"

"I just want to know all I can about a potential enemy," he replied.

"My mother never shared her plans with me, Chief Gyfford," the boy assured him. "The only piece of information she wanted me to be certain of was that I was to rule the world. What a disappointment I turned out to be."

"I apologise, son," David said, sensing the other's anger. "I wasn't accusing you of anything. I just thought you might have overheard something."

"I told the council everything I remember from my childhood," he told the giant man. "I was as helpful as I could be. I don't like the stigma that clings to. They look at me as if some fell creature is going to tear through my flesh, revealing my true form.

"I thought you, of all people, would be a little more open and understanding. But little questions and comments from you prove you refuse to think of me as anything but the son of the White Witch."

"That's not fair, Takmel."

"You harbour a deep scar, David," the boy continued. "I can sense it. There is much pain in you. It started before Tomas died. Way back before you liberated Blackrock Haven, you lost Ivo, my father. That was the beginning.

"Then your closest friend, a *brother*, Tomas, left you. And most recently Martha and Isabel, your wives, and your infant daughter, slipping into the icy waters of the river last winter, leaving you and Arthur alone."

"Takmel," Catherine warned him in a low voice.

"And now your hurt is guiding your thoughts in a manner most inappropriate for a leader." Takmel pursed his lips. "You accuse anyone different to you as being a danger to the *fair* community of Woodmyst."

David glared at the boy.

"Who have you been talking to?" he barked.

Takmel shook his head. "No one. But I know your mind, Chief Gyfford."

"What are you talking about?" Catherine asked.

"You should tell her, Chief."

David stared angrily at the lad for what seemed a long time.

"Tell me what?" Catherine piped up.

"The chief is afraid of your sister," Takmel told her. "Even more than he is afraid of you and me."

"David?" The girl peered at him, pleading for an explanation. "It's not true."

"Of course, it is," Chief Gyfford replied sheepishly. "I'm afraid of all of you. I'm afraid of the Seven. I'm afraid of your mother and the Erilian women. I'm afraid of you and him. But I am most afraid of your sister."

"But we love you, David." She wept.

"And I love you too," he replied earnestly. "But it doesn't change the fact that I am afraid."

She shook her head, not understanding how he could feel this way about her family.

"Why?" she asked. "What did we do to lose your trust?"

"Nothing yet," he lied, tears welling in his eyes. "But my son is in love with your sister, I think. One day, he will leave me for her. She will take him from me. He's all I have left."

"We are here," Catherine told him. "We'll always be here."

"She's dangerous," he said suddenly, changing his argument and wiping his eyes on the back of his sleeve. "The people fear her."

Takmel stepped towards him slowly. "If you drive her away, he will follow her. But he will not be the only one you will lose, Chief Gyfford. The crew of the *Adelandria* will follow her as well. The entire Warde family will leave. The six coven members will follow their prime, taking their husbands with them.

"The council will split in two and the city will be divided. This is not the place to be when an enemy is breathing down the back of your neck. Are you too blinded by your prejudice to see that Alice is the asset you need right now?"

David looked at the boy with sad eyes. His chin quivered, causing his plaited beard to shake. He turned his gaze to Catherine, who was still crying.

Eventually, he lowered his stare to the ground and turned away.

"Leave me alone," he grumbled as he moved towards the sawmill.

Eight

Its talons raked at the fallen leaves, digging at the ground to unearth large bulbs that grew by the roots of the oak trees. The giant bird was busying herself with finding food as a larger, more colourful male performed a dance, hoping to gain her affection.

It wasn't working.

The male fluffed his feathers and stamped his feet, turning in circles as he dipped his head up and down in a repetitive pattern. Fine yellow and red plumage flashed from beneath his black covering feathers, drawing her eye momentarily.

Thinking he had her attention, he squawked loudly.

She cocked her head and returned to digging.

"What is it?" asked a soft whisper from above.

Arthur peered up from his hiding place behind a thick cluster of shrubbery.

"By the gods," he gasped. "I think I soiled myself. How did you get up there?"

Alice grinned down at him. She sat comfortably on a broad branch, her back resting against the trunk of the tree.

The male spun again, flashing the bright colours as it turned.

The girl dropped to the forest floor silently, crouching beside Arthur, who had returned his attention to the two birds.

"Are they about to have sexual relations?" she asked, teasing him.

"Mate," he hissed. "The word is *mate*."

She smiled playfully.

He continued observing them, engrossed in the behaviour both the male and female were displaying.

"So?" Alice eventually asked.

"So, what?"

"So, are they about to mate?"

"I'm uncertain," he answered. "He certainly wants to. But she seems indifferent to him.

I'm not sure if her attitude is part of the quedia ritual or not."

"So, the female is playing hard to get?"

"Yes." He fixed his eyes upon the animals. "That's generally the case with most species."

"Not all species, though?" She placed her hand on his thigh.

"Alice, please," he said, frowning. "This is important."

She retracted her hand and flopped down upon her rump disappointedly.

"Definitely not all species." She shifted her attention to the quedia. The male ducked his head again, emitting another loud squawk.

Within seconds, he was back into a spin and flashing his red and yellow under-feathers.

"He's a persistent one," Arthur observed.

"How long has he been doing this?"

"I don't know," the boy replied. "A few hours."

"A few hours?" she breathed. "And nothing?"

"Not yet," replied Arthur.

"He's not going to be mating with this one," Alice told him. "She either thinks he's unattractive or she's old and dried up."

"Alice!" He glared at her with wide eyes.

"Come on," she urged him. "I've got something for you and I don't have a few hours to wait."

"Alice…" He tilted his head, raising an eyebrow warily. "I told you I'm not ready for that yet."

"Not that, you idiot," she chuckled. "I've got meat for you. I can't leave it hanging from my saddle all day. Come on."

He looked over to the quedia again. The female was scratching at the ground, as she had been all day. The male was spinning, spinning, spinning.

SQUAWK!

"All right," he surrendered. "I'm coming."

She jumped up and clapped her hands excitedly.

The giant birds recoiled and peered over towards her. They both started honking and screeching loudly in objection to the intrusion.

"Oh, be quiet," Alice called back.

"Now look what you've done." Arthur lifted himself to his feet. "There's no chance for him to complete the mating ritual."

"He didn't have a chance, anyway." She took his hand and led him back through the forest, away from the annoyed quedia.

Holding his hand, she took him to a clearing where her stallion waited patiently for her, munching on the grass in the middle of the small glade.

"Did you install the windows and door to the cabin?" she asked.

"Yes," he replied. "I put another door at the back, facing into the cave, just in case a draught could somehow work its way through..."

She suddenly pulled him into her and planted a kiss on his lips. Her hands wrapped around his shoulders and held him tight.

He had no choice but to reply in kind. She was too strong for him to attempt any escape, not that he wanted to.

He moved one of his arms around her waist, sliding his hand beneath her swords. The other moved to the back of her neck.

"Thank you," she managed.

"You're welcome." His voice cracked as he smiled bashfully.

***

"I think it was a rukyul," Alice said to Arthur as he clung to her waist by wrapping his arms around her. He sat precariously on the back of the stallion, uncomfortable because of where his arms were situated.

She felt the tension emitting through his rigid body as she told him about the encounter with the strange beast outside her cottage.

"That's unusual." He frowned, keeping his head from banging into the pommels and grips of Alice's swords strapped to her back.

"Are you calling me a liar, Arthur Gyfford?"

"I would never do that," he answered. "You would beat the snot out of me if I did."

"Yes, I would." She grinned.

"I just mean that the rukyul are known for keeping to the lands by the Eastern Sea," he informed her. "I don't remember anyone mentioning one venturing this far west or south."

"Its appearance reminded me of the tales my mother told me," Alice said.

"Perhaps it's a rogue," he suggested.

"A what?"

"A rogue. Maybe it was exiled from its pack."

"Maybe," she surmised. "It seemed pretty hungry."

"And it didn't attack you?"

"No." She steered the horse out of the forest and onto the old road that eventually led to the ruins of Oldcastle. She turned left instead, leading the stallion towards Woodmyst. "I didn't want it to."

"Nobody wants to ever be attacked," he remarked.

"I know," she replied. "It's hard to explain. It was as if I could tell it what I wanted, but without words."

"You could control it?"

"Not quite." She scrunched her face, trying to think of the words. "It was more of a mutual understanding. All it really wanted was to eat. I offered it something so it wouldn't have to hurt my horse or me."

"It could have killed you and your horse and then would have been able to have its pick of a meal."

"Animals don't think like people, Arthur," she informed him. "They don't look for a way to benefit through manipulation and murder. They just act on instinct."

"I know." He smiled. "A lot like you."

She reached around and slapped his thigh.

He yelped as the stinging pain shot up and down his leg like wild fire.

"That hurt," he complained, half crying and laughing at the same time.

She smiled, returning her hand to the reins.

"Hold on," she told him, touching her heels against the stallion's sides.

The horse lunged forward and set off into a gallop.

Arthur tightened his grip around Alice as she raced her steed along the old road. Trees passed by on either side in a blur. Arching limbs stretched above them, forming a tunnel of red and yellow leaves.

The chestnut stallion thundered along the passage, his hoof falls echoing loudly through the trees as they neared the end of the forest.

They burst out of the woods, continuing to race along a straight section of road that stretched over the grounds to the west of Woodmyst, leading to the iron gates set into the wall.

A long horn blew from the tower, signalling for the gates to be opened.

As Alice drew nearer to the wall, the massive iron doors screeched and clunked loudly as they opened.

She slowed the stallion as they approached, giving the tower guards a friendly wave. Arthur risked losing his balance momentarily, lifting a hand to the soldiers above. He quickly returned his arm to the girl's waist, fearing he would topple off.

"It's all right." She placed her hand on his wrist. "I won't let you fall."

"I know," he replied. "I'm just not fond of being a passenger. I prefer to be in control."

"No, you don't," she said, laughing. "You haven't ridden since you were nine."

"I drove the wagon last week, thank you," he argued.

"Drove a wagon?" She giggled. "That doesn't count."

"Why not?"

"It's a bloody wagon," Alice remarked. "My four-year-old half-brother can drive a wagon. He can hitch one too." She laughed, mocking her passenger. "Drove a wagon?"

"Fine." He sounded upset. "Not everyone is as good as you, Alice."

She lowered her head as they passed through the gate. Her hand tightened around his.

"I'm sorry," she told him. "I didn't mean to be so insensitive."

He took a deep breath and sighed.

"It's all right." He tightened his grasp on her. "I wish you would find somewhere else for these swords when you carry me like this. It's hard to hold you with them in the way."

She bit her lip gently and grinned.

***

With the stallion unsaddled and placed in his stall, Alice groomed him from tip to tail with a coarse brush. He nickered contently as the thick bristles ran over his skin.

She had left Arthur at his house, handing him one of the stag's legs before taking her steed to the stable house for the night. After a quick wipe down with a wet rag, removing clumps of mud from his legs, she used the brush to work out any knots in the stallion's muscles.

She placed the brush on a small shelf to the rear of the stall and lifted a blanket from the partition separating her steed's stall from the one next to it. After draping the covering over the beast, she placed a long caparison made of tattered grey linen that she had sewn together herself. She laced it together near his breast and rubbed his muzzle.

Finally, Alice reached for a large pail of oats sitting on the pen's floor underneath the small shelf. She poured the contents into one half of a dual trough to the side of the stall. The other half already filled with water.

She set the pail on the floor, expecting the stallion to nuzzle her thankfully. Instead, it pushed by her and buried its nose into the oats.

Alice smiled and rubbed the horse's shoulder.

"All right," she said. "You enjoy your meal. I'll see you in the morning."

The stallion crunched the grain noisily as the girl collected her belongings and exited the stall.

She hung her saddle to one side, over the door to the pen. Her bridle was slung from a hook jutting from a beam that supported the partition between the pens.

Lifting her swords from the floor outside, the stall in one hand, and the stag's leg lying nearby in the other, she set off back to the entrance of the stable house, nodding to a few of the workers as she passed them by.

With haste, she made her way along a wide road that ran along the side of the training yard. The sun was sinking towards the forest and the afternoon shadows grew long and dark.

She had promised her mother she would be home for the night. She'd hoped to be there a little earlier, as she wanted to surprise the household with the offering of meat.

Eventually, Alice turned right into a street that led towards the river. It was a short walk from there to her family's house, where she saw her mother and Simon Bell seated on the front porch in deep discussion.

Alice felt apprehensive about approaching, afraid to interrupt something that she had no right to interfere with. But they had already seen her and waved as she drew nearer.

"What have you got there, little huntress?" Simon called.

"A leg," she replied, stepping onto the porch. "I killed a stag."

"And where is the rest of it?"

"I gave another leg to Arthur," she answered. "I offered the rest to a rukyul. At least I think it was a rukyul."

Simon gaped at her as Emily rose to her feet.

"What do you mean by *offered*?"

"It came out of the woods," Alice explained. "I think it smelt the blood from the stag. I persuaded it to let me take my portions and gave it the rest."

"You saw only one?" Simon queried.

"Only one."

"Alice…" Emily stepped towards her and placed her hands on the girl's shoulders. "Rukyul are pack animals. They're very dangerous. You need to be careful."

"There was only one," she assured her mother. "It was hungry, so I fed it."

"Where did it appear?" Simon got to his feet.

"What?" Alice didn't want to say. She worried Simon would take a party to hunt the poor creature down and possibly inadvertently discover her cabin.

"You said it came out of the woods," he explained. "Where?"

"Not here," Alice told him. "I should get this meat inside and prepare it."

"Was it near to the caverns?" he persisted.

"I don't want you to kill it," she argued. "It was alone. It was hungry, and I fed it my kill. And that is that. I won't tell you anything more. I should have just stayed out there tonight."

Alice turned and entered the house in a huff.

"Wait," Emily called after her. "Alice, please."

The girl ignored the appeals and continued through the house, passing her aunt and half-brother in the sitting room as she moved into the kitchen.

"Sorry, Simon," Emily apologised.

"It's not your fault," he said. "I shouldn't have pushed her. I'm the one who should apologise."

"She's changing." The auburn-haired woman shook her head. "I don't know how to talk to her anymore."

"Some of what David said at the council meeting is right," said Simon as he resumed his seat. "She's unpredictable, yes. But danger-ous? I don't think so. She's still your daughter, Emily. She's just going through the change that all girls go through at her age. Give her time. Give her some space, but not too much."

"You think I should spy on her?"

"By the gods, no! That'll just push her further from you. Find out what she enjoys and offer to accompany her."

Emily sat in the chair beside him and pursed her lips.

"If David banishes her," she said to the man quietly, "I would say that we'll all find out what she enjoys and accompany her. I will need to go with her, Simon. All of my household will."

"I know. I've spoken to Tricia. We both agree to join you if it comes to it."

"What about Thedric?"

"He's only four." Simon smiled. "He wouldn't understand. Besides, he'll agree to do anything you ask him. You could ask him to wear a pile of horseshit for a hat and he would."

Emily snickered, picturing the little boy with a lump of manure resting upon his mop of dark hair.

"Oliver and Agnes have also told me they will join us," he continued. "So have the rest of the Seven and the crew of the *Adelandria*. They can all see that something has changed in David. Ever since the incident that took Isabel and Martha from him, he has been an unhappy soul."

"This could split the community." Emily shook her head. "I don't want this. I know Alice wouldn't want this either."

"You may not have a say," said Simon. "There is a strong allegiance to Tomas. So many believe that they still owe him."

Emily opened her mouth.

"And before you say it," he said quickly, holding his finger up to her, "I know he wouldn't want that. In fact, I know he would say that nobody owed him anything. But some of us can never forget the sacrifices he made. He meant so much to us, Emily. And because he isn't here to receive our gratitude, we have transferred our allegiance to your household."

"It isn't necessary," she whispered.

"Too bad." He smiled. "You have it."

***

Alice removed the skin from the leg and cleaned it with water, removing grit and grime that it had collected on her journey home. She threw the pelt into a large pail that contained food scraps such as vegetable peelings and egg shells, collected during the day.

After cleaning her hands and the dagger in her belt, she used the knife to score the meat. She poured a small amount of oil and vinegar over it before sprinkling rosemary and salt onto the flesh. Using her hands, she rubbed the spices into the markings she had made with the blade.

"I'll fix some potatoes," Joanne told her, leaving Antony on a seat by himself in the sitting room.

"Fine," Alice grumbled, still in a mood as she prepared the leg for baking.

"All right." Joanne peered at her as she reached into a pantry for the vegetables. "You're not happy. What is it?"

"Nothing," she replied with a grunt. Suddenly, she ranted. "They just interrogated me about where I was, all because I saw a rukyul and fed it."

"And you think that was unwarranted?"

"I told them it was hungry, so I fed it," she answered. "What else do they need to know?"

"A rukyul is a dangerous animal, Alice," her aunt explained.

"That's what they said." She pointed towards the front door.

"Have you ever encountered one before?"

"No." She creased her nose. "But I was in control of the situation."

"You're a little girl and a rukyul is a large predator."

"I persuaded it to back off," Alice informed the other.

Joanne looked at Alice for a seemingly long time.

"What do you mean, you *persuaded* it?"

"I don't know," she answered. "I can just do it. I can will myself upon creatures."

"For how long have you been able to do this?" Joanne placed several potatoes on the kitchen bench.

"Since..." Alice thought about it for a moment. "Since forever. I think I've always been able to."

"Been able to, what?" Emily asked, moving through the sitting room.

"Where's Simon?" Alice asked.

"He's gone home," she answered, moving around the table to the girl. She took Alice's face in her hands and kissed her daughter on the forehead. "I'm sorry for upsetting you. I was just worried when you mentioned about the rukyul."

"I know," the girl said, leaning into her mother's embrace.

"Now." Emily looked into Alice's eyes. "You've always been able to what?"

"Your daughter has discovered a power that she possesses," Joanne explained as she slid a small blade over a tuber, removing its dirty brown skin to expose the white flesh beneath.

"She can communicate with beasts."

"Is this true?"

"Yes," Alice nodded. "But it's more than that. It's like they recognise me as one of their own, only stronger."

"You used this ability with the rukyul?" Emily asked.

Alice nodded as she reached for an oven tray from a low shelf.

"And it responded?"

"It submitted itself to me," she replied.

"You've tried this with other creatures?" Joanne questioned, picking up another potato to peel.

"Yes," the girl answered. "I tried with my stallion when I was train-ing it. To this day, no one else can get near him unless I'm around. I remember trying it with the water fowl when I was younger. They followed me around the water's edge for most of the day. The cattle and sheep are the easiest. They're so stupid that they would submit in half the time it took to convince the birds."

"For what purpose could this power be yielded?" Emily asked her sister.

Joanne shrugged as she picked up another spud.

"Well," Alice said, "it prevented a rukyul from eating my horse and me. That must be worth something."

Nine

"We make for that rise between those two spires," Greil hollered through the wind.

Yuri squinted; his eyes almost closed as he tried to see the point of land his leader described. The dust was thick and the howling wind was almost a gale. Anything beyond a few feet in the surrounding distance was barely visible.

"We're close to the Haigok," he called to the Kayl'sro. "We should leave the females and younglings here, out of harm's reach."

"Some of our females fight more fiercely than you," Greil replied.

"A great number are still giving suck," Yuri reasoned.

Kayl'sro Greil turned his head slowly, peering at the many Agrodien drew together in the chilly wind. He could see several children hugging tightly to the legs of their mothers, their faces hidden from the elements.

"Fine," the leader conceded, turning towards the giant towering spikes. "Those with children remain. All others will fight."

"You should be careful, Yuri," a young female quietly jeered to his side. "You question the Kayl'sro too much."

"I *advise* my Kayl'sro, Zeveera," he corrected. "That is my role as advisor. You'll do well to remember your role, *female*."

She opened her mouth and hissed defiantly before moving after her leader with a long blade in her hand.

"Be careful, old friend," another said, approaching Yuri from the side. His eyes followed Zeveera warily. "She has his ears."

"Amongst other parts of him," Yuri observed. "Don't worry, Gharnef. He won't execute his best warriors, no matter who is whispering words of discord to him."

"Still," the other said, frowning, "I don't like where this is heading. The uprising against our elders. Talk of eating human flesh. Now, this attempt to take from the Haigok. None of this will pan out well for us. I have concerns for my children."

Yuri pulled his sword free of its sheath.

"He is our Kayl'sro," he replied. "He has the allegiance of most of our warriors. That means he has the power and support. What can we do?"

"We can stage a coup," Gharnef said softly. "You could be our Kayl'sro. The others respect you."

Yuri shook his head, lowering his eyes to the ground.

"We would be cut down before anyone had a chance to offer their loyalty," he told the other. "We would be bound and allowed to live long enough to watch Greil disembowel our children, rape our wives and slit their throats."

With that, Yuri started after Greil, heading into the lands of the Haigok.

With little else to do, Gharnef followed, taking the armed Agrodien with him.

***

The Kayl'sro peered down into a vast valley from atop of a high precipice. His army crouched on the dusty ground behind him, awaiting instruction.

Far below, he saw a green valley floor covered with thick vegetation. There was a stream running from north to south, disappearing into a large cavernous mouth on the southern wall of the valley's steep rock walls.

A sizable community stood on the western side of the valley, closest to the Agrodien's position. There were crude houses built of rock, timber, and clay.

The valley, shaped much like a bowl with natural formations at its lip, protecting it from much of the onslaught that the weather brought.

As the winds relentlessly flung dust and silt into his face, the Haigok were shielded from it all. Only a small amount of sand fell to the valley floor.

Carefully, the Kayl'sro scanned the perimeter.

There were no signs of guards or watchers on the rim. For all he knew, they believed themselves to be safe and sound inside their homes.

More importantly, he saw no dragons.

Many caverns dotted the walls of the valley, giving the possibility of dens for the large-winged beasts. But he had doubts.

The stories he had heard of the dragons kept by the Haigok were told by others who were told the same stories by others again.

Perhaps the tales were exaggerations.

Perhaps they were lies intended to frighten and excite children.

His eyes moved towards the southern edge of the community, pausing when they came to a large building within a wide and long fenced yard.

Several Haigok were there, attending to horses. Greil could see their grey flesh on their heads and arms as they moved through the yard, interacting with the beasts. Their bond seemed intricate and strong. The larger steeds followed the Haigok trainers without leads attached, keeping in pace with their masters.

Stealing the animals may prove difficult.

But not impossible.

Greil moved his gaze farther to the south, to a section of the wall not far to the right of his position. He saw a winding road, not much wider than a steed, that climbed the rock face. It zig-zagged back and forwards to the top, exiting the valley a few yards away from where he hid.

"Over there," he pointed with his sword.

Yuri followed the blade to where the track appeared on the lip of the rock wall.

"I told you there would be a way in," the Kayl'sro told him, moving away from the lip of the bowl, back to where the warriors waited. "They need to get their horses in and out, and there it is."

Yuri looked at the sky. The sun rested upon the horizon, emitting a deep red glow across the expanse above them.

"We should wait until dark, Kayl'sro," he advised. "With one way in and out of that valley, we should be as stealthy as we can."

"Agreed," Greil nodded. "There are many caverns and while I did not see any dragons, there is still the chance that they have them hidden away. There is also a chance that they have more warriors than I could see. The fewer of their kind we encounter, the better."

Yuri met eyes with Zeveera, who crouched beside the Kayl'sro, watching him indignantly. He kept his stare fixed upon her until she moved her eyes away, yielding to his authority.

"You may need to watch my back tonight," he whispered to Gharnef.

"I already am," the other assured him, his wary eyes locked onto the female.

Ten

With a rekindled fire blazing in the stonework to the side, flickering light filled the room as David and his son sat opposite one another at the dining table. Arthur baked the leg Alice gave him, serving it with a side of taters and corn.

"Where did you get this?" David asked. "It tastes fresh."

"Alice made a kill today," Arthur replied, stuffing a morsel of meat dangling precariously on the tip of his fork into his mouth.

The bearded giant glanced up to his son.

"Alice?"

"Mm-hmm," the boy grunted.

"How big was the deer?"

"She said it was a stag."

"She *said* it was?" David cut into the meat. "You didn't see it?"

"No," Arthur replied, detecting his father's inquisitiveness was more than simply trivial. He moved his gaze from his plate to the man across the table from him. "She carried two legs with her. One sits here on our plates and partially in the oven. The other, I would guess, is sitting at her table as we speak."

"And where was the rest of the beast?"

"She had a run-in with a rukyul and offered the rest to it," the boy answered, realising too late that he may have said the wrong thing.

"A rukyul?" David put his knife and fork down. The sound of metal scraping against ceramic made Arthur wince a little.

"She assures me she was safe," he said.

"Of course, she was," David replied. "She probably controlled it somehow. Made it dance in circles for her."

Arthur stared at his father, surprised and confused by the statement. "How did you know?"

"That she can control beasts." David clarified. The boy nodded. "Because, I remember. I remember little things people do. And I remember her controlling wild things as a babe. I can only imagine what she is capable of now. She could control an entire pack of those things and set them upon the people of this community."

"She wouldn't do that," Arthur argued.

"Her aunt and her mother, even her sister, are powerful in their own way," David continued, ignoring his son. "I should have guessed she possessed some trait like them. What's next? Perhaps she can squeeze the life from someone like the Sovereign could. Maybe she could tear them apart or set the sky on fire like the Seven."

"Even if she could, she wouldn't do such a thing to any of us."

"She's dangerous." David got to his feet. "I knew she was. I should have acted sooner. I should have listened to that little voice telling me it was so."

"What are you talking about?" Arthur put his cutlery down and leant back in his seat. "What little voice?"

"She needs to go," his father said. "She needs to leave Woodmyst."

"No." The boy sprang up. His fist thumped on the table, causing everything upon it to vibrate loudly.

"You don't get a say in this." The giant moved to the fireplace. "I'm the chief. It's my decision."

"No, it's not," Arthur challenged. "It's the decision of the council. You cannot remove any member of this city without their approval."

"Then I will get the approval of the council," David barked.

"And I will leave you, Papa," the boy told him.

"What?" David turned to face his son, remembering Takmel's warning. "Why?"

"I am promised to her," he answered. "And she to me."

"You're too young to understand what that even means," the man said, turning back to the fireplace to stare into the flames.

"No," he replied. "I'm not."

David placed a hand on the stonework above the hearth and turned his face towards the boy.

"You won't just be exiling Alice Warde," Arthur said. "The daughter of Tomas Warde, a hero of Woodmyst You'll be exiling her entire family and friends that support them.

"You'll be dividing a community and losing valuable people that have stronger bonds with you than most families do.

"And you'll be losing me. I love her. I always have and I always will. Don't make this foolish decision."

"You're a smart lad." David turned his eyes back to the flames. "You stepped up and have done quite a lot for me since your mother and Martha were taken from us. But this city is bigger than you and I. Even bigger than all the people you say would leave for her.

"My concern is for the safety of Woodmyst's civilians. I see her as a danger, a potential threat. She must leave, son.

"She won't need to go far. She has her cabin near the caverns. The soil is good there, and a spring flows nearby. We'll give her some seed and livestock. She'll be looked after. I just don't want her inside the walls."

"You're making a mistake," Arthur replied, tears streaming down his cheek. "She loves you like a father and you reject her because she is different from you. What happened to you? What made you hate her so much?"

David saw a picture in his mind of the old narrow bridge that crossed the river to the eastern edge of the town. It seemed to dance in the flames for a moment before vanishing into the recesses of his mind.

"The safety of this community comes before our own selfish needs, Arthur," the man answered. "This has nothing to do with me, or my feelings towards her. It is about Woodmyst."

"So, you've made up your mind?"

"I'm afraid I have no choice in the matter," the chief said. "I will call a council meeting and table this proposal."

"Then I have no choice either," Arthur replied, leaving the table and retiring to his room.

Eleven

The wind continued to howl, sweeping dust and sand across the sky above them, intermittently concealing the Agrodien from the moonlight. The silver orb hung low in the sky, casting a deep, dark shadow into the valley of the Haigok.

Yuri peered up to the great spires, the Pillars of Mohaa. Something about them sent a shiver down his spine, from neck to tip of tail. A feeling of impending doom swept over him as he contemplated what might come of this attack upon the dragon keepers.

This is a mistake, he surmised. *We shouldn't be here.*

He continued after his Kayl'sro, creeping down the narrow path and into the valley.

Torches had been lit and posted high on poles, stationed at intervals along a path that led from the horse yard to the village. Light flickered from within the crude huts, spilling into the night through tiny cracks in curtains and shutters that covered the many windows.

Greil moved onward.

He kept low to the ground and moved swiftly towards the fenced yard.

His eyes darted about, searching for signs of life. Apart from the sound of those inside their dwellings, he couldn't find anyone within view.

The horse yard was empty, and the stable appeared dark.

With another quick glance around, believing it to be safe, he leapt over the high fence and signalled for the next in line to follow.

They left twenty warriors behind to guard the perimeter as the Kayl'sro led the rest to the large building on the far side of the yard.

Upon reaching the large doors of the stable, Greil stopped to address his advisors.

"We take all we can," he hissed. "Quickly and quietly. I want to be out of here before they realise their horses are gone."

Yuri reached for the beam that held the door shut and lifted it away silently. He placed it on the ground as Gharnef pushed the doors slowly. They opened with a squeak, stirring the beasts inside.

A few soft snorts protested at the disturbance.

"Harness them only," Greil commanded. "We won't need saddles."

The Agrodien warriors swept into the dark building, finding the harness equipment and fastening it to the steeds as quickly as they could.

Most of the steeds were compliant, but a few tossed their heads in objection. The Agrodien had to force these temperamental beasts to comply, gripping the animals' muzzles with their cold, leathery hands.

A few horses squealed, sounding an alarm that would have reached their masters in the dwellings nearby.

"We must go," Yuri called to his leader.

"Take what you can," Greil shouted. "We leave now."

The warriors jumped on top of the chargers and rode in haste, out of the stable and across the yard, each leading at least two other beasts by the reins.

Those watching along the fence line started knocking palings free, creating access for the riders to escape through.

A loud cry resounded from the village as a few of the Haigok ran from their huts towards the horse yard.

"Hurry," Yuri called to the warriors surrounding him. "They know we are here."

The Agrodien by the fence leapt upon riderless steeds being led by their comrades. Steering for the road that rose from the valley floor, the warriors increased their pace in desperation to escape.

Risking a look, Yuri peered over his shoulder and saw a few war-riors struggling as they crossed the horse yard. Their steeds were not cooperating in the slightest. They bucked and tossed their manes as the riders did their best to maintain some element of control.

The Haigok numbers were increasing as they drew nearer to the yard. More and more spilled into the night to investigate the clamour.

A few of the dragon keepers hurdled the fence and closed in on the struggling riders. Yuri understood at that precise moment; not all of them were going to escape with their lives. His feeling of dread was not just his doubts manifesting themselves. It was a premonition.

The riders at the rear of the pack fought to keep their horses on task, but it was useless. Within moments, the Haigok were on them, leaping into the air and knocking four of them from the beasts.

Dust and flesh flung into the air as Agrodien and Haigok tussled on the ground. Yuri wanted to go back to help.

Sensing his thoughts, Gharnef called over to him.

"We must go," the other shouted. "You have a family."

Yuri watched another five of his warriors fall to the dirt behind him.

"So do some of them," Yuri replied. But he knew the warriors were all but dead. He heard their cries of agony as the Haigok tore flesh from their bones.

"Not a good way to die." Gharnef frowned as they started up the narrow road.

The going had slowed significantly, as the steeds needed to move along the track in single file.

Greil raced his steed along the straight stretches of road, slowing only to turn the beast for the next section of quick running. They followed suit, but the corners still proved a problem as it took careful navigation to pull the unridden horses through.

"We must move faster," the Kayl'sro called down the rock face to the warriors below.

Yuri peered back into the valley; only a few warriors were behind him. The rest of the Agrodien were on the road ahead.

Many Haigok raced towards them across the ground between the horse yard and the path, closing the gap between them rapidly.

"A lot faster," he called back up to his commander.

Zeveera smirked when she peered down at the valley floor, seeing Yuri's predicament.

A long trumpet call sounded from the village.

Suddenly, the Haigok stopped charging.

They stood motionless, staring up to the Agrodien who were still climbing the road as fast as they could.

"Why did they stop?" Zeveera asked. "They have them. They're right there."

Greil glanced over his shoulder at the female before moving his gaze down to the valley floor. He saw the stationary Haigok standing in the open, only a few yards from the path.

"You seem displeased that our warriors aren't being torn apart," he surmised.

She sneered a little, keeping her eyes upon Yuri as she wondered why the Haigok weren't advancing.

Thunder rumbled from the far side of the valley. Her eyes flickered in the direction from where the sound had come. A deep, guttural roar followed, sounding from the northern end of the vast gorge.

Great, winged beasts burst from caverns that dotted the valley's rock walls.

The Kayl'sro's eyes widened as he counted three, four, five and rising.

"So!" he gasped. "The tales are true."

"Go," Yuri called from below. "Go now. Go!"

Greil didn't feel the need to remind the advisor of who was leader here. He saw the threat. He knew exactly what to do. He urged the steed forward with a jab into its ribs with his heels, and the beast lunged forwards and galloped towards the next turn.

The warriors behind him increased their pace, climbing the road carelessly.

One of the flying creatures called across the valley. Its roar thundered through the air, bouncing off the rock walls and filling the ears of the Agrodien escapees.

One rider turned sharply. His steed lost its footing and slipped over the edge of the path. It tumbled over the ledge, taking its rider and two unmanned horses with it.

Yuri watched the tragedy unfold before his eyes as he pulled his steed to a halt. The plummeting horses and rider continued to fall, crashing into another rider on the section of road below it, then another, and another. By the time the horses had smashed to the valley floor, the Agrodien losses had increased by another eight.

The riders stared after the fallen warriors and the steeds, lying lifeless on the ground below.

"What are you waiting for?" Yuri hollered to those ahead of him. "Move!"

The line of riders increased their pace again as the dragons drew nearer. The cries from the giant creatures rumbled through the sky with great ferocity. Yuri felt each call vibrating through his chest into his bones. His stomach tightened into a knot as he bellowed command after command to the riders in front to hurry.

Intense heat streaked over his head, causing him to wince and raise his arms to shield his face. The flare was so bright that he could do nothing but close his eyes and hope to Q'sharh that it wasn't his own flesh that he could smell burning.

High-pitched screams from Agrodien and steed resounded from above him as the riders and their chargers on an upper-level burst into flame.

"We're trapped," Gharnef called over his shoulder to Yuri. He was a few riders in front of the other, staring up at the flaming bodies of his comrades.

The ground shook as one of the flying creatures thudded against the rock face above him, burying its head into the flames to feast on its burning prey.

"Keep moving," Yuri hollered.

"It blocks our path," called a warrior.

"Charge it," the older Agrodien bellowed.

With a shout, all the riders raced their steeds up the incline, turning onto the next stretch of road and charging towards the dragon.

It appeared confused by the sudden action of the little lizards on steeds, lifting into the air with a sweep of its giant membranous wings, still holding a burning horse and its rider in its jaws.

***

Greil stared over the ledge towards the flames lapping at the rock wall of the canyon. The last of the riders were reaching the lip of the bowl and racing across the flat land, back to where the females and children awaited them.

"I counted twenty-five," Zeveera said, sitting high upon her steed to his left.

The Kayl'sro kept his eye on the dragon nearest to the wall far below. The others, at least seven, continued to circle above the valley floor.

Apart from the flames dancing upon the road, Greil saw no other movement. At least eighty of his own kind were slain in that one attack.

"I don't see Yuri," he told her.

"He was below the flames," she told him. "Surely he is being torn to pieces as we sit here. We should move on before they send their dragons after us."

He sighed and turned his steed away from the valley.

Zeveera peered one last time over the edge and smirked before following her leader into the wind-swept desert.

***

Yuri raced his steed through the fire, hoping he would see the sharp turn in time before lunging into the air.

Luckily, his horse knew the road and turned just in time.

A loud trumpet call resounded from deep in the valley.

The dragons hooted a thunderous reply, rising into the sky.

Yuri thought the worst, believing the creatures intended to block the path from above, thus trapping them on the rock face where they would surely perish.

"Keep moving," he hollered.

The team of horses galloped higher and higher, making their way through the flames and onto empty road once again.

"We will need to check these horses when we reach the top," Gharnef called. "I fear they may have received too much of a lashing from these flames."

"Forget the flames," Yuri yelled back. "Worry about those dragons."

His eyes followed the giant beasts as they cleared the rim and started towards the north, away from them and into the night sky.

"Where are they going?" a warrior behind Yuri called after them.

"To our home," the other replied. "They go to attack the Canyons of Terikith."

"Why?" the warrior asked. "We're not there anymore."

"No," Yuri answered, steering his steed around another sharp bend. "But they don't know that."

With one last dash, the fifteen remaining riders emerged on the surface of the vast expanse, back into the strong gale that tossed dust and grit through the air around them.

"Where are they?" Gharnef asked, peering about.

"Perhaps they believed we were dead," another warrior suggested.

"Perhaps," Yuri nodded. "We're on our own for now."

"They wouldn't wait," said a rider. "They will move on in the night to keep ahead of the Haigok."

"My guess is, they have continued onwards," Yuri said.

"Even with so many of us taken by fire?" a warrior asked.

"We can't go back. Our homelands will be ash before long," Yuri answered, reminding them of the dragons.

"We should move on," Gharnef put in.

"Agreed," said the other. "We continue south. With luck, we will be reunited with our families by sunrise."

Twelve

He paced back and forth along the aisle through the centre of the assembly hall. His boots thudded faintly against the stone floor with each step. The guards by the door watched curiously as he strolled to the far end of the room, turning on his heels at the base of the stairs leading up to the platform before returning.

Tugging at the plait dangling from his chin, David gave deep thought to how he was going to persuade the other council members of his intentions. It would not be easy, considering that so many of them owed their lives to the Warde family. To make it even more difficult, a few of them related by blood.

He reached the guards' position and turned again, making his way back towards the platform. His hand continued to rub at his whiskers as his eyes followed the lines between the stonework.

The sound of soft footfalls climbing the steps outside caused him to stop and turn.

He saw Richard using a staff to help him navigate the climb. Assisting him by holding his other arm by the elbow was Becka. She carefully guided him to the top step before lowering her hold, placing her hand in his instead.

"You're early," the chief said, peering into the dull morning light outside.

"Good morning, David." Richard smiled. "I was on my morning walk... *Our* morning walk when your runner found me."

The old man grinned as he looked at his wife. "She won't let me go out on my own anymore and I refuse to sit at home wasting away. So Becka has accompanied me on my early wanderings around our budding city."

"Why call such an early meeting, David?" Becka asked, eyeing the man suspiciously.

"We should wait for the others before we discuss town business," he replied.

"Come, come, David." Richard shuffled along the aisle towards the larger man, his wife keeping close to his side. "We're all friends here. I practically raised you. You can speak freely with us."

The chief scratched the back of his head. "The Agrodien are approaching and I think we need to get our defences in order for an attack. Our wall surrounds us on three sides, making us vulnerable to any advances made to the east."

"That's it?" Richard questioned, stopping a few feet from the other. His eyes moved up the giant's frame and locked onto the other's gaze. "The Agrodien?"

"You don't believe this to be an important issue?" David asked.

"I don't believe that *you* believe it to be an important issue," Richard answered. "Why did you really call this emergency meeting, David? No more horseshit."

The chief lowered his brows. He didn't expect to be caught off guard so easily.

His heart raced, and his throat seemed to tighten. His eyes flickered from Richard to Becka and back again. Both awaited a response.

"She's a threat, Richard," he finally said. "She needs to go."

"Why?"

"She can control beasts," Chief Gyfford explained. "I always knew she could. But now she has exercised this power on a rukyul. I've seen what those animals can do. If she can harness this ability to manipulate a whole pack of them, she will soak this city in blood. I can't risk that, Richard."

"Ability?" Richard spat. "We have seven women with abilities more powerful than anything that I have ever seen. And you fear one little girl."

"I've seen what she can do without even trying," the other argued. "She hasn't even reached maturity yet, and she exhibits such power."

"But you're not even willing to give her a chance?" Becka asked, gazing at him in disbelief.

"The people fear her," David told them. "They have said as much to their representatives on this council."

"They are newcomers to Woodmyst," Richard said. "They are yet to understand this place and its people. We come from here, David. She comes from here. She is one of us. She belongs here."

David shook his head, turning away from the two standing before him.

"I can't risk the people of this city," he maintained. "If she turns, has a bad day, gets into a foul mood, she could hurt people. I will put the petition to the council to have Alice Warde exiled from the city limits."

"You would throw a little girl out to fend for herself just as winter approaches?" Becka fumed. "You are a pig, David Gyfford."

The chief stopped walking and frowned as tears rolled over his cheeks.

His mind filled with an image of his two wives standing upon the old eastern bridge, resting their elbows on the guardrail as they watched smaller versions of Alice and Arthur playing in the snow by the river bank. The sound of racing hooves filled his memory as he fought his way back to reality again.

"I've made my mind up," he said, wiping his eyes with his large hands.

"Go," Richard instructed his wife.

Becka turned and hurried back along the aisle and back out of the assembly hall in haste.

"Where is she going?" the chief asked, following her with his eyes.

"Where do you think?" the elder put in, moving past the larger man to begin the climb to the platform.

"You think warning Alice about this decision will accomplish any-thing?"

Richard took each step one at a time, carefully leaning heavily on his staff.

"Word travels quickly through our community, David," the old man said. "She goes to inform the family. From there, she will send word to the Seven. It will be only a matter of time before the whole of Woodmyst is aware of what you wish to do regarding a little girl."

"It won't change anything," the chief replied, following Richard up the steps to the platform. "The city will continue to grow and the council will continue to meet."

"Perhaps." Richard waggled his head a little, considering the other's words. "Perhaps not."

"What would you have me do?"

"Let her stay." The elder turned and faced the chief. They stood atop of the platform, facing one another near the tables set up for the council meeting.

David held his ground. "I cannot."

"Then make sure she has provisions to get through winter," Richard commanded.

"I had no intention of abandoning her," Chief Gyfford replied, moving around the tables to his seat. "She will receive all the supplies she needs."

"And if her family leaves with her?" Richard sat down in his seat. "Or anyone else who may wish to follow her? What of them?"

"Then we'll divide the stores," David answered. "I won't let people go hungry. I won't let them freeze to death. She is still one of us. I just can't have her here."

"And so…" The elder leant on the table, his attention fixed upon the other. "Where do you expect her to go?"

"She has a cabin," David replied. "It's sturdy and well-constructed. She will be fine."

Richard shook his head.

"What happened to you, David?" he asked. "You've changed."

David pictured the snow-covered bridge again. He lowered his gaze to the table and frowned. "I know," he whispered.

***

Joanne closed a small wooden chest and slid it back under her bed before racing for the door as quickly as she could. The sound of thudding from the other side had woken everyone in the household, all except for her.

Antony stirred from his sleep. He would soon demand her attention for the rest of the day until he placed his head back on his pillow that night.

She opened the door and faced Becka, red-faced and puffing heavily.

"Becka!" Joanne gasped. She stepped back to allow the other woman into the house. "Are you all right? Can I get you some water?"

"I'm fine," Becka wheezed as she entered the warmth of the sitting room. "I have terrible news."

"Who was it at the door?" Emily asked, entering from a door to the side of the room, wrapping a gown around herself. Her eyes landed upon the visitor. "Becka? By the gods. Are you hurt? What's wrong?"

She moved across the room in haste and placed her hands on the other's arm.

"You should sit down." Joanne took Becka by the other elbow and guided her to her own seat.

"What's going on?" Catherine asked, wiping her eyes with the back of her hand.

"It's Becka," Joanne replied.

"Becka?" The girl was suddenly wide-eyed.

"Bloody heck," said a deep voice from behind the girl.

"Put some clothes on," Catherine said over her shoulder.

"Some warning would be nice," Takmel offered.

"I'm sorry for intruding," Becka told them. "But I have some terrible news. Is Alice here?"

"She left early this morning," Joanne informed them.

"Do you know where she went?" the woman asked.

"No idea," the other replied.

"I barely see that girl anymore." Emily shook her head. "What is this all about, Becka?"

"David has called an emergency meeting," she answered. "He intends to exile Alice."

The room fell silent.

Soft crackles emitted from the fireplace as each of them waited for another to speak first.

"What's all this?" Lucy asked, carrying her daughter on her hip.

"I put my pants on," Takmel announced, entering the room. He peered around the room, looking around to each of the women quizzically. "What happened?"

"Chief Gyfford wants to exile Alice," Catherine explained.

"On what grounds?" Emily asked the woman seated in the chair.

"He claims she poses a threat to the people of Woodmyst," Becka replied. "He said something stupid about her possessing the ability to control animals. Did any of you know about this?"

"She told me about a rukyul she encountered yesterday," Emily answered. "But I wasn't sure if she even had any powers. I hoped she would be more like her father."

"I think she is, by nature," Becka told her. "But she is your daughter, too. Your blood runs through her veins as much as Tomas'."

Emily lowered herself into another seat.

"What do we do?"

"We pack," Joanne told her sister. "We find somewhere else to take our family."

"We can't just move." Emily shook her head. "We have a life here. This is our home."

"Mama?" Catherine lowered herself to the floor by Emily's chair. "We can make a new home."

The girl laid her head on her mother's lap. Emily ran her fingers through Catherine's deep auburn hair and wept.

"Your father is here," she said.

"His remains are here," Lucy said, moving into the room. "But he will always be with us."

Emily wiped her tears on her sleeve as she continued to stroke her daughter's hair. She looked over to Takmel, who was watching the interaction between mother and daughter with interest.

"I never had the type of relationship with my mother that you have with your daughters," he said, sensing her thoughts. "I wish I did, but that wasn't to be. And as much as I mean to have a life with Catherine, I could never ask her to be apart from you. You should all go together."

"Thank you, Takmel." Emily smiled. "I know you two love one another."

"We can hear it through the walls." Joanne giggled.

"Nevertheless," the older sister said, laughing, "I don't want to be apart from either of my daughters. Not yet.

"Tomas took you in before he passed. That makes you as much a part of my family as anyone else in this room. You will come with us."

"Whether you like it or not." Lucy smacked him on his bare shoulder, moving past him to claim another chair for herself.

"I'm so sorry to bring this news to you," Becka said.

"It's not your fault," Joanne told her. "It's David's."

Emily shook her head. "He's suffered a significant loss. People never think rationally when they go through something like he has."

"It was a long time ago." Catherine looked up at her.

"To you," Emily agreed. "Yes. But not for him. He loved his wives more than life itself, Catherine. That's something that both you and Takmel are only beginning to understand."

The girl nodded, looking over her shoulder at the boy standing near the doorway to the bedrooms.

"We'll need tents and wagons to load our belongings," Joanne suggested.

"I'll talk to the Erilians." Emily rose to her feet. "There's so much we need to prepare. But I think some breakfast and a mug of hot tea is the best way to begin."

***

Alice steered her stallion through a thicket, making her way towards a clearing as she followed the foot of a round hill. She was slowly making her way to the higher country that rested upon Woodmyst's borders, exploring ground she rarely ventured upon as she gradually made her way to the caverns.

Most of the trees were bare now, losing their dry foliage to the surface below. The stallion's hooves crunched the red and yellow litter as he plodded forwards, twitching his ears around to tune into the calls of birds fluttering about the bare branches.

Alice moved her eyes about, sniffing the air periodically. Something didn't seem right to her as she pulled her cloak about her, readjusting the straps on her shoulders.

She checked her bow, tethered to her saddle, just behind her on the left. Her quiver, loaded and stuffed full of arrows, strapped to her right, within easy reach if needed.

As she entered the clearing, she smelled the distinct aroma of smoke.

Someone had a camp set up nearby.

Someone was cooking meat.

Someone was near her cottage.

Edging her steed on, Alice made her way through the clearing and back into the woods, redirecting the stallion towards the caverns.

The steed sensed her mood; realising they were now on the hunt, he softened his hoof falls in an attempt to lessen the sound of their approach.

Ducking beneath branches and guiding her horse, Alice reached for her bow. With a quick tug with her thumb and finger, the cord holding the weapon in place came loose.

Releasing the reins and allowing the stallion to have control, she took an arrow from the quiver and set the notch onto the string.

They were close, approaching the caverns from the north.

She had the high ground, an advantage from a tactical point of view.

But she didn't know how many they were. They could number one or one hundred for all she knew.

She crossed a small stream that would eventually snake its way down the hillside and pass near to her cabin in the cave. The trees parted ahead of her, allowing a view of the open ground surrounding the caverns.

A small campfire had been lit near to the structure. Surrounding the hearth were twelve or so men and a few more women, seated upon logs and stones the intruders had moved into place. She saw no children, but assumed these people were vagrants, homeless by the way they dressed. Dirty rags would look better than the attire they wore. Their hair appeared unkempt and their skin stained with grit and dirt.

A deer, skinned and set upon a spit, hung above the flames. One man sliced at the meat with a long dagger, handing some to a woman nearby. Another pushed him aside, a larger man who cut deeper into the flesh of the roasting beast.

Alice smelled the blood dripping from the fresh slice. The kill was fresh.

A low growl to her side made her head turn.

The rukyul was still here, watching the people below, hiding beneath a cluster of shrubs.

Its eyes turned to meet hers momentarily before returning to the gathering below.

She followed its gaze to her cabin.

They'd broken the door.

Her mood changed from curiosity to anger.

She needed to inform them of whose land this was and that vagrants were not welcome.

With a slight dig with her heels into the stallion's sides, she edged forward, raising her bow and taking careful aim.

She pulled the tightly upon the string and released the arrow.

It whistled loudly as it shot through the air, zipping between two of the men seated by the fire and into a support pole for the makeshift spit.

The deer fell into the flames, landing on kindling and ash, surprising all near to it.

The men pulled rusted swords and axes to the ready as they turned to face the newcomer.

"You're on my land," Alice called from atop of her steed as she rode into the clearing. "You broke my door."

She leapt from her steed, letting her bow fall to the ground as she pulled her two swords from their sheaths and over her shoulders.

"I demand payment for the damages."

Thirteen

"What is this?" laughed the largest of the vagrants, pointing to the little girl with his broad axe. "Something new for me to play with?"

"Leave her be, Zael," another chided. "She's just a child."

"You shut it," the first barked. He glared at Alice with hungry eyes, parting his lips in a crooked smile filled with yellow teeth. "She looks old enough to me."

Alice moved her eyes over each of the men, measuring them by observation as they formed a line on either side of their leader.

"What do you say, little one?" the big one called to her. "Are you ready for a taste of Zael?"

"Why don't you come over here and see for yourself?" Alice teased.

Some men standing near the large man laughed as four of the others stepped away, returning to the fire.

"What?" Zael questioned them. "Afraid of a girl?"

"I'm not fighting children," replied one.

"Me either," said another.

"Cowards," the leader spat, returning his eyes to the girl standing on the ground before him. "I'm going to strip you bare and force myself onto you."

"Of course, you are," she smirked.

"When I'm done with you," he said, pointing his axe to the men beside him, "I'm going to let my men take turns with you. If you survive that, I'll split you in two with my axe just for disturbing my breakfast."

"You're all talk and no action," Alice goaded him. "You're boring me with your words. Pay up or die."

Zael's eye twitched. His face turned red with anger as he gripped the handle of his axe tightly, causing his knuckles to whiten.

"There will be no payment, bitch," he hissed.

He raced forward, raising his axe above his head.

She moved swiftly, sprinting into his attack and ducking beneath his swing.

The strikes were quick, sweeping across his belly and neck.

His axe cut deep into the soil as he stumbled forward.

Alice stood to her full height as she faced the line of men between her and the hearth.

Behind her, Zael staggered to the right, his intestines spilling onto the ground and dragging along behind him.

"Who's next?" she asked as the large man crashed to the surface in a twitching heap.

The remaining seven men standing in the line looked to one another in disbelief.

Suddenly, three of them lunged towards her, raising their rusty swords in anger.

The other four didn't wait to see what was about to transpire. Instead, they raced for the tree-line on the northern boundary of the clearing and disappeared from view.

Alice blocked each blow made by the three vagrants. Her blades flashed brightly in the morning light as she twisted and turned them around her body.

The four men by the fire stood with the women, watching the girl in awe as she played with her prey like a cat would with mice.

They stepped forward to view the battle as the fight moved away from the campsite.

A low growl from the undergrowth nearby warned them to stay where they were. The rukyul kept low to the ground as his eyes moved over the gathered women and men by the fire.

"Oh shit," one man gasped as the beast moved between them and the scuffle on the open ground.

Alice parried and blocked blow after blow. The blades clashed loudly, sending piercing ringing of steel upon steel into the air.

As one man attacked from the front, another tried for her back. Her blades held them at bay. Her legs, swinging in wide arching kicks or jabbing sharply to the side, caught the third attacker off guard.

Slowly, the men tired.

Their blades became heavy and their breath short.

The more they grew weary, the more they realised that this little girl was in absolute control.

They were about to lose, and there was nothing they could do about it.

Alice continued to block their blows as they became desperate to finish the skirmish. She knew the three men wouldn't last much longer unless she showed them mercy.

But she couldn't risk letting them survive.

These men wanted to rape and kill her.

Why should I allow them to breathe?

She lunged her left sword into one man's neck and twisted the blade, opening a wide wound beneath his chin.

In one rapid move, she retrieved her blade and turned, jabbing both blades into the stomach of the man directly behind her. She ducked just as the third man swung his sword, intending to strike her across the back. Instead, his rusty blade dug into his comrade's chest and stuck there.

Alice used the moment to retract one of her swords from her second victim, thrusting it deep into the third man's gut. She angled the blade upwards, directing it to the organs beneath his ribs.

At that moment, the first of the three hit the dirt, landing clumsily on his face.

The second stumbled backwards, carrying his friend's sword in his breast. His eyes moved from the girl before him to the third man, confused and befuddled.

The third stood motionless as Alice lifted herself upright. She pulled her swords free of the two men and wiped them clean by sliding the blades across their raggedy clothing.

Both dropped to the ground as she sheathed her blades over her back.

"Anyone else?" she asked, turning to face the four men and the women being kept in place by the rukyul.

Their fear-filled eyes flickered from beast to girl, not knowing which one to be afraid of more.

"W-w-we have no quarrel with you," a man eventually blurted. "We'll repair the damages and be on our way."

"Your name?" Alice asked, approaching them assertively.

"Glaun." He lowered his head. His eyes kept moving to the rukyul. The beast snarled at the man.

"Don't look at him directly," she warned him. "I don't think he likes it when you do that."

Alice ran a hand along the beast's flanks as she moved from its tail towards its head. It looked over at her quickly, tilting its head to allow her to rub behind its tiny ear.

The fur was thick and coarse. Beneath it, she felt the solid frame shielded by thick hide and muscles. Alice had touched nothing so powerful before. Not even her stallion, standing on the grass a few yards away.

"Please don't make it eat us," one woman bawled.

The girl moved her eyes to the other, keeping her face neutral.

She was young. They all were.

Not one of them looked older than her aunt.

There was no way they would survive the winter the way they dressed.

"Repair my door and anything else you have broken," Alice told her. "Replace all of my property that you have taken and used, then I might consider feeding him something other than weeping women for a change."

"We'll do anything you say," Glaun offered. He dropped to his knees. "Anything."

"All right." Alice frowned, rubbing the rukyul's snout. It offered a pleasant grunt. "First thing. Pull that doe out of the fire and reset the spit. No fun in wasting good meat."

Fourteen

Arthur rode beside another, an older man upon a dark steed. They entered the clearing from the east and pulled to a halt when they viewed the strangers near the caverns.

The four men were busy stacking wood at the far end of the clearing. Several women, Arthur counted at least fifteen, gathered near the cabin.

Standing by the dwelling, tethered to a support beam, stood Alice's stallion.

The two riders couldn't help but fear the worst.

The man suddenly pulled his sword from his sheath and shot forward on his horse, leaving the boy behind in a flurry of dry leaves.

"Where is my niece?" the man called. "What have you done with her? I'll have all of your heads if you have harmed her."

The rukyul bounded from the porch where it had been resting, snarling as it raced to intercept the approaching rider.

"I'll have you too, you foul demon," the man hollered, steering the dark steed for the creature.

A sharp whistle broke the air.

The rukyul skidded to a halt and turned to the source of the sound.

Alice stood on the porch of the cabin with a steaming mug in her hand.

"I'm fine, Uncle Lor," she called.

He pulled his horse up and stared at her, confused.

"What is all this?" he asked. "Who are these people? What are those men doing over there? What the hell is that thing?"

"I've made tea," she said to her uncle, waving for Arthur to approach. "Come and sit with me."

The rukyul climbed back upon the porch; the boards creaking under his weight as he lowered himself, curling up comfortably by Alice's chair.

Lor approached warily, keeping a watchful eye on the beast. It did the same, not even blinking as the newcomer alighted from his steed.

Arthur trotted up, clumsily trying his best to stay upright before pulling to beside Lor's horse. He dropped to the ground and tethered his charger beside the others.

The girl moved towards him, wrapping her arms around his shoulders.

Alarmed by the action, the rukyul raised his box-shaped head to observe the exchange. After a moment, he lowered his chin, offering a disapproving grunt as he moved his eyes to the men at the far end of the clearing.

"And what do you call this one?" Lor asked, approaching the creature with an outstretched hand. It growled a warning, causing the man to recoil a little.

"I wouldn't do that, Uncle," Alice told him. "He's not tame by any standard."

"Then how is it he is here?"

"He has submitted to me," she replied, resuming her seat on the bench that ran along the veranda.

"A new pet?"

"No." She shook her head as he sat beside her, examining the dark beast carefully. It was sleek and muscular. He had never seen such a creature before, but he had heard of them from those who had journeyed with Tomas to Blackrock Haven.

"Strange that he would have travelled so far to the south," Arthur commented as he sat on the edge of the porch, resting his back against a support beam.

"How do you know it's a he?" Lor asked.

"He has the largest set of balls I've seen on any creature," Alice pointed to the rukyul's nether region. "These people came from a settlement on the range to the north. One of the men, Glaun, told me the game is disappearing and crops aren't taking to the soil like they once did."

"So, they came here?" Lor questioned.

"Zael brought them here," she replied.

"Who is this Zael?"

"One of the men they build the pyre for." She pointed to four bodies lying face up on the grass near to the stacked timber that the others were piling.

"Alice?" Arthur blurted, alarming the rukyul enough for it to raise its head again. "What happened?"

"Zael thought he could rape me," she answered. "I showed him he was sadly mistaken. His three friends tried to take me down after his demise, but I was too good for them."

"And these people?" Lor asked as a woman handed hot mugs of tea to him and Arthur.

"Zael broke my door and intended to steal my belongings," Alice answered. "These women are returning it all and are tidying up after themselves. The men over there are going to burn the dead."

"And then what?" her uncle pressed. "What will they do after that?"

"Look at them," she said. "They're hungry and covered in rags. I can't send them away. Perhaps Woodmyst can take them in. If not, there are many caverns here. They won't survive the winter in the open, Uncle."

Lor turned to look at the women about him.

They were young and emaciated. Their hair was scruffy and their clothing soiled and worn by weather and time.

He understood why his niece had compassion for them; it was easy to see that they were a people in desperate need. But he didn't know them, and therefore wasn't sure whether they could be trusted.

"I'm not sure about this," he said. "Your family is on their way here. I don't know how they will take this."

"What business is it of theirs?" Alice asked.

"They are coming here to live with you," Arthur informed her. "They are bringing tents and timber and all of your belongings and theirs."

"What do you mean, *coming here to live?*"

"I'm sorry, little one," Lor said, placing his arm around her. "The council has moved for you to be exiled."

"Exiled?" she furrowed her brow. "Why? What did I do?"

"A great number of the new people are afraid of you," Arthur replied. "My father is one of them."

"David?" she stood suddenly to her feet. The rukyul lifted his head again, looking to her quizzically. "I don't understand."

"He hasn't been himself since Martha and Isabel—" Lor stopped himself. "I know you know that. But he has given his ear to the new-comers and they are afraid of all things that they perceive as unnatural. They are afraid and so is he."

"So," she peered across the clearing to the men, lifting the bodies onto the pyre. "I can't return home?"

"This is your home now." Arthur stood and moved to her side, taking her hand in his.

"What about you?" she asked. "Will I be able to see you again?"

"This is my home now," he answered.

The kindling was lit, and the flames took to the pyre quickly.

"I'm so sorry, Arthur," she eventually told him.

"I'm not," he said, and smiled.

Thick smoke lifted from the clearing, far into the bright morning sky, as the bodies of four intruders burnt.

***

Alice was strapping her bedroll to the saddle as the first of the wagons appeared at the eastern edge of the long clearing. Her stallion tensed, shifting its weight as she used a stirrup to lift herself over his back to lace the cord through a metal ring attached to the back of her seat.

Grabbing the horn, positioned on top of the pommel, she leapt down to the ground to grab her bow and quiver. Her eyes moved to the approaching cart, drawn by two steeds and driven by Simon Bell. His wife Tricia and their son Thedric seated beside him. They gave a friendly wave as

Alice moved around her horse with the weapons in her hands.

She slung the quiver over her shoulder and waved back as the rukyul stepped off the porch to investigate the new arrivals. Simon pulled the cart to a halt immediately, recognising the type of creature.

"Alice," he hollered. "Call your pet, please."

She looked towards the wagon and saw the terrified looks on the passengers' faces. She snapped her head around to glare at the beast. It was moving low to the ground, slowly, as if stalking.

"No," she said to it calmly.

It peered over to her and reluctantly complied, lowering itself onto the grass, emitting a deep huff of displeasure.

Alice strode over to it and gave it a loving rub behind the ear, to which it grunted happily.

"Why are you preparing to leave?" Lor asked her, stepping out of the cabin. He moved his gaze to the far end of the clearing to where the vagrant women had gone, joining the four men who stood by the burning pyre. "You have people arriving and others here who should be leaving."

"They are not going anywhere," Alice told him. "This is *my* land and I'll decide who should stay and who should go."

"We just arrived and your family is coming," he stepped off the porch and approached her. "You can't go now. We need you. We came here for you."

"I've waited too long already," she replied. "Glaun told me that the four who ran off are loyal to Zael. They may return or they may find others who are just as desperate as they are. I need to track them while the trail is fresh."

"And what then? What will you do when you find them?"

"Kill them," she said blandly as she tethered the bow to her saddle.

"At least wait until we get everyone settled," Lor pleaded. "We can form a party to go with you."

"I hunt better on my own, Uncle," she said, smiling. "Besides, you have a wife and a son."

"I wasn't suggesting myself," he corrected her. "There are others coming. Younger men."

She put her hand on his shoulder. "If I wanted to take younger men, I would take Arthur to keep me warm. But he's staying here, too. Has he set himself up yet?"

"He was placing linen on the bed a moment ago," Lor replied. "I think he's under the impression that you will share the bed with him."

"I would if I were staying." She lifted herself over the stallion, reaching across from the left side to strap the quiver to its position high on the right of the saddle.

The wagon creaked as Simon drove up to the cabin.

"One of those things killed your father's horse, as I recall," he said, jumping down from the cart.

"It wasn't this one," Alice told him as he made his way around the fully laden vehicle to help Tricia down from her seat. He then lifted Thedric in his arms and placed him on the ground beside his mother.

Tricia wrapped her arms around the girl.

"Hello, Alice," she whispered. "I guess you've heard the sad news."

"I have," Alice replied. "And I'm grateful for what you are all doing for me."

"Why don't you take those off for once in your life?" Simon blurted, pointing to the swords strapped to her back.

"I'm about to take my leave," she answered.

"What?" He looked at Lor questioningly before returning his eyes to the girl. "Now?"

"Men have escaped and I need to track them down." She lifted herself into her saddle.

"And what of them?" Simon pointed to the visitors at the far end of the clearing. "Who are they?"

"They're my guests," she told them. "And you will please treat them as such."

"You be careful," Arthur said, standing by the door. "Come back in one piece."

"I love you too, bookworm." She smiled before steering the charger away. She started off across the clearing, heading to the north. Turning her head, she called over her shoulder to the rukyul. "Come."

It jumped to its feet and raced after her, leaving the seven standing by the cabin to stare after the huntress as she disappeared into the forest.

***

"How many?" David asked, leaning back in his chair at the council table.

"Numbers are sketchy," the guard answered. "We know that the Warde family, including Lor Verney, Simon Bell and their wives, have gone. They were first to set off taking five wagons and ten horses. Others followed shortly after, Oliver Weston, the crew of the *Adelandria*. All gone."

"My father?" Henry Cunningham peered across the table to the soldier.

"He went with them, yes."

Henry lowered his eyes, shaking his head sadly.

"What of the Seven?" Chief Gyfford asked.

"They have followed their prime," the guard offered.

"And their families too, I suppose," David grumbled as he stared at the table before him. His eyes darted to the messenger. "My son? Did Arthur go with them?"

"He was riding with Lor Verney on horseback last we saw. I would have told you sooner, but it isn't unusual to see him coming and going."

"You're not to blame." David held his hand up to the young man.

"She has beguiled him," Seamus Harling put in.

"No." Chief Gyfford shook his head. "He's in love."

"What about horses and wagons?" Harling asked the guard. "What are our losses?"

"We've lost around sixty horses from the stable house and twenty wagons, my lord."

"We should send men to retrieve them," Henry Cunningham suggested.

"The horses are their own," David told him before turning his attention to the guard.

"Were they not?"

"They were, my lord," he replied.

"Then they are entitled to take their own property as they wish," Chief Gyfford told the other men seated nearby.

The guard continued with his report.

"They took supplies of grain, seed, some livestock, tents, building supplies…"

"Thank you." David signalled for the soldier to stop. "That will be all."

"My Lord." The guard turned and retreated along the aisle between the seats of the assembly hall.

"That will be all?" Henry questioned. "They've obviously taken from our supplies."

"I practically gave them permission to do so," David replied.

"Winter is on the way," the other argued. "We could very well need those articles for our own survival."

"And what about them?" the large man asked. "The same snow will land upon the ground where they shelter. I won't have one of them starve or freeze to death over a few sheep or tents that they may have taken with them.

"They are still our people. They are *my* people. My son is amongst them. Your father is amongst them. Sending an armed force after them will only drive them further from us.

"I know the men who have gone with them to be furious warriors. I've seen their capabilities during battle with my own eyes. We do not need to make enemies of these people.

"Besides," David continued, "we have more than enough in our stores to last out the winter. And, there is more being added each day."

"This is all because you banished that girl," Harling mumbled.

"You wanted that." David pointed to the other. "So did you. You told me your people feared her."

"You fear her too," Chief Harling added. "I've seen it in your eyes. You embrace her with a smile, but I see it, David."

"Aye," he nodded. "She's dangerous. That I can state with all certainty. I love her like a daughter and fear her all the same. The decision to exile her stands."

"But it has split this council," Cunningham observed. "It may yet cause further divisions in the community."

"I suspect it will. There are many still loyal to Tomas, even after all this time. She is his daughter, after all."

"Are you having second thoughts, David?" Harling asked.

The sound of hooves thundering onto the tiny bridge filled his head. The memory of crunching timber and groaning iron as the crossing broke caused his stomach to tighten. The distant screams of his two beautiful wives echoing through his mind brought tears to his eyes. The image of the little girl standing upon the snow, her face towards the disaster, fixated, focused.

His anger returned.

"No." He shook his head. "The decision stands."

***

"Still no sign of them," Gharnef said, scanning the horizon to the south and west. "We've reached the borderlands and have not even seen a track or an overturned stone."

Yuri peered towards the mountains to the east. Tall, brown, dry grass stretched in all directions. With a party the size of the Agrodien group, they surely would have noticed a trail, but there was nothing to signal where Greil had taken the others.

"We know he intends to make for the old lands of our people," Yuri told the others. "We make for the foothills of the mountains and follow them south. Eventually, we should come upon their trail."

"Or get there before them," one rider offered.

"We need to find them first, Yuri." Gharnef sounded desperate. "I don't trust Zeveera. She despises you and me. What she could do to our wives and children worries me."

Yuri nodded.

"It worries me too, old friend," he replied. "This whole expedition worries me."

Fifteen

"We should move into the forest," an Agrodien warrior suggested, looking at the trees that covered the mountainsides nearby.

Kayl'sro Greil peered across the plain to the west. His eyes scanned the horizon, occasionally searching the sky for any sign of life.

They had ridden hard, doubling the load upon horseback to carry all the females and offspring as far and fast as they could before the horses tired. They reached the foothills before the horses slowed substantially. From there, they led the beasts by the reins and walked through the grasslands as the sun climbed higher into the morning sky.

Occasionally, Greil pushed the horses further and harder, mounting them on and off to increase the distance between themselves and the Haigok. The threat of the dragons attacking was constantly on his mind.

He needed to get his people off the open ground and under the cover of the woodlands he could see in the distance.

"We ride again," he shouted. "We don't stop until we reach the trees."

The Agrodien adults leapt upon the chargers, reaching for the younglings with outstretched arms.

A low cry from far above caused one warrior to turn his head. He peered up to the sun, squinting against the bright orb that hung high in the midday sky.

There, barely visible, was a dark shadow.

The dragons had found them.

"Your mother had best keep up, little one," Zeveera hissed to a small youngling clutching to an adult female's back. "Or else you may be food for the demon in the air."

With that, she rode off in haste, chasing Greil across the plain.

"Mama?" the little one cried. "Will the dragon catch us?"

"Don't listen to her, Donhran," the adult told her. "Zeveera is a wicked, spiteful one. Her words are always nasty. I will let nothing harm you."

"Did the dragon catch Papa?"

The female couldn't find the words to respond. "I don't know," she managed.

"Of course not," another interjected, speaking to the youngling as she reached over from her steed to touch the other adult female on the shoulder. "Your father and my Gharnef are brave warriors. I believe they are on their way to us right now."

"Thank you, Evalad." The first female frowned.

"Don't give up on our husbands yet, Galonia," she answered, stroking the head of an infant strapped to her breast. "They've always found their way out of the worst of situations."

Galonia stared after the other Agrodien, following their Kayl'sro to the east.

A great guttural cry from the sky caused her stomach to tighten.

"This one feels different," she said. "This one feels bad."

"Mother," a young male called from another horse. Clinging to his back were two more infants, a small female positioned between the rider and one slightly larger male. "We must flee."

Galonia nodded.

"Hold on to Koryn tightly, Unonia," Evalad called. "I don't want you falling off again."

"I'm holding on," the little one hollered.

They started across the grassland as fast as they could, picking up speed as the horses increased their pace from canter to gallop.

A thunderous cry from above them shook the ground as the sky seemed to open up, sounding like thick fabric tearing open as the creature swooped by them and over the retreating Agrodien.

Risking a look, Galonia saw a rider on the back of the great winged beast as it tore back into the air, turning to the left as it climbed higher and higher.

It trumpeted another loud call that echoed through the blue expanse above them.

"Faster, younglings," she called to the riders beside her as another beast answered the call of the first.

It streaked across the sky from the north, briefly casting a shadow that covered the Agrodien upon the ground.

Galonia looked to the left, where her friend was using one hand to keep the reins and the other on her tiny son strapped to her chest, shrieking.

"Both hands on the leads, Evalad," she called. "Your son is not going anywhere."

The other complied, moving her leathery hand away from the infant and to the reins.

Behind her, Galonia observed, a dragon swung around in a high arc and started back towards them from the north-west. It made its way towards the surface, opening its mouth as it approached.

"Hurry," she screamed. "Hurry!"

The beast shot a jet of flame from its throat, setting the grass ablaze.

She felt the heat, even from this distance, as the creature drew nearer and nearer, spewing fire onto the ground behind them.

She knew, no matter how fast the horses could go, there was no way they were going to outrun the speed of a flying dragon.

The flames grew larger and larger; the heat intensified.

At any moment, she and her family would be no more.

Suddenly, the dragon swooped back into the sky and moved away to the north.

"It's getting ready for another attack," Koryn called from his steed.

"No," the other male youngling seated on the back of his charger corrected, pointing into the air before them. "The other dragon attacks from the south. Look."

Sure enough, the other creature dived towards the lead riders, a streaming flame engulfing the ground, barely missing the Kayl'sro and Zeveera.

The Agrodien riders swerved to the right, moving around the flames and continuing towards the woodlands.

Hooves thundered against the dry grassland as they fled for their lives.

The tree-line was growing larger in their view and seemed within reach. But the dragons were quick and were already turning around to make another attack run.

The dragons approached from their flanks, setting the ground on fire, funnelling the Agrodien.

Herding them like livestock.

The grassland behind the riders quickly turned into an uncontrollable blaze as the winds sweeping down from the mountains fuelled the flames. There was nowhere else to run but towards the forest.

Kayl'sro Greil was the first to enter the woods, steering his steed deep into the cover and slightly towards the south.

"We should make for higher ground," Zeveera called after him. "The wind pushes the flames away from us and back into the plains."

He kicked hard, causing his horse to lunge forwards, climbing into the highlands hidden beneath the trees.

The beasts in the sky turned for another approach.

As the last of the Agrodien riders entered the cover of the woods, the dragons closed their escape with a blanket of fire.

"We have made it!" Zeveera grinned. "We have escaped."

"Then why do I feel we are still the prey?" Greil grumbled as he urged his steed to continue to climb further into the rising lands.

**

Alice sat high in her saddle, peering across the mountaintops and into the north. The wind was chill, and she had resorted to wrapping her cloak around her tightly.

Far away, she saw the thin line of smoke rising from behind a distant peak. It was too far and too large to be a campsite for the four runaways she sought. It was also something that didn't particularly interest her.

But she thought it odd and there was something unsettling about it.

She lowered herself to the ground and crouched beside the stallion, inspecting the fallen leaves and freshly upturned soil. The rukyul sniffed the ground near her, grunting as it picked up the scent of men.

The trail was at least an hour old. She didn't expect the four escapees to move so quickly. They had scaled the peak of the highlands nearest to her clearing and had followed the ridgeline of the range back towards the north.

Her suspicions told her they were heading for familiar territory, possibly to recruit more men for a return visit to her home. She knew those she loved, now moving into the glade near the caverns, could handle themselves. But she was not about to risk their lives, particularly the children.

Jogging ahead of her, keeping his nose to the ground, the rukyul followed the trail a short distance before turning back to face her. He kept turning his head back and forth impatiently, looking at her and then back to direction of the man's scent.

"All right," she told him, climbing back onto the stallion. "Give me a moment."

The sleek creature kept its nose close to the ground as it wound its way around trees and clusters of shrubs, all the while leading Alice farther along the range. Here and there, the girl saw clear signs of the four men, where they had slipped on soft ground or scraped against the bark of a tree. A few places bore the recent imprint of boots.

Keeping to the high ground might have appeared to be a wise choice for the men, allowing them to hurry on the relatively level surface of the smooth crests that were reminiscent of rolling hills.

But Alice knew better.

Not too far ahead, the mountains broke into craggy peaks that jutted out of the ground like crooked teeth. The only way to navigate the land would be to move further east, well into the middle of the range where the land was easier to move upon, but filled with countless climbs and descents that would drain their energy. Otherwise, they would need to move to the west and try for the foothills that ran along the edge of the mountains.

She couldn't imagine they would try for the rocky peaks ahead. Not when she considered their physical state.

They were hungry and tired. The ease at which she defeated her attackers in the clearing had told her that.

Then again, she had believed they would have been within striking distance by now.

Perhaps they might try for the harder route.

The rukyul kept ahead of her, pausing momentarily to make sure she was following. Alice observed his demeanour as he took her farther along the trail.

Alice perceived contentment from the beast. She imagined he appreciated the new purpose she had given him. Possibly, he felt he belonged with her. She sensed that his understanding was that she, her stallion and he together were a pack.

Perhaps they were.

Compared with the other people she had met, she felt more like this rukyul than any of them.

A hunter.

Wild.

Untamed.

An animal.

She couldn't understand why the creature was alone, an animal that her elders had told her travelled in large numbers. But here he was. Alone.

What Alice recognised was that he submitted to her, recognising her as the leader. He needed to belong, and he chose to belong to her.

She didn't comprehend the ways of her own people in the same manner that she understood the wild. Out here, under the sky and amongst the trees, this was home.

The rukyul stopped ahead of her and waited for her to pull up alongside.

"What is it?"

It slowly started away from the ridge, moving down a slight slope leading to the left.

She followed cautiously as it sniffed the ground again, finding the trail a few feet from the crest.

The men were heading for the lowlands.

Sixteen

They spaced the wagons into neat rows, stretching from the cabin to the northern edge of the glade. Simon busied himself with pitching temporary barriers made of canvas, assuring some level of privacy, as the plan was to convert the vehicles into temporary living quarters.

As cargo was unloaded and camp established, Emily and three of the Erilian women approached the strangers, keeping to themselves at the western edge of the clearing. They were standing around what remained of the pyre, allowing the remains of ash and embers to settle and slowly die. One of them, a small man, saw the women approaching and signalled the others to turn away from the hearth.

"My name is Emily," the auburn woman announced. "These are Rhydra, Sharek and Akasati. I am the mother of the young lady you met earlier today. I am sorry for your loss and hope you don't hold any resentment towards my daughter."

Emily looked briefly to the dying flames before moving her eyes over each of their faces.

"No resentment." The man shook his head. "My name is Glaun. The men that your daughter slayed were not kind people. They attacked her. In all honesty, none of us will miss them."

"They weren't your kin?" Sharek asked.

"Only Kygra here is kin to me." The other pointed to another scrawny man standing nearby.

"Hello," he said politely.

"My wife, Lilen." Glaun touched a young woman by his side on the shoulder. "And Terix, my brother's wife."

117

Emily looked over at another smallish female standing beside Kygra.

She noticed through all the muck and silt that covered them, a red tinge in their hair.

"Where do your people come from?" she asked.

"We came from a settlement high in the mountains to the north," Glaun replied. "Before that, the four of us grew up in Freymoor, near the horn."

"My family came from that way also," she said. "I have not been that far south since I was a child."

"There was a witch there," he told her. "We left some years ago when she killed the magistrate."

"She's dead," Akasati informed them.

"There was another in Linport," one of the other women blurted.

"They're all dead," the Erilian said. "Only one remains in Newholt, and she is our ally."

"You are friends with the witches?" Kygra asked them before turning to his brother. "I told you we should have headed west."

"Not all of those who possess power are the same," Emily told him. "My sister and six of the other women over there defeated their leader many, many years ago."

"You're talking about the Sovereign," one woman said, stepping forward. "I have heard the tale of seven little girls dressed in coloured robes, like a rainbow. They overpowered the Sovereign with lightning from their eyes."

"It didn't happen that way." Emily shook her head slightly. "I was there."

"Then how was she defeated?"

Emily remembered Yasmeen Svoboda, the Green Mistress, being flung through the air and torn apart. The image of blood and intestines hitting the floor, covering the throne, running into the crevasses between the stonework flashed through her mind.

"It doesn't matter," the auburn woman answered. "All that matters is that they were all defeated."

"Why did you go north?" Sharek questioned. "It's cold up there."

"It was as far away from the south as we could get," Glaun replied. "Our fathers and mothers decided it was best to get away from all the cities. So, they pooled their resources and bought passage on a ship to Oakbeach. From there, we trekked into the mountains for weeks."

"We heard Oakbeach is gone now," Lilen put in. "Very sad. There were some very nice people there."

"Yes, there were," Emily said, recalling the faces of James and Anya Halle, the innkeepers who had been so kind to them. She looked the northerners over carefully. "You're all young. Where are your mothers and fathers now?"

"Dead," Kygra replied bluntly. "The first few seasons were harsh and winter stocks were frequently low. Our fathers were first to go without so that their children could eat. Our mothers soon followed. Sickness took most of them from us and they always said it was simply the will of the gods. But we all knew that it was because they were giving their meal portions to us and taking very little for themselves.

"We tried our best to give it a go up there," he continued, "but the winter always won in the end. After a few more seasons with little prosperity, we considered returning to the south."

"Zael led our expedition," Glaun said. "We set out with fifty and moved into the highlands with twenty steeds loaded with supplies and a small herd of goats. We intended to buy more livestock from Newholt when we settled.

"Eventually, after a few days of walking, we came upon a sheltered vale, not unlike this. There were no caverns though, but there were some steep rock faces that we built our first shelters against.

"There was water from a spring, plenty of game and trees as far as the eye saw. We busied ourselves and created a nice little hamlet.

"Zael, however, got greedy and made himself lord of our tiny community. He gave himself and his supporters the right to take whatever he wanted.

"Food, clothing, women." Glaun's eyes welled with tears. He instinctively wrapped his arm around his wife. Emily understood where the story was heading.

"The first two years were hard, but we managed. If we just gave him what he wanted, he left us alone. It wasn't much of a life, but we were alive."

"Then about a month ago," Lilen interjected, "strange things started to occur."

"Strange things?" Akasati furrowed her brow.

"The livestock disappeared first," Lilen told her. "We mistook the missing animals to be the work of predators, like your daughter's rukyul. But it wasn't.

"Some of us even suspected Zael and his men to be responsible, but then they also vanished one by one."

"Zael suspected foul play," Kygra put in. "He pointed his finger at every one of us because he knew we despised him."

"The newborn babes were taken through the night," Lilen said. "Some mothers with them. The one that Zael counted as his wife was amongst those taken. It was then that he decided it was time to flee. It was the only decision that he ever made that I fully agree with."

"We headed south, leaving everything we could not carry behind, sticking to the ranges all the way," Glaun told the women. "We lost a few more of our companions during the first few nights of travelling."

"Did you ever see your attackers?" Sharek asked them.

"No." Glaun shook his head. "Not even a footprint or shadow."

Emily looked the strangers over again, noticing how dirty and worn their raggedy clothing was.

"You need to bathe," she said. "All of you. And you need a change of clothing. Those rags you wear are only fit for the flames. We'll see what we can scrounge up for you."

"Thank you." Glaun bowed slightly, showing his appreciation the best way that he could. "We have vowed our servitude to the young Miss, your daughter. I guess this means we should naturally extend it to you as well."

"We don't take slaves, sir," Emily told him. "Each of us contributes our worth."

"Your daughter told us the same," he replied. "Nevertheless, we are in her debt and yours."

***

"Fire," Gharnef called, pointing to the south. His steed stood upon the crest of a rise that Yuri and the others slowly climbed.

The horses were tiring after a long night of continual riding. They needed to rest. So did the Agrodien.

But the urgency to find their families pulled them onwards.

A wide, black haze lifted into the sky before them. As the other riders sidled up to Gharnef, they saw the enormity of the blaze.

Far in the distance, the grasslands blazed. The flames were being pushed away from the mountains to the west by the winds sweeping down from the mountains.

It was a haunting sight. Almost mesmerising.

"I would wager the others are over there somewhere," one warrior stated.

Yuri moved his eyes to the rising smoke. He had spotted something moving amongst the dark clouds, weaving in and out of shadow in the air not too far from where the woodlands met the open plains.

"What are those things?" Gharnef asked, seeing the same objects. "Birds of some kind?"

"Dragons," Yuri answered. "They tracked the others."

"Are they dead?" a warrior blurted.

"My eyes are good, young one." Yuri frowned. "But not that good."

"What should we do?" Gharnef asked.

"The horses are too weak to outrun dragons," the other replied. "We should dismount and climb into the mountains a little. We can use the cover of the woods to sneak by them and see if our families are among the flames or not."

"You don't appear too concerned, Yuri," a rider observed. His tone disrespectful towards the elder.

Yuri shot him an angry glare.

"This is your commander," Gharnef rebuked the young warrior. "You will do well to remember that."

"My apologies." He lowered his head in respect.

"No need." Yuri softened his demeanour, returning his eyes to the circling dragons. "I am worried about my wife and children, just as you are yours. But something tells me they are not in that inferno. I believe they are on the mountainside moving to the south."

"Why don't the dragons pursue?"

"I think they may be heading into a trap," he replied.

"Then we should move with haste," another warrior suggested.

"And have our horses die underneath us along the way?" Gharnef asked the younger Agrodien.

"There is nothing we can do," Yuri told them, dismounting his horse and leading it towards the tree-line. "For now, we need to be concerned with ourselves. If you believe in Q'sharh, now is the time to pray to him for their safety."

***

Alice pulled alongside the rukyul. Its hackles were up as it growled warily at a gap between some trees.

She saw a rocky ledge overlooking the plains to the west. Surrounding this was thick scrub and swooping terrain.

The girl dropped from the stallion and placed a gentle hand on the rukyul. It continued to face towards the north.

Even with the strong wind crossing the mountains to blow the blaze away from them, Alice smelled the powerful scent of smoke. It was hard to believe they had moved so far. She was so fixated upon tracking down the escapees that she had lost track of time and distance.

Her attention moved away from the smoke. She found what had caused the rukyul to behave so strangely.

The smell of fresh blood.

Edging forwards, leaving her steed where it stood, she pulled her swords free and stepped cautiously over the leaf litter covering the ground. The rukyul stayed by her side, stealthily, softly placing its paws.

Alice moved around a cluster of trees and into a small clearing where large, craggy rocks protruded from the ground.

Lying on the stones were the four bodies of the runaways.

Their skin removed and hung precariously in the tree branches nearby. Alongside the human pelts, the men's intestines were wrapped around the limbs in a macabre display.

She had seen blood many times before during her hunts, where she skinned and disembowelled her prey. But nothing had prepared her for this.

Seeing a human treated in the same manner that she would handle a deer or rabbit was unsettling.

Her gaze moved to their skinless faces, settling upon eyeless sockets and mouths opened in endless, silent screams.

The blood was still moist.

The kill was fresh.

The hunters were still here.

Seventeen

Hastily, Alice turned on her heels and raced back to the stallion. The beast stood where she had left it, but her path was now blocked by five hooded figures cloaked in dark garb.

Each of them held curved swords at the ready, waiting for her to make the first move.

She recognised them from the stories Richard had told her. She remembered the tales of the dark warriors that brought so much death to Woodmyst.

"I always wanted to meet a Night Demon." She smirked, crouching slightly, preparing to spring into an attack.

A sudden flurry of leaves and snapping twigs burst to life beside her as the rukyul lunged for the warrior farthest on the right.

As quick as lightning, it shot across the small clearing and snapped the figure into its jaws, shaking it wildly.

It reminded her of a rag doll as it let its blade go in the violent outburst.

Dark blood sprayed across the ground as the rukyul clenched its teeth closed, crunching bone and slicing flesh in its giant, sharp teeth.

With a great hurl, it flung the warrior over the ledge, its top half separating from the lower as it toppled through the air. An ear-piercing screech emitted from the figure as it fell away.

The remaining four warriors stared in disbelief as their comrade disappeared from view. Alice didn't wait for them to snap back to reality, using the moment to strike.

She lunged at the two figures on her left, plunging a blade into the hidden face of one warrior as she swung the other sword down and onto the second one's shoulder.

The blade cut deep, slicing through bone and sinew, stopping low in the warrior's rib cage.

The first warrior fell limply on the ground. The second screamed noisily as she pulled the blade from its chest.

It slumped onto the forest floor, writhing in agony like a cut snake.

The remaining two figures returned their attention to her, arcing their swords through the air.

She blocked both of their attacks with her own blades. With a swift kick, she sent the warrior on her right flying through the air. His back met the trunk of an oak tree, knocking the wind out of him.

As he fell to the ground to recover, Alice focused on the remaining warrior.

The figure was already attacking, swinging his blade from his side horizontally, as if he was using an axe to cut down a tree.

She sprang high into the air, over the blade and over the attacker.

Landing on both feet behind him, Alice pivoted, ready to strike.

Without warning, the rukyul swept in and ripped the warrior from the ground. He shook the cloaked figure in his jaws ferociously.

Alice heard the bones crunching as the fighter dropped his blade noisily against the stone ledge.

This time, the giant beast didn't throw the attacker over the cliff's edge.

This time, it feasted.

Alice didn't feel the need to stop the rukyul.

She patted it with gentle slaps against its shoulder as she moved by it towards the winded warrior, rising back to his feet.

He saw her approaching and frantically reached for his sword.

She was too quick.

Her blade plunged deep into his chest. He let out a scream that caused her ears to ring.

As the shrieking died down, a new sound gripped her attention.

A trumpet call.

It came from down the mountainside, somewhere between her and the fire on the plain.

She moved to the ledge and peered over towards the north, but saw nothing.

The trees were thick, still covered with enough foliage to prevent her from seeing through to the ground.

Thunder from above made her look up.

Apart from the smoke rising into the sky, there was not another cloud to be seen.

Then she saw them.

Four great winged monsters glided towards her.

She thought of running, but they would have her even at a full gallop.

Moving her eyes over them, scanning quickly, she saw four cloaked figures on the creatures' backs.

Dragon riders.

Alice sheathed her swords and raced back to her stallion. She removed her bow and quiver from the saddle before returning to the ledge. There, she notched an arrow onto the bowstring and took careful aim.

Lifting the arrow tip slightly above her target, she took a deep breath and released the shaft.

It whistled through the air as it shot towards the closest dragon.

TWACK!

The arrow struck the rider in the head, causing him to slip from his seat, only to plummet to the ground far below.

The great monster pulled to the right and moved away into the sky.

Alice was already preparing to shoot a second arrow at the next when the rider spotted her and steered the second dragon away.

The third, however, didn't notice her. Instead, he came in hard and fast.

She fired.

The arrow struck the warrior in the chest; a fatal wound, but not an immediate death.

As the third dragon continued towards her, the fourth turned to join the second in the air above. Together, they circled like giant carrion birds.

The third was still coming in too quickly. The rider slumped forwards on the beast's back, seemingly confusing the dragon of what it was meant to do.

Instead of shooting a blast of fire, it crashed through the treetops and attempted to land on the ledge.

Alice leapt backwards as the giant beast smashed into the rock face, shaking the ground about her violently. It scraped the ground with its enormous talons as it tried to push itself up and over the ledge with its powerful legs.

The rider slipped from the beast's back and tumbled down the mountainside, clutching at the arrow sticking from his chest. The dragon, however, committed to the task. Even without its master to guide it, the intended prey was clearly visible.

It snarled and snapped at the young girl with its massive jaws. Alice stepped back, keeping out of the creature's reach.

The dragon roared in frustration as it pushed with its massive legs, attempting to climb higher to get a better reach with its long neck.

Alice quickly turned to check upon her animals. The rukyul had placed himself between the monster and the stallion. Its hackles were standing on end as it bared its razor-sharp teeth at the giant attacker.

Alice returned her gaze to the dragon in time to see its teeth snap shut a few inches from her face.

She jumped back just as the creature lost its footing, sliding a few feet down the rock face.

The beast inhaled a deep breath.

There was no time to act.

She wouldn't be able to move her stallion and the rukyul out of danger before the jet blast of fire engulfed them all.

Racing forwards, placing herself between her animals, Alice dropped her bow and held her bare hands palms out to the beast.

Something instinctively took over, and she knew this was the only thing she could do.

You're going to die, girl.

The dragon exhaled, blasting fire from its jaws.

"No," she said calmly as the jet of fire reached her fingers.

The flames burst to the sides and high into the sky, as if striking an invisible wall before igniting trees and leaf litter along the edge of the rock face.

"Inferno," she breathed softly, sending the flames into the sky, directing them to the two circling dragons above.

While the creatures were unharmed by the blast, the flames instantly engulfed both riders, who fell like shooting stars to the ground.

The dragon stopped spewing fire and glared at the girl.

Alice lowered her arms and locked eyes with the beast.

It inhaled again, preparing to hit her with another barrage of fire.

She kept her eyes fixed, driving her stare into it, invading its mind.

The beast held its breath and closed its great mouth, blasting her with a harmless breath from its nostrils.

It kept its eyes on her for a moment longer, emitting a strange chirp before slipping from the ledge.

Alice raced forwards and peered over the edge to see the creature spread its wings and swoop back into the sky.

The horn blew again from somewhere below.

The dragon thundered a cry, but not an answer to the trumpet, rather a call to the other three dragons.

She watched as the flying giants regrouped in the sky. They swooped around each other playfully as the trumpet called again and again.

Eventually, the dragons fled to the north, away from their masters on the ground and out of view.

Turning to see both the stallion and rukyul staring at her, she nodded with a frown.

"I know," Alice said to the two animals. "I don't understand what happened either."

The rukyul turned and headed back towards the south, the direction from which they had come.

"We're not leaving yet," she told him, causing the creature to turn around. "There are Night Demons on our borders and I need to know why."

***

"I saw it up there." Zeveera pointed into the sky. "Fire spiralling from the ground and hitting two dragons from beneath."

"Perhaps one of the other dragons had poor aim," a warrior suggested.

"It was clearly an attack," the angry female hissed. "Not an accident. All four dragons have fled to the north."

"Were the riders still on the beast's necks?" Greil asked her.

"I saw something ablaze fall from the backs of two," she reported. "I cannot say about the others. They were too far for me to see."

"What of the rest of you?" He turned in his saddle to face the other riders nearby. "Did any of you see?"

The Agrodien warriors looked sheepishly to the ground.

"Not one of you saw?" he growled.

"Begging pardon, Kayl'sro," one rider near to the female said. "We were busy following you through the forest. We didn't have time to look to the sky."

"Yet, Zeveera did," he grumbled.

"She was the only one who did," the warrior blurted without thinking.

Suddenly, his body stiffened. His eyes moved down to his ribs, where he saw a blade pushed to the hilt, sticking from his flesh.

The hand attached to the handle belonged to Zeveera. The warrior looked at her, confused.

"Why?" he asked.

"You accuse me of lying and expect that I should be forgiving?" She smirked as she twisted the blade, feeling resistance as it scraped against bone. "I am the first mate of the Kayl'sro. I demand more respect."

She retracted her blade and watched him fall from the steed, thumping upon the ground.

"Are there any others who doubt my words?"

The rest of the warriors remained silent, moving their eyes to the fallen Agrodien, still twitching upon the ground.

"We move on," Greil commanded. "Keep watch. I heard a horn ahead. The Haigok are waiting for us."

**

Yuri scanned the skies as he led his steed through the woodlands. The smoke was much closer, still to the south of them. But that wasn't his primary concern for the moment.

"Have you seen them again?" Gharnef asked, walking behind him and peering into the air now and then.

"No," he replied. "I thought it might have been a ruse; sending the dragons north, only to have them sweep back around and attack from another direction. But they continued on for at least as far as I could see."

"They may still return, Commander," a warrior suggested.

"Indeed, they may," Yuri agreed. "We'll pause for a moment up ahead. I can see a small glade where the horses can eat, if they wish to."

"Won't the others get farther away from us?" another Agrodien asked.

"Perhaps," he answered. "But the horses aren't ready for another bout of intense riding yet."

"Why do you care so much for these creatures?" Gharnef questioned. "You know what Greil has planned for them."

"I've never been one for horseflesh," the commander answered. "I intend to release mine before we reach the ancient homelands. There will be enough game for us without resorting to eating these beasts."

"Do you think Greil really will eat the humans?" a younger female warrior queried.

Yuri turned to look at her. She appeared sickened by the thought.

"Did you side with him at Tirikith?" he asked her.

"Only because I was afraid," she admitted.

The others all turned to face her as they walked on. She lowered her head, ashamed of her actions and fearful for speaking her mind.

"Who else acted out of fear?" Yuri probed. "I know I did."

The younger travellers turned their attention to him, listening intently to his words.

"The old ways were enough for us," he began. "Kayl'sro Marrok was correct. We were satisfied in Terikith. We had everything that we needed right there."

"Yuri," Gharnef warned. "I don't think you should say these things. We don't know who we can trust."

"I killed an elder," Yuri told them, ignoring the warning. "I bit into his neck because I left my sword in my home. I wasn't expecting there to be a hostile takeover that night, so I left my blades by my bed. So, when Greil acted in the way he did, and after seeing the multitude supporting him, I was afraid.

"I was afraid for my family and what may happen to them if I didn't show support to the majority. So, I used my teeth to kill an elder I'd respected for all of my life and watched him die slowly, bleeding out upon the ground by the fire.

"Greil named me a commander for my actions. He gave me a position of authority for my loyalty towards the cause.

"Now, I fear for my family again because of Greil's actions," he continued. "They are far ahead of us, possibly dead. I can't be sure. If they are, then all of this is for nothing.

"One thing is certain. I've been thinking about it more and more since we escaped from the Pillars of Mohaa. I am a coward.

"I should have stood for what was right. I should have defended the elders and what they stood for. I should have been brave. Instead, I acted out of fear and look where we are now."

They stopped in the middle of a small clearing. The horses lowered their heads to bury their noses in the long, lush grass.

"I'm a coward also," another admitted. "I have no family, but I feared for my own life."

The warrior wept profusely, dropping to his knees.

"It's all right." Gharnef moved to the young Agrodien.

"I killed my mother," he blubbered. "Why did I do that?"

Yuri sighed as he closed his eyes.

Gharnef laced his hand upon the weeping warrior's shoulder.

"We all did shameful things," the commander offered. "I don't know how many of you acted to support Greil or out of fear, but I intend to rectify my mistakes."

"You should be the Kayl'sro, Commander," one of the other Agrodien suggested. "You have my sword."

"And mine," said another.

Before long, the entire gathering had pledged their allegiance to him, bowing their knees and producing their blades in offering.

"Rise," Yuri commanded. "All of you. We can concern ourselves with such matters later. For now, I suggest we take a small rest while the horses feed."

They lifted themselves to their feet and moved off in different directions, leading their chargers by the reins to various locations about the glade.

"You're taking a risk trusting them," Gharnef told him. "I, too, acted out of fear. But I would only confide in you with this information. What if they tell Greil when we finally catch up with him? Or, what if they decide to unite and take you themselves?"

"I have you by my side, no?"

"Of course," the other replied. "You need never ask."

"And there are at least two others who will side with me," Yuri nodded towards the young female and the weeping warrior.

"Four against ten," Gharnef shook his head. "Good odds. I think your ability to count needs improvement."

Yuri smiled as he rubbed his horse's neck.

"We'll be fine, old friend," he replied.

Their heads turned to the south as three long trumpet blows echoed from higher upon the mountainside.

The Haigok were manoeuvring.

"They attack Greil?" Gharnef queried. "They attack our families."

"We can't know for certain," the other replied. "But I think we need to risk another ride."

"Mount up," Gharnef called to the others.

Within moments, the Agrodien were upon their steeds and racing through the woods, making for the higher ground to the south.

As hoof falls thundered through the trees, three more trumpet blasts resounded through the air.

Eighteen

Racing towards them head on, Alice crouched upon her saddle, ready to pounce. There was no use in trying to be stealthy. Their trumpet blasts were enough for her to realise that they knew exactly where she was.

She counted eight cloaked figures. Their wide, bulbous, yellow eyes told her they were surprised to see her. A few of them looked to the region behind her in search of more, only seeing the rukyul charging through the undergrowth by her side.

With a great cry, Alice lunged into the air, pulling her blades free of the sheaths on her back. Turning them in her hands, she angled the blades downward as she locked eyes with her target; the one with the twisted ram's horn in his hand.

Her blades sank deep into his breast, causing him to drop his curved sword and trumpet in shock.

One of the Night Demons lunged at her from the left.

She responded with a high kick to his face, sending the figure sprawling onto his back.

Spinning to the right, Alice pulled her blades free in time to block a thrusting blade from another cloaked figure. She held his blade with her left blade as she plunged the right sword into his neck.

The figure tried to scream, spewing dark blood from the gash in his throat instead.

Another raced towards her from behind, arcing his curved blade over his head and towards her crown. She pulled her weapon free from her victim, but knew that she wouldn't be able to defend against the new attacker in time.

He was within inches of making contact when the giant, black form of the rukyul appeared before her, gripping the Night Demon in his teeth and shaking him ferociously like a toy.

Alice turned to the remaining cloaked figures. The one she had kicked away had returned to his comrades. He staggered, holding his head as he locked eyes with hers.

One of them said something to the others in a deep, rumbling voice. She didn't understand the words, but she got the message.

As they fanned out, she knew they intended to surround her before attacking.

The rukyul dropped his prey and lowered his head, growling angrily at the figures.

The one on the right, still rubbing his face, moved his gaze to the dark creature. He slowed his approach, clearly concerned for his life.

Alice seized the opportunity and lunged for him, piercing him in the belly. Her other sword swung upward, knocking the blade of an attacker on the other side.

She spun on her toes, sending an arcing kick into the jaw of another before stabbing upwards, into the chin of the fourth. The blade crunched through bone and popped out the top of his head.

"Go," she barked to the rukyul. Alice signalled with her eyes for him to move to where the stallion stood.

The beast raced around the skirmish and placed himself between the horse and the enemy.

Three cloaked figures remained.

They regrouped and started debating their next move.

One of them slapped another on the back and pointed to the girl, urging him to attack first. The figure was reluctant, stepping back as it warbled something in reply.

They both turned to the third and gestured for him to attack. It shared the sentiment of the second, stepping back and protesting loudly.

Alice sighed as she waited for them to make up their minds.

"Hurry, lads," she taunted. "The sun will get low soon and I've still got to find a place to set up camp for the night."

They stared at her in silence, perhaps understanding her words as much as she understood theirs.

"I'll make it easy," she said, smiling.

Like a flash, she darted forwards and hacked into the neck and shoulder of the centre figure, sending a spray of dark blood over the two standing on either side.

Realising that there was no escape, no time to retreat, the one on her right attacked, bringing his blade down again and again and again.

She blocked and parried each blow, drawing her foe away from the other.

The third glanced around, looking for an escape route while the girl was busy with the other cloaked figure. Seeing the rukyul, he knew he would be run down and mauled to death within moments if he tried to flee.

Instead, he raced into the fray, swinging his curved sword through the air as he drew near to the girl.

She blocked the blows, one after the other, swinging her blades this way and that. The loud clang or steel against steel rang out across the woodlands as both Night Demons fought with all their strength.

With each thrust, she parried.

With each hack, she blocked.

She felt their strength with each attack. They were stronger than any man that she had skirmished with. Even stronger than David.

But with each blow, they weakened.

Their assaults had turned into an attack of desperation. They had seen what she did to the others of their kind. They made sure they kept her on the defensive, never giving her a chance to become the attacker.

Or at least so they thought.

Alice noticed their breath becoming more rapid. Their arms were not raising as high as they did earlier in the skirmish. She surmised their muscles were becoming sore and their bodies exhausted.

Enough was enough, she thought.

She blocked a blow from the figure on her right as she slid her blade across the throat of the one to her left. In one swift motion, she brought the sword across her and into the sternum of the other, angling the weapon into the cavity beneath the figure's ribs.

Both Night Demons crumpled to the ground, lifeless.

She crouched to wipe her blades clean upon the cloaks of the fallen figures before returning them to the sheaths on her back.

Rising to her feet, she noticed the rukyul staring past her. Its hackles were still on end and its teeth bared.

She turned to see horses.

Many, many horses.

Each had riders that reminded Alice of large lizards.

The one on the lead horse, wearing a black bearskin over his shoulders and long iron claws about his neck, lifted his sword and pointed towards her with it.

He called something to the others that she didn't comprehend, a language she had never heard before.

Whatever he said, she knew it wasn't good news.

She spun to the animals behind her. They were standing some distance from her. Her mind raced with different options.

Should she try for the stallion and escape?

Should she stand and fight with the rukyul by her side?

Both choices could end with her animals injured or dead.

Instead, she chose a third option. Perhaps not the wisest.

"Run," she hollered to the animals. "Go home. Go!"

The horse, knowing the girl better, didn't hesitate. It turned and galloped away in haste. The rukyul looked after the horse and back to the girl, not wanting to leave her.

Alice was already racing up the side of the mountain and away from the riders.

Noticing the sheer number of horses approaching, the rukyul turned and raced away, following the steed's lead.

The lead rider pointed his blade at Alice as she climbed the mountainside.

The others directed their attention on her, climbing after her towards the top of the ridge.

The girl pushed hard with her legs, feeling the burn in her thighs as she leapt over large stones and fallen logs.

Behind her, the sound of hoof falls and crashing shrubbery grew louder as more and more horses joined the chase.

The ridge was within sight.

Once there, she would follow it south and try for the Kyhur Circuit.

As long as they didn't catch her first.

Nineteen

"There," Gharnef pointed to a distant slope. Barely visible, moving beneath the trees were many steeds breaking in two directions. The bulk of them moved steadily along the face of the mountain, to the south. A smaller quantity raced up the slope at full pace.

"Where are *they* going?" one of the younger warriors asked.

"They give chase to something." Yuri squinted, moving his eyes to a ridge above the charging horses. "Something small moving like the wind above them."

"A deer?" The young female ducked her head, leaning to the side to see past a low limb of a nearby tree.

"A human," Yuri replied. "I think. Only, I've seen no human move like this one."

"Have you seen many humans?" Gharnef queried.

"A few," the commander answered. "From a distance."

"Do we pursue?" asked a warrior.

"We go after the larger group first," Yuri told them. "When I know my family is safe, I will go after Greil. You're all welcome to join me if you wish."

"I've pledged my sword to you, Commander," the female said. "I go where you go."

"I hold none of you to any vow," he said, urging his steed forwards. "You are free to choose your own paths."

He galloped through the trees in haste, ducking and weaving beneath branches and around thick trunks of oak and pine.

Behind him, sixteen riders followed his lead.

***

Simon made his way back to the large circle of people surrounding the hearth in front of Alice's cabin. He resumed his seat beside his wife, Tricia, and picked his mug of tea up from the ground. She stared at him, waiting for him to say something. Her eyes quickly scanned the faces of all others sitting around the fire. They, too, waited for him to speak.

He sipped noisily from his cup, exhaled a long, loud breath, and leant back in his chair. Tricia smacked him on the arm.

"What?"

"What did they say?" she asked.

"Who?" He pointed with his thumb over his shoulder to another campfire at the far end of the glade. "Them?"

"The Chief Squire of Dendadia," she retorted. "Yes, them. Who do you think?"

"I invited them to join us," he replied. "They all felt they would be intruding and didn't think we were entirely comfortable with them around just yet. Their leader, Glarn..."

"Glaun," Emily corrected him.

"Glaun," he repeated. "Right. He said he'd be more willing with Alice here before he joined us."

"We should have gone with her." Lor threw a small stone into the blazing fire they had made in the middle of the encampment, sending a few small sparks into the air. All the other family and friends who left Woodmyst had gathered about the hearth after setting up tents and shelters near Alice's cabin. They sat upon stools and chairs brought with them as pots of water sat steaming at the edges of the campfire.

"As if you would be able to keep up with her," Oliver quipped. "She moves too quickly."

"Then we should go after her," the other suggested.

"No." Emily shook her head. "The sun sinks to the west. It will be dark soon. The land out there is rough. You could find yourself stepping off a ledge before you knew it."

"This is your daughter we are talking about, Emily," Linet, her sister-in-law, said.

"Ay," the auburn woman agreed. "And I'm worried about her more than all of you combined. But she knows those mountains better than any of us. As much as I want to go after her and bring her back, I know I'll be placing myself in danger if I do."

She peered around at the faces of the gathering. Catherine and Takmel were missing.

"Where is Catherine?" she whispered to Joanne, seated beside her.

"She and Takmel ventured into the woods to the east some time ago," her sister answered. "Don't fret. They've probably just found some quiet place to... Well, you know."

"That's the last thing any mother wants to picture her daughter doing." Emily sighed.

"We wait until first light," Jeremy Schoenbach, former captain of the *Adelandria* offered, continuing the conversation concerning Alice. "I don't expect many of us will sleep well tonight.

We all fear for her safety. Some more than others."

He peered over his shoulder at Arthur, who sat on the porch by himself. The boy stared worriedly into the mountains, waiting, hoping for a sign of her return.

"I can't believe she just left like that," Lucy said, nursing her daughter Holly on her lap. "She should have waited for us."

"Have you ever known that girl to do anything we think she should?" Joanne asked, watching her son who was venturing too close to the hearth. "Don't touch the fire, Antony."

"Yes, Mama," he said, plonking himself onto the ground by a large stone, part of a circle of rocks that encompassed the fire.

"She'll be fine," Karlena told them. "She has training. Each of us has shared something with her. Alice is a quick learner. We can't teach her anything more."

"She could teach us," Akasati added. "She surpassed everything she has learnt. Her weapons skills are better than ours. She can skirmish better than us. She's stronger, faster and more cunning than anyone I know."

"I don't fear for her safety," Baldwyn said, staring blankly into the flames. "Not one bit. If anything, we should be concerned for anyone, or anything that tries to cross paths with hers. I don't believe they will last the night with her out there."

"That may be so." Emily smiled as Antony walked over to her, raising his arms to be picked up. She lifted him onto her lap, grunting slightly. "You're getting heavy, boy."

He kissed her on the cheek before pressing his ear against her chest.

"She's still my daughter," the auburn woman continued. "It's my place to be worried for her, even if she can fend off who knows what might be out there. A wild rukyul by her side and the power to control animals is not enough to bring me comfort.

"I don't think I'll get much sleep tonight, Jeremy. But I need to be a member of the search party in the morning."

"I had a feeling you would," the captain replied.

The sound of the cabin door closing gently made Emily turn her head. Arthur had quietly moved inside.

"Look." Simon leant forward, nursing his mug in both hands. "I don't understand why we are all so worried. The sky is still light. She may be sitting on some knoll somewhere, twisting the stems of daisies to forge a crown with them for all we know."

They all looked at him questioningly. Even the two infants, Holly and Antony, furrowed their brows at his words.

"Well..." He lowered his gaze to the fire. "She could be."

***

Racing side by side, the two creatures wove their way around trees and leapt over fallen branches at great speed. They kept to the route they had followed on their way to search for the escapees earlier in the day.

The shadows were growing long, and the air was cooling as the sun made its way to the western horizon.

Occasionally, the rukyul turned and peered back, wanting to return to Alice. But the girl had urged him to go. He knew, deep inside, that he was the protector of the steed.

Torn between devotion and instinct, he chose duty instead.

Reluctantly, he raced after the speeding horse towards the south.

***

"Keep going," Greil bellowed as he urged his horse to charge faster.

The other warriors were struggling to keep up with him as he pushed and pushed them through the forest as they gave chase after the small human.

Their steeds' hooves thundered as they crunched through shrub and crushed the undergrowth in their path.

They raced across the crest of the mountain, following the trail of the girl that fled far ahead of them.

With their eyes darting to the left and the right, the warriors watched for her, searching for the girl on the slopes in case she tried to escape off the trail.

But Greil knew she was ahead of them, locking his gaze forwards.

He jabbed the horse's sides with his clawed feet, hissing angrily as the steed lunged again to increase its speed. It was tiring, and he knew it.

He ducked under a low branch, clipping some dry leaves with his long tail.

Ahead, at the top of a rise, he glimpsed her before she disappeared over the edge and out of sight.

He thought he saw her turn, but wasn't certain.

Is she taunting me?

He gritted his teeth, keeping his eyes on the peak where he had seen her.

How is she able to move so quickly?

He dug his claws into the horse again.

It protested loudly with a squeal.

"She's just ahead," he called to the others. "Keep going."

***

She sprinted hard along the ridge, kicking up leaf litter and dust as she sped through the forest. The wind in her face had grown cold as it swept down from the high, jagged peaks in the distance to her right.

The steeds giving chase were far enough behind her to be out of view. But her ears told her they were still following.

Their hoof falls were slowing, signalling that the horses were tiring. The reptilian riders had pushed the chargers too hard. Their exhaling breaths were loud, emitting a noise like a raspy cough.

They would need to rest soon.

Alice planned to use this to her advantage.

She was far from weary.

When the reptilian ones eventually stopped, and they would, she would leave a trail for them to follow.

Somehow, she knew these creatures had ill intent, not just for her, but for others of her kind.

For now, however, she kept running.

And running.

Twenty

David stood atop the western wall, peering across the open ground and into the dark woods beyond. The moon had crept over the eastern horizon, spilling a silver haze over everything in sight.

His mind raced with hundreds of things ranging from mediocre needs that were required to be done in the city, such as supply distribution, to the positioning of men after hearing about the threat of approaching Agrodien.

But chiefly, above all other thoughts, his mind kept returning to his son and the others with him in the wild. It was the first night he was truly alone and sitting in his home made him feel restless.

"David," a low, soft voice called from his side. The chief turned to see Ruttger Harrow standing on the walk. "There is a chill in the air. Why don't you come and have supper with Courtney and me?"

"I'm not completely sure I would be great company tonight," David replied.

"You shouldn't be on your own," the other said, moving to the wall's edge. He placed his hands on the battlements and scanned the ground below.

"I've never been on my own before," the chief admitted. "Not since I took Isabel and Martha for my wives. And now, my son has gone too."

"It was bound to happen one day, David," Ruttger replied. "You can't keep him forever. He needs to find his own way, and that usually starts with a young and pretty girl."

"But her?" David closed his eyes and shook his head. "Why her?"

Ruttger eyed the man for some time.

"You know," he began, "I've never understood your disdain towards her. She's always seemed a pleasant lass whenever I've encountered her."

The sound of thundering hoof falls filled David's mind.

"She's dangerous," he muttered.

"How?" Ruttger asked, turning to face him, leaning his shoulder against the nearest merlon.

He recalled his wives standing upon the bridge, peering back to Arthur and Alice playing in the snow by the riverside.

"She's uncontrollable." He moved his eyes to the river, turning away from the other man to hide the tears that were forming there.

"I've seen her in action," Ruttger pressed. "She appears to be in full control of her abilities."

In David's mind, the horses crowded upon the tiny stone bridge, running at full pace towards his beloved Isabel and Martha, who held his infant daughter in her arms. Their combined weight and the increasing vibration caused the bridge to convulse, to buckle and break.

"My thoughts exactly," the chief said. A deep pain formed in his heart as he remembered. The imagery was vivid and clear.

The girl stood facing the bridge, transfixed and focused.

"I don't want to talk about it anymore, Ruttger." He wiped his eyes with the palms of his hands.

The screams of Martha and Isabel filled his thoughts; the image of the tiny bundle wrapped in swaddling cloth falling with stone and iron, tumbling into the icy water.

"What did she do to you?" the other inquired.

David shook his head. "Don't."

"How could this little girl have caused you so much pain?" Ruttger probed.

"Please..." the chief sobbed.

"What did she do to make you hate her so much?"

The girl, Alice, stood motionless, her eyes black as pitch as the crossing crashed into the deep water, taking both women and fifteen steeds to the bottom with it.

"She murdered my wives and daughter," he cried. He turned to face the other man. His face twisted with rage and sadness as tears streaked down his face. "She murdered my baby daughter."

David dropped to his knees and bawled uncontrollably.

Ruttger moved to him and placed a gentle, comforting hand upon the chief's head.

"She made those horses charge," David blubbered. "Why did she do that?"

"I think you've been holding this for too long, David," Ruttger said, frowning. "This injury needs to mend."

"I loved her like she was my own," he sobbed. "Why did she take them from me?"

Ruttger, knowing full well of Alice's ability to control animals, understood that she was capable of the act. But knowing the girl as he did made him feel confused. The act didn't reflect the personality of the child.

It made little sense.

"Why did she do that?" the chief cried.

"I don't know, David."

***

"Galonia," Yuri called as he raced his steed along the sloping face of the mountainside. They had reached the tail end of the Agrodien riders. The bulk of them were female and younglings.

"Yuri?" she replied, turning her steed to approach him.

The other riders in the pack stopped to let her through to him. Both pulled their horses alongside one another and dropped to the ground, where they embraced.

"I feared you dead," she admitted. "I thought the dragons had you."

"As did I," he said, smiling, remembering his escape from the Pillars of Mohaa. The two touched foreheads and stayed like that for some time.

Gharnef and the other riders following Yuri dismounted and reunited with their families, as well. Only two of the warriors, the female and a young male, remained with the steeds, holding the reins while their comrades embraced their wives and children.

"I cannot stay long," Yuri told them.

"Why?" Galonia asked. She looked him up and down.

"I must find Greil," he told her. "This madness needs to end. Do you know where he went?"

"They gave chase to a little human," Koryn, his son, answered. "A female, I believe."

"You saw her?" Gharnef asked.

"Briefly," he replied. "She killed all the Haigok on the mountain."

"Are you certain?" one warrior queried.

The youngling nodded.

"She must be a witch," the young female offered.

"Perhaps," Yuri said. "It doesn't change what we must do. We need to stop Greil."

"But you just got here," Evalad, Gharnef's wife, stated. "Your horses are tired and you need rest."

"We'll exchange horses," Gharnef told her. "We can't rest yet. We pledged our service to Yuri. Greil must be stopped."

"Then what?" one of the female riders asked. "We return home? Is that even possible?"

"No," Yuri answered. "The dragon riders have destroyed our home, no doubt. We cannot return. We must attempt to treat with the humans. We must try to make peace."

"They drove us from our lands," said a youngling.

"Are you over a thousand years old?" asked a warrior.

"No," the other answered.

"So, you weren't there when our ancestors were driven from these lands, were you?"

The youngling pouted, offering a small hiss as he looked down at the ground.

"These lands are not ours," the warrior announced, loudly enough for all to hear. "They never were. Our forefathers once inhabited them. But not us.

"We don't know how many men now live beyond the forest. It has been more than a thousand years. They breed quickly. Their lifespans are not as long as ours. This we know.

"Perhaps they number in the hundreds, which will be more than us. But I think they will number more than a thousand. Maybe more than a thousand-thousand.

"Yuri proposes peace," the warrior continued. "This could allow us to live amongst them, or maybe they will grant us lands of our own.

"Greil offers war. Perhaps we will have victory at first. But I think we will be wiped out. If one little human girl can easily kill the Haigok, a race we fear, then what chance do we have against all humans?"

A thick silence fell over the mass of riders as they gave the warrior's words some serious thought.

"Will you take the Iron Claws of Agrodia, Yuri?" asked a female mounted upon a steed.

"If that is what fate presents me," he answered.

"Then may Q'sharh be with you," the rider said. "We should try for peace before any other possibility. It would be what Kayl'sro Marrok would want."

"Yes, it would be," Yuri agreed.

***

Huddling against the rock face, nestled comfortably in a recess with her cloak wrapped around her tightly and her hood pulled over her head, Alice tucked her knees against her chest as she peered down upon the reptilian encampment far below.

The riders had finally stopped their pursuit, realising their horses needed to rest. Now, the beasts were tethered to trees a short distance from the fire the riders had made for themselves.

Alice counted twenty-seven steeds. As she watched the riders positioning themselves around the hearth, she formed a plan.

One rider, she assumed it was their leader, hollered and barked at them before turning his attention to the horses. Some steeds jumped at his outburst.

She surmised they had no better luck with understanding his words than she did. Still, it made entertaining viewing for the night.

Eventually, another reptilian approached him. This one was smaller. Alice assumed it was female.

When she touched the leader's chest and shoulders, he seemed to calm down.

"Definitely a female," Alice whispered.

She observed the two as they moved to the hearth. They sat down and embraced. The female removed her garments. The leader watched her for some time before taking his own clothing off.

Alice found the behaviour interesting.

She couldn't believe that these beings could be so intimate within plain view of the other riders.

As she watched, the other riders lay down, turning their faces away from the two lovers. It wasn't long before the two lovers were coiling their arms, legs, and tails around one another's naked flesh.

Alice settled against the rock face, keeping out of the wind that swept from overhead towards the west. She needed to wait until the lovers had fallen asleep.

The moon continued to climb over the range and was high in the sky before the reptilians appeared to all be slumbering.

Carefully, quietly, she climbed down the cliff, making sure her hands and feet touched each hold silently.

With her boots back on the ground, she approached the steeds slowly, keeping her eyes on the sleeping riders by the fire. The reptilians' eyes remained shut tight as they rested.

The lovers were now sleeping in an embrace, covered in a thick black bearskin she had seen the leader wearing beforehand.

A steed nickered softly as she drew near.

"Shhh…" She placed her hand gently on its muzzle.

Her fingers unthreaded the leather strappings of the bridle loose so she could remove the apparatus from the steed's head.

Peering deep into the horse's eyes, she rubbed its nose and tilted her head, signalling the beast to move away.

As it quietly moved towards the south, she started removing the bridle from the next steed.

After releasing all twenty-seven beasts, she followed the horses away, peering back momentarily to the slumbering reptilians. They were none the wiser.

Alice smiled as she rubbed the shoulder of the nearest horse, slowly walking away into the night.

Twenty-One

The morning sun had not yet breached the horizon, sending a soft pink light into the sky. A few birds nattered in the trees, playing amongst the coloured leaves and knocking a few to the ground below.

"Shut up," Greil hollered angrily at them.

He turned as the sound of approaching horses grew louder. He saw seventeen Agrodien trotting over an embankment towards the camp-site by the steep rock face. The first in line was Yuri.

"You were dead," he called to the approaching riders.

"We got better, Kayl'sro," Yuri replied with a smirk.

"She was here," one of Greil's men called, following hoof tracks towards the south. He pointed to the distinctive outline of a small boot-print in a patch of dirt. "The horses went with her."

"Little bitch," Zeveera snapped.

"Give me your horses, Yuri," Greil barked. "She can't have got too far."

"I'm afraid not, Kayl'sro," the other answered, pulling his blade free of its sheath. "This ends now."

"Traitor," hissed Zeveera. "We should gut you and feed your intestines to your children."

"Try it," Gharnef taunted, pointing his sword at her.

"We outnumber you, Yuri," Greil snarled. "You don't stand a chance."

"You don't need to follow him," Gharnef shouted to the other warriors standing about on the ground. "Put your weapons down or join us."

155

Greil laughed at the futile attempt to win his followers over.

"Didn't you wonder why this faithful few rode closest to me?" he questioned. "These Agrodien were loyal to me long before I named you two my commanders. I should have listened to Zeveera after I thought you had perished in the valley of the Haigok. I should have slit the throats of your wives and children. Now, get off those horses and give them to me."

"No," Yuri barked.

"Take them," the Kayl'sro commanded.

His warriors bolted for the steeds, leaping into the air, knocking the riders from the beasts' backs.

Sword clashed against sword as seventeen Agrodien warriors battled against seventeen Agrodien warriors.

Seizing the opportunity, Greil signalled for Zeveera and the remaining eight loyalists to take steeds of their own.

They leapt upon the horses and charged for the south with the Kayl'sro in the lead.

"He's getting away," the female warrior called out.

"A little busy right now," Yuri replied as he blocked a thrusting blade that missed his belly by an inch.

Gharnef blocked and parried blow after blow, continuously being driven back towards the rock face. The younger warrior he faced was faster and stronger than he, and was already wearing him down so early in the skirmish.

Frustrated, Gharnef threw himself upon his attacker and sank his teeth into the warrior's neck, tearing a sizeable chunk of flesh away. The warrior screamed in agony as dark blood spilled from the wound.

He thudded on the ground, holding the gash with both of his leathery hands. With one thrust, Gharnef slid his blade through the warrior's skull and deep into his head.

The warrior went still, leaving the older Agrodien to retrieve his blade by placing his foot against the fallen one's chest and yanking hard on the hilt.

Yuri was having similar problems. His foe was much younger, and more agile than he.

His sword was not as much use at slicing the other as it was with blocking blows. The sound of steel against steel rang loudly in his ears as he kept swinging his blade to the left, then the right, preventing the other from hacking into his flesh.

The commander found a moment now and then, choosing to kick his opponent in the stomach or punch him in the face.

The young warrior stumbled back, dazed. But he quickly regained composure and came tearing back to attack Yuri again and again.

Another warrior fell to the ground, one of Yuri's. His stomach torn open and his guts spread out on the ground. The loyalist charged for Yuri; sword held high.

Gharnef intercepted him, slicing his blade across the other's chest.

It cut deep, but not enough to slow the attacker.

Instead, he turned and started hacking his blade towards the new target.

Not again, Gharnef thought as he blocked blow after blow.

With her teeth buried deep in the throat of her opponent, the female warrior clenched her jaws and turned her neck. The gargling sound of blood filling the other's windpipe filled her ear as she stood to her feet, leaving the warrior on the ground beneath her.

She retrieved her sword from the dirt and peered around to see where she was needed.

Gharnef was closest. Yuri was just a little farther.

She bent down and took her foe's blade from his dead fingers and charged towards Gharnef.

With a single move, she lunged and knocked the loyalist off his feet, plunging one sword deep into his flesh where his neck met shoulder. Before he could hit the dirt, she was already sprinting to help her commander.

Yuri continued to block blow after blow. His challenger had learnt from previous mistakes and wasn't letting up this time. There were no opportunities for the older Agrodien to punch, push, or kick.

Block and parry.

Block and parry.

Block and...

The loyalist went suddenly still, staring at Yuri with questioning eyes.

The commander stepped back, watching as a thin line of blood appeared across the loyalist's neck.

Slowly, gradually, the line grew wider and wider as it grew into a gash.

Dark blood spilled over the loyalist's chest and onto the ground, pooling by his feet.

With a deep thud, the warrior's head slid from his shoulders and bounced on the forest floor.

The body seemed to stand for an exceedingly long time.

Eventually, Yuri pushed it over with his outstretched hand, to crash into the leaf litter.

"Glad to be of service," the young female said.

The commander peered around to see the battle was over.

"We lost three," Gharnef offered.

Frowning, Yuri looked to the ground before raising his eyes to the young female nearby.

"You fought well," he told her. "I never asked your name."

"Nola'ee, Commander." She bowed.

"We have seven horses," he said. "Gharnef and I will take two. You will ride a third."

"And the other four?" Gharnef asked as he strode over to them. "Who will ride them?"

"I could ask for volunteers," Yuri suggested.

"They would all volunteer," Nola'ee told him.

"She's right." Gharnef said. "You should request seven volunteers remain for burial duty instead."

Yuri agreed, nodding as he looked over the bodies of the dead.

***

Emily opened the tent flap quietly to peer inside. Her elder daughter was curled up asleep with Takmel's arm over her waist.

She's here.

The woman lowered the flap. The morning sun still sat below the horizon and the autumn sky was just turning a faint blue.

"Mama?" Catherine mumbled, stirring awake. Her eyes were half-closed and her movements were groggy. "What's wrong?"

"I missed you last night," she replied in a whisper, intending to let Takmel sleep on. "I just wanted to see you are safe."

"We just went for a walk in the woods." Catherine lifted the boy's arm off her body. He grumbled as he rolled away from her to face the wall of the tent.

"A *walk* in the woods?" Emily smiled.

Wiping her eyes, Catherine smiled before pushing the covers away.

"It was a pleasant night," she said, lifting herself from the bed, "for a walk."

"I bet it was." Her mother smirked. "Get dressed and come help me fetch water."

As the tent flap closed, Catherine turned to the slumbering boy. The corners of her mouth rose again as she watched him sleeping.

***

Arthur was returning from the nearby stream, carrying two pails of water back to the cabin. It was his second trip.

He had emptied the first load into a large pot that sat upon the stove, heating over a low flame. The second, for a barrel that sat upon the kitchen counter, where he could access the fluid through a small tap Alice had fixed in place.

He was halfway across the ground between the stream and the campsite when he noticed movement in the woods to his right.

Something large and dark approached the glade.

His heart raced as his mind took him to two places. He hoped it was Alice returning from her expedition. As he lowered the pails of water to the ground, he prepared himself to race to her, to embrace her.

He also readied himself to run for the encampment, to raise the alarm if a stranger appeared on the edge of the clearing.

Crunching leaves and heavy footfalls grew louder and louder as the dark form drew nearer and nearer.

The muzzle of a horse appeared between a tight cluster of trees. Arthur glared at the animal as it plodded into the glade.

The chestnut stallion.

Alice's chestnut stallion.

Its saddle was bare, and its reins dangled loosely from its neck.

Another figure followed it into the glade.

It was almost as large as the horse in height. It growled, baring its teeth as it placed itself between the steed and the boy.

Arthur's heart stopped.

His eyes flickered to the woods and back to the angry rukyul.

He hoped Alice was following the animals. That she would call the snarling beast away.

But she was nowhere to be seen.

The stallion shook his mane and turned his head towards the boy.

Ignoring the rukyul's protective gesture, he brushed by the creature and made his way over to Arthur. The horse pressed his nose against the boy and nickered softly.

Keeping his eyes on the rukyul, Arthur observed the creature relax his posture. The boy rubbed the stallion's nose and jaw.

"Where's Alice?" he asked in a low voice.

The rukyul unknowingly answered the question, turning to face the woodlands he had just exited. Soft, deep growls from the beast informed Arthur that the girl was still out there.

The creature wanted to go back into the wild after her.

Arthur led the stallion back towards the cabin, leaving the pails of water on the ground where he had placed them. It was then that the boy saw the loyalty of the rukyul in action. It followed the steed, watching Arthur warily, still protective of the horse as they moved to the side of the encampment. Every now and then, the creature stopped to peer back to the trees.

***

She stood atop a rise in plain view. The windswept around her, casting the tail of her cloak to the side as she wrapped the upper portion tightly around her chest.

The horses she had freed during the night before were long gone. They had continued south at a run after they'd ventured far enough from the reptilian camp to be out of earshot.

She had covered their tracks as best as she could in the short time available. A good tracker, however, could still pick up their trail.

Alice had no intention of letting that happen.

Expecting to see twenty-seven angry reptilians on foot chasing after her, it surprised her to hear hooves echoing over the highlands.

She tightened the straps over her shoulders that held her swords on her back, and upon her thigh that kept her dagger in place.

Listening intently, blocking the noise of the wind whistling through the trees and the pleasant chirps of playful birds, she counted the hoof falls.

By her reckoning, there were at least eight, perhaps more.

She prepared to run, placing her weight on her left foot.

As soon as they saw her, and when she was sure they had, she would flee.

They needed to see her.

She couldn't let them track the horses to the south.

She couldn't let them find her home.

Glaring towards the rises and falls of the land below her position, she saw movement beneath the canopy. Breaks in the foliage where autumn's bite had prevailed exposed the approaching riders.

Ten.

She counted ten racing through the woods.

They pulled to a halt in a small clearing on a rise within view of hers. A few of the riders looked to the ground. She surmised they were searching for tracks.

It seemed to take them some time, considering that Alice could almost see her trail moving through the clearing all the way from her position on the rise.

Pursing her lips and curling her tongue, she let out an ear-piercing whistle.

The female was the first to spot her, pointing towards her so the others could see their intended prey.

The leader raced towards her first, disappearing beneath the trees and out of view. His followers were on his tail within moments.

Alice didn't wait to see if they would find her again. Instead, she sprang from her left foot and darted into the woods to her right.

She passed a waist-high post with a dragon's head carved upon it; one of the many markers that were positioned along the Kyhur Circuit.

Sprinting into the forest, she made sure her tracks were easy to follow.

She needed them to find her.

She needed them to track her down.

She needed them to believe they had a chance.

Twenty-Two

Simon strapped his sheathed sword to a leather flap just in front of the left knee roll of his saddle. As he tightened the fastenings, Arthur brought him a canteen of water for the journey.

"I should go with you," the boy said.

"We have enough," Simon replied, attempting to be polite about the matter, looking around at the other five horses being prepared to leave.

"She and I are..." Arthur stopped speaking, peering to the ground momentarily. "It should be me."

"Listen, lad." The other placed his hand on the boy's shoulder. "She loves you. We all can see that as clear as day. And that's why you can't go."

"That's why I should go," he argued.

"Let's think of the worst scenario that enters our heads," Simon said. "What if she's under attack? This is something I believe is the case. She sent the animals away, possibly persuading that demon dog to protect her horse instead of staying with her. More likely, wanting to get the both of them out of harm's reach.

"Now, if we go out there and find her, and you're with us, don't you think she will be concerned for your safety more than any animal? Of course, she will. And that means she won't have her mind where it ought to be. Understand?"

Arthur nodded, frowning as his eyes moved to the ground again.

Simon was right.

"Worse than that," the elder continued. "What if she's injured? Or what if she's dead?"

163

The boy raised his eyes to lock with those of the man.

"You don't need to be there to see that, son."

"What should I do?" Arthur asked, his eyes welling up. "I can't just sit here and wait."

"Then keep busy," Simon replied, returning to preparing his horse. "Tend to the stallion.

Make sure everyone has tea. Sweep the porch. Anything."

The boy nodded, stepping back from the horse as Tricia, Simon's wife, approached with Thedric, his son.

"Papa," he called, and a wide smile appeared beneath the dark mop of hair upon his head.

"C'mere boy," Simon called, reaching out to pick the little boy up in his arms. "You need someone to cut your hair."

"No." He shook his head wildly as his father lifted him from the ground.

Simon chuckled as he moved his son upon his hip, holding him in one arm.

"Husband," Tricia said, coming to his side to embrace him.

"Wife," he replied, wrapping his free arm around her, placing his lips on hers.

Arthur took that as his cue to leave. He walked back through the encampment towards the cabin.

The stallion stood on the grass at one end of the porch. The rukyul sat on the platform nearby, his eyes fixed upon the mountains to the north.

"You want to go after her?" Arthur said to the creature.

It looked at him and groaned before returning its gaze to the peaks.

"Me too," the boy said, sitting on the edge of the porch near the creature.

"Daylight is wasting away," Akasati called out from the back of her steed. "Kiss your wives and let's go."

"Give them some reprieve." Sharek smiled, sitting on her steed beside the other. "The sun is still low in the sky. We've got hours before dark."

Rhydra joined them, ready to leave. Simon, Oliver and Lor started over to them, peering back at their wives and waving children.

"Anyone else feel like they're reliving old memories?" Oliver asked as they crossed the glade.

"Not really," Rhydra replied. "For one thing, there were more of us then."

"Also," Simon said, smiling, "it was bloody freezing as I recall."

"I wasn't even there," Lor said.

"That's because you were too busy shagging Linet behind her brother's back." Oliver chuckled.

The Erilian women peered quizzically at Lor.

"It's true," he said, smiling. "Tomas would have killed me if he knew."

"Oh, he knew," Simon put in. "He just knew he'd have Linet to contend with if he slit your throat."

The party laughed.

"I'm not joking," Simon added.

As they climbed into the woodlands, the sound of heavy feet paced up from behind.

Rhydra turned to see a dark form moving towards them in haste.

"Shit," she spat as the beast overtook them, racing ahead a few feet.

"Bugger me," Oliver gasped as he caught sight of the rukyul.

"Should have known he would come along," Simon said. "There's a bond between this creature and Alice."

"That thing scares me to death, Simon." Oliver pointed to it. "Do you remember what those things can do to horse and man?"

"Ay," he replied. "I remember seeing one of those things pick a whole horse up in its jaws and shake it like a dog shakes a rabbit. But I wager that thing has a better nose for scent than you, me, or any of these steeds. He could take us all the way to Alice."

"Do you think it will lead us to her?" Lor asked. "There's a better chance it will simply take off and go after her on its own."

"Possibly, but I don't think so." Simon frowned, peering at the beast. It stood facing them, turning its head to the north and back again. "Lead on, ya bastard."

The rukyul turned and trotted up the embankment, keeping within sight of the riders.

"I hope she's safe," Akasati said, as they followed the creature.

"Somehow, I don't think it's her we should worry about," Sharek said. "If there is anyone out there trying to hurt her, then may the gods be merciful."

"You know what she would say to that, don't you?" Lor smiled. "There are no gods."

"There are no gods," Sharek agreed.

"Just like her father." Simon smiled.

***

Emily watched as Catherine and Takmel carted water back from the stream. They were walking slowly, smiling and talking as they approached the camp.

She supposed their love for one another was a welcome distraction from the fact that her younger daughter was missing. Only, it wasn't working for her.

While the two young lovers occupied themselves with their feelings for one another, her thoughts were consumed with Alice.

She wanted to be in the party with the others, riding to the north to search for her younger girl, but that would mean leaving her elder one. One thing she couldn't bear to live with would be the accusations of abandonment if she left Catherine behind.

Catherine was old enough, and quite capable of surviving without her. She had Takmel, and there was always Joanne and Lucy for her to turn to in Emily's absence. Even so, she was missing her sister at the moment. She didn't need to be missing her mother as well.

Others had passed by the two love birds several times, bringing pails of water into the camp. In any other circumstance, on any other day, Emily would reprimand the couple for moving too slowly. She would tell them to increase their speed and focus on the task.

But not today.

They were each the distraction that they needed. The fetching of water was simply an action to fill the time.

"Young love," Lucy said, holding Holly by the hand as they approached the auburn woman.

"Seems to be going around." Emily gestured to Arthur, seated on the porch, still staring up at the mountains.

"Should one of us speak to him?"

"No," Emily replied. "I think he would prefer to be alone right now. I'll speak to him later."

"The Seven have gathered at the eastern edge of the glade," Lucy reported.

"Why?"

"Something about guiding energy." The other shrugged. "Who knows? Only the Seven, I suspect."

"Or others like them, possibly." Emily returned her gaze to the young couple returning from the stream.

"Have they ever shown signs of..." Lucy searched for the right words. "You know..."

"Abilities?"

"Mmm."

Emily shook her head.

"Not since the night when Tomas..." She stopped speaking, feeling her throat tighten. It had been about five years and she still had trouble speaking about it.

Lucy wrapped her arm around the other's shoulders.

"I miss him too," she admitted, placing her head onto Emily's shoulder.

"Who do you miss, Mama?" Holly asked, scrunching her face as she looked up at the two adults.

"Your papa, my love," Lucy replied with a smile.

"I wish you met him," Emily said to the child. "One day, when you're a little older, I'll tell you all about him. Would you like that?"

"I don't know..." She shrugged.

***

Greil pulled his horse to an abrupt halt. He looked to the ground as one of his warriors raced by, slowing down as he approached what looked to be another trail leading back into the mountains.

"The path splits in two here," he called back to the group.

"What of her trail?" Zeveera questioned.

"She continues to the right," he pointed out. "She follows the markers."

"Markers," Greil hissed, looking at one of the wooden posts with a dragon's head on top, snarling back at him. "What purpose do they serve?"

"Perhaps they follow the border of their lands," another warrior suggested.

"Then why does she not just enter instead of following them?" the female asked, moving her eyes from one post to another along the trail.

"This is just a goat track, Kayl'sro," a rider announced, turning his steed towards the path moving off to the left.

"There are no signs that she went that way?" Greil glanced to the left.

"None," the other replied.

"We should continue to follow the markers," Zeveera advised.

"And fall right into her trap?" He frowned. "She wants us to go this way."

"She's one little girl," the female growled.

"Who could wipe out an entire Haigok squad," he snarled.

"Perhaps she had help with that."

"Then she's not just one little girl." He glared at her. "She's leading us this way. We need to use caution."

"Should we go back and find another way?" Zeveera asked.

"No," he said, shaking his head. "We can't allow her to escape and tell others of our approach."

He dug his heels into the horse's sides and raced off, following the markers to the right.

***

The circuit crossed diverse terrains. One such place was a section known as the Cat's Eye. It was a narrow fissure set into a massive vertical rock face, barely wide enough to allow a horse to pass through. To do so successfully, the rider would need to dismount and lead the beast through the narrow path.

There were other ways around the obstacle, but it would take time to detour off the path and navigate back to the trail on the other side of the steep elevation. Alice knew the alternate paths could prove tempting to her pursuers. She knew; however, they would eventually surrender to the Cat's Eye.

There were two other options available to the pursuers. One was a three-mile trek through the thick woods to her right over some very rocky terrain layered with loose stones and boulders, upon which they would need to take care with the steeds. The other was a nice leisurely stroll to the peak of the mountain, almost five miles before a safe place to climb over the elevation would present itself.

Alice looked at the two dragons' heads, one on either side of the passage. She then peered up to the thin sliver of light high above her, inside the passage. Moving forward, she entered the Cat's Eye, leaving clear footprints in the dust behind her as she went. With a quick look over her shoulder, she listened intently and scanned the woods to her back.

She had made a lot of ground between herself and the reptilians.

There was no sign of them yet.

She still had plenty of time.

Moving deeper into the passage, she peered up at the slice of sky far above her.

She had much to do.

Twenty-Three

Chief David Gyfford sat in his seat at the council table. His eyes slowly moved about to the many empty seats that were once filled by his closest friends.

"I'm surprised you stayed," he said to Richard, seated directly opposite to him. His wife Becka waited in the front row of seats before the platform, glaring at the large man speaking to her husband.

"Where else would I go, David?" the old man replied. "My knees hurt. My back aches. I can barely shuffle from place to place without someone assisting me. And it has been getting worse with each passing season. I fought for this land when I was younger and watched all my friends die. I fought for it again not that long ago and lost those I considered daughters and sons. I think I've maintained the right to still live here. Don't you?"

The chief nodded, moving his eyes to the table.

"I didn't mean anything by what I said," he replied.

"I know exactly what you meant," Richard told him. "You knew what would happen if you sent her away. You knew it would split this council. Now, this poison filters into the community.

"We are a blossoming city. We are larger and more populated than we have ever been. People look to Woodmyst as a beacon of hope. Now, we face the possibility of losing, not only friends and family, but others who can see how divided we are."

"And what would you have me do?" David thumped his fist against the table.

"Bring them back," Richard stood. "All of them."

171

"No," he replied.

Ruttger raised an eye, examining the chief.

"David," he began. "Perhaps you should consider telling..."

"Telling what?" the other quickly interjected. "That I was wrong when I wasn't? Cunningham and Harling both agreed with me. They can see what I can see. The girl cannot stay in this city."

"And where are Cunningham and Harling now?" Richard asked, gesturing to the empty chairs with his open hand. He sat back in his seat. "Did they betray you also? Have they gone to the caverns too?"

"I don't know where they are," David answered, looking along the table to Andris Hill, dressed in his leather armour. "Commander, if you could."

"I'll send a guard," the young man replied, rising from his seat at the table to approach a soldier standing at the top of the steps.

"This council is barely a tea-party, David," Richard said. "Six members. Four, if you count those of us who have shown up. Why bother?"

"We still have matters of concern to discuss," he replied. "The walls still need to be constructed."

"A little difficult when the foremen of the quarry are stationed with the rebels," the old man said.

"We will need to appoint new foremen," Ruttger explained.

"Why not keep the ones we have?" Richard asked.

"They won't return to Woodmyst," David answered. "They're loyal to the Wardes. And I don't like you referring to them as *rebels*, even if it is in jest. They are still our friends."

"Except for the little girl, of course," the old man chided.

David glared at him.

"I've sent two men for Chief Harling and Henry Cunningham," Andris told them as he resumed his seat.

"Thank you, Commander," David said. "I think we need to consider sending transports to the quarry to bring the loaded pallets of stone back to the city. We need to finish paving the streets and get the walls built."

"Agreed," Richard conceded. "But the walls should take precedence. Muddy roads are survivable. A defenceless city fighting against an enemy may result in peril."

"Richard is right," said Andris. "We need to complete the walls. There is still a large section to the north and east that needs constructing."

"What do you propose, David?" Ruttger asked.

"We close the sawmill for now and employ the men to aid in construction under the guidance of the masons. We use what military personnel we can to transport the stone and restart the building immediately."

"We also need crop pickers and reapers," Richard put in. "The farmers are a little short-handed and our granaries need topping up before winter reaches us."

"It's not ideal, but we need the men on the wall and the women in the fields." He saw Richard's wife move in her seat, protesting silently at the remark. "I know what you're thinking, Becka. I totally agree. But we are a little desperate."

"Closing the sawmill will present more problems," Ruttger told them. "We also need timber supplies for our hearths. The nights are getting colder. Fires are being lit earlier and earlier. We need to fill the stores. I think we have to rely solely on the military to construct the wall."

"We can stretch out our guards on the tower," Andris added. "One man per shift instead of three on each tower."

"Make it two per tower," David replied. "And only the towers on each corner of the wall and the four gates."

"Sixteen men per shift?" Andris asked, confirming the instruction.

"Ay," the chief confirmed.

"Better make sure they have good eyes, boy," Ruttger said to the young commander.

Andris placed his elbow on the arm of his chair and started scratching at the stubble on his face.

"We still need to speak to the masons about cutting stone," Richard said. "We can bring every piece of rock back here, but the supplies will eventually stop if we don't find someone to man the quarry."

"Perhaps the military..." David began.

"No," Ruttger interrupted him. "Those men are soldiers. Not rock cutters. All have their own distinctive skills. You wouldn't leave it to a rock cutter to fill in for a trained soldier. Likewise, you wouldn't leave it to a soldier to fill in for a trained rock cutter."

"You're right," David agreed.

"We've got the rock cutters," Andris told them. "We're only missing the overseers and foremen."

"Perhaps some of the rock cutters can stand in?" Ruttger asked.

"No." David shook his head. "Baldwyn and Gustav are good at what they do. We need them in the quarry."

"Send an envoy to treat with them," Richard suggested. "They're not our enemy. Promise them equipment, supplies, whatever they need for the winter and beyond in return for their services."

"Supply a whole settlement for the work of two men?" Ruttger questioned.

"Two men who are very good at their work," the old man said, smiling.

"They are still part of us," David said. "And they always will be. Richard is right. We'll send a messenger to bring our requests to them."

"I'll go," Andris volunteered.

The others looked at him questioningly.

"I'm a member of this council," he said. "I was once the servant of the Black Miss. Who better to go?"

"They'll be angry and may take it out on you because you are a member of this council," Richard told him.

"I know," he said. "But Joanne will listen. "I'll take Sevrina with me. Maybe they'll receive me a little more openly if my wife comes along."

"My lords!" a shout from the large doors of the assembly hall reverberated along the aisle. "My lady!"

"What is it?" David stood to his feet as a guard walked briskly through the room towards them. He was puffing heavily and his skin appeared pale and clammy.

"Chief Harling..." he wheezed. "Henry Cunningham. His wife and children."

"What?" Chief Gyfford moved around the table. "Talk to me, man."

"They're all dead," the guard blurted.

"Dead?" Ruttger and Andris sprang to their feet. Richard turned to see his wife standing with her hands covering her mouth in shock.

"How?" the old man asked.

"I don't know," the guard replied. "I found the Cunninghams in their beds. I had to break the door to get in. Someone had torn them apart. There is so much blood."

"How do you know the same fate befell Chief Harling?" Andris asked.

"The other guard you sent informed me before I came to report."

"Where is this other guard, son?" David asked.

"He's outside," the young man replied. "He couldn't contain himself, my lord."

"I need to see the bodies for myself," Richard said, standing.

"No, you don't," Becka argued.

"I'm not a child, wife," he grumbled as he started slowly down the stairs. "I've seen many terrible things in my time. I need to see if there are any clues who did such a terrible thing."

"They are both councilmen," she reminded him, stepping forwards to take his arm. "You are a councilman. What if the person responsible wants to do this to all councilmen?"

Richard stopped moving and turned to look at David.

"Retribution?" the chief asked.

"For what?" Ruttger queried.

"For exiling the girl," Andris surmised.

"It makes little sense," Richard replied.

"Couldn't be any of those who left," the young commander added. "None has returned since they left early yesterday morning. The wall guards would have noticed them."

"Then it was someone still in the city," Richard said.

"Agreed." David nodded. "But who?"

***

Richard and Becka rode upon a horse-drawn carriage. As one of the horse guards drove them to the Cunninghams' house in the southern sector of the city, Becka pleaded with Richard to reconsider going into the house.

"I need to see with my own eyes," he told her again. "I need to make sure."

"Make sure of what?" she asked. "That they are dead? Don't you believe the words of the guard?"

"I do," he replied, holding her hand in his. "But I need to make sure it wasn't…"

"Alice?" she asked. "That it wasn't Alice?"

"I know it wasn't Alice. The girl wouldn't do such a thing. It's not in her nature. No, I need to make sure *they* haven't returned."

"Who?" she pressed. "They, who?"

"The Night Demons," he told her. "I need to see."

"How will seeing Henry Cunningham and his family's remains help you know if they have returned?" She placed her hand on his jaw and forced him to face her. "I don't want you to see them like that."

He smiled, soaking her in as he placed his weary hand on her cheek.

"Why did you choose me?" he asked. "Why did you stay? You're still young and more beautiful today than you ever were. You could have any man you want."

"I want you, Richard Dering." A small tear slid down her cheek.

He kissed her.

She held him there as the driver pulled the carriage to a halt.

"I don't want you to go into that house, though," she whispered.

"I must," he replied. "David is too young to remember the things we saw. So are you. But I still see them in my sleep."

He exited the vehicle; the guard offering his hand to help the old man down to the ground.

"They promised you," she reminded him, remaining in her seat.

"Some break their promises, my love," he said, using his walking stick to help him shuffle to the door.

A guard stood on either side of the entrance, keeping people passing by or potential visitors from stumbling upon the carnage inside.

"It's not pleasant in there, my lord," one of them said, opening the door for
Richard.

"I didn't expect it to be," he answered, moving into the house. "Please don't let my wife in."

"Yes, my lord," the soldier bowed slightly.

Richard moved slowly into the sitting room, the first room of the dwelling. Several chairs sat around the fireplace that sat neatly against the far wall to the left. The room was not dissimilar to the one in his own home. Places to sit, some tables for objects, some shelves for articles.

Nothing extraordinary.

Nothing out of place.

On the mantel above the fireplace sat a well-fashioned tea set. Floral arrangements over a cream glaze adorned the ceramic pieces. The handles on the cups and pot trimmed with real gold feather. It was an expensive heirloom, one of the few things they had brought with them from Oldcastle.

One of the few things that had survived Oldcastle.

Richard turned and shuffled along the hall towards the bedrooms. He passed an open door to his right, the privy, before pausing outside the closed door of the next room.

Placing his hand upon the handle, he wondered if Becka was right. He wondered if he truly wanted to see what was behind the door.

All he had to do was turn around and leave, but his hand had already started turning the knob.

The door opened with a soft squeak before thudding dully against the wall inside the room.

Streaks of thick, deep red blood covered the walls on all sides of the room. Tiny chunks of flesh had stuck in places, appearing as if they were about to fall. Pools of red had soaked into the rug beneath the beds and formed little streams across the floorboards where more portions of flesh lay.

The two beds each held the bulk of the chaos. Streamers of skin and tissue strewn out and over the edges of the mattresses, dangling so they just touched the floor. The ribs of the victims broken outwards, giving the impression that something had burst from their bodies.

The arms and legs looked to be untouched except for the splatter of blood over the pale skin. The faces of Mercy and Ronald, Henry Cunningham's children, held an unending silent scream of agony.

Richard felt the corners of his mouth pull down, as he didn't know whether to cry or be sick.

Twenty-Four

"I want you to teach me," Arthur said.

Karlena and Jeremy gave the boy a quizzical stare. They were skinning a doe they had just hung in a tree. Its nose dangled a few inches from the ground, slowly dripping blood onto the leaves below. A few of the dogs that had come with them from Woodmyst waited patiently to the side, salivating heavily as they watched the captain slide his hunting knife through the skin on the abdomen of the kill.

"Me or her?" he asked.

"Both of you," the boy replied. "But I don't want anyone to find out. Especially Alice."

"She would be a far better teacher than either of us," Karlena told him as she cut a deep ring into one of the hind ankles of the beast with a small blade.

"Please," Arthur said.

"Can you ride yet?" Jeremy asked.

"I'm getting better," he answered. "I've been trying to practise every chance I get."

"Which is how often?"

"I don't know." Arthur furrowed his brow. "Maybe once a week."

"Maybe?" the captain snorted, stifling a laugh. "You're going to have to do better than that."

"I don't understand what my riding has to do with hunting and fighting," the boy objected, looking at Karlena and Jeremy.

"You need a horse to carry you, your bow, your sword and your kill," the Erilian woman explained. "How do you think we carried this doe back here?"

"Besides," Jeremy said, moving towards Arthur. "It gives us a good reason to tell the others why you will spend most of your days with us for the next few weeks."

"Months," Karlena interposed, moving her gaze over the lad.

"Months?" Arthur scrunched his face up as he peered over at the woman. She cocked her head and slid her blade effortlessly from her cut in the doe's ankle to the groin.

"How old are you, boy?" Jeremy asked, standing in front of him. "Twelve?"

"Almost thirteen," he replied.

"And you don't know how to ride?"

"I'm getting better."

"Alice, I'm told, could ride without help from the age of three," the captain told him. "Most of the other children in Woodmyst could ride by the time they turned five or six. What hindered your ability?"

"Books," the boy replied. "I was constantly reading books about how to do things."

"But never doing them." Jeremy turned the knife over in his hand, offering the handle to the boy.

Arthur peered quizzically at the hilt and then at the captain.

"It's never too late for a more practical approach," the man told him. "First lesson. Skinning a deer."

Jeremy led him by the shoulders over to the dangling beast.

"What do I do?"

"Carefully cut into the white tissue where the skin meets the meat," he explained as he pulled the fur with his hand, exposing the pink flesh beneath. Arthur saw the pale, membranous layers of fat and fascia beneath the pelt. He placed the tip of the blade on the tissue.

"Here?"

"Careful," the captain reminded him. "If you do this right, we can use the pelt for something else."

"No pressure, boy." Karlena smiled as she moved around the back of the doe to cut a ring into the other hind ankle.

It was slow going, but with a little guidance here and there, he stripped the animal bare of its outer layer, all except for a portion from neck to nose and four tiny sections near the hooves.

"Shouldn't we remove the head?" Arthur asked, staring at the blank, dark eyes peering back at him. He suddenly felt like a terrible person.

"Not yet," Jeremy told him. "Now comes the messy part."

The dogs lifted themselves from their haunches and started wagging their tails. Their tongues flicked from beneath their noses as strings of foam dangled in the corners of their mouths.

"Make a deep cut into its gut," Jeremy instructed. "Not too deep. You'll feel the blade pop through."

Arthur heeded his teacher's words and slowly pushed the blade into the flesh near the beast's privates. He felt the pop, just as the captain told him he would.

"Now," Jeremy ran his finger in a line along the doe's lower abdomen all the way to the sternum. "Cut along here. Keep it shallow. If it's not deep enough, we can retrace it with the blade."

Arthur used tiny sawing motions to move the blade through muscle, fat and fascia. Before he could reach half the distance of the intended incision, raw tissue appeared through the hole.

"A little faster," Jeremy told him.

The boy applied his weight into the cut, slicing through the flesh quickly until the knife hit bone.

Without warning, the doe's intestines spilled upon the ground, emitting a great sucking and slurping sound as they evacuated the body cavity.

Lower intestinal tubes and attacked Arthur's arm with slimy, discoloured liquid.

"By the gods," he spat, the mess thumping onto the ground by his feet.

The hounds came racing in suddenly and snatched up the organs in their teeth, dragging them across the dirt and playing tug-of-war with the longer pieces.

Arthur, still holding the knife in his hand, observed the dogs growling and snapping at one another over the discarded flesh. His eyes were wide and his skin was pale. He felt his stomach turn as two of the dogs tore open a large grey bulbous sack, spilling thick, green fluid over their muzzles.

"Well done," Jeremy said, patting the boy on the back.

Arthur buckled over and threw up.

Jeremy snickered.

"Well done indeed."

***

Greil stood motionless, staring into the narrow fissure, waiting.

Waiting.

The sound of an approaching horse from his right made him turn, momentarily locking eyes with one of the wooden dragon heads sitting upon the marker post by the passage.

"There are no tracks, Kayl'sro," the rider announced. "This wall seems to go on for a long way to the south. I couldn't see any place to take the horses over, under or through."

Greil shook his head, peering back into the gap.

"She went through here. So must we."

"We could abandon the hunt," Zeveera offered. "We could continue to the south and reclaim the homelands."

"She will inform them of our approach," he snarled. "We need to kill her before she makes it back to them."

"This will take time," the female argued. "We will need to lead the horses through on foot, one by one."

"I am the Kayl'sro," he barked. She cowered, half crouching with her hands over her head. "Me. Not Zeveera. Kayl'sro Greil."

"Forgive me, Kayl'sro," she begged, placing her hands upon his feet before licking them with her long, forked tongue.

"Get up," he grunted.

She clambered back to her feet, keeping her head low as he strolled over to an awaiting warrior who was holding their horses. Taking the reins from the rider's hands, Kayl'sro Greil led his steed towards the narrow fissure and past the two wooden dragons.

Zeveera watched as he moved farther into the passage, shadow sweeping over him like a veil. She stormed over to the rider and snatched the leads from his grasp before following her leader into the gap.

One by one, the other eight Agrodien loyalists moved into the passage.

Deeper and deeper they moved.

Farther and farther into the thin channel in the rock.

Greil kept his eyes upon the dusty floor, following the footprints the girl had left behind.

Around bends and along straight stretches, they continued to lead their steeds, taking the corners slowly so their beasts could navigate the turns.

A sudden loud rumble and terrifying crash filled their ears.

Something terrible had happened behind them.

A large dust cloud swept through the passage towards them, engulfing the steed and warrior at the back of the line.

"What was that?" Greil shouted, moving to see past his horse.

"I don't know, Kayl'sro," the warrior cried. "I cannot see past the horse. I think it was something near to the entrance to the passage."

"Go back and see," Greil commanded.

"The horse is too big to turn," the young Agrodien replied.

"Go back and see," the Kayl'sro bellowed.

The warrior understood the command, crawling beneath the horse's stomach and rising to his feet after clearing the tail. He raced as fast as he could back through the twists and turns of the fissure. The tinkling of tiny pebbles bouncing off the rock walls filled his ears as he drew nearer.

The dust was still thick, but transparent enough to see through.

A magnificent pile of rubble blocked the entrance.

There was no going back.

"The way is shut," he called back along the passage. His voice reverberated along the walls.

"What do you mean *the way is shut?*" Greil hollered.

"A rock slide," the warrior replied.

A deafening clunk from far above made him peer up to the tiny sliver of sky.

A black dot appeared in the thin patch of blue, growing bigger and bigger and bigger.

The warrior screamed when he realised it was too late to run.

His voice fell silent as the boulder crushed his head into his body cavity.

"Now what?" Greil grumbled.

"Kayl'sro," another warrior called from behind Zeveera. "I think we should move on."

"I'll decide when we should move..." he began, pausing when he noticed the countless stones falling over the ledge far above them, tumbling noisily as they crashed against the walls of the narrow passage.

"Q'sharh," Zeveera hissed as she started pulling her horse towards her leader.

Greil was already moving, tugging on the reins and heading forwards to escape the rock slide.

***

Alice ran as swiftly as she could along the top of the fissure, peering over now and then to see the position of the reptilian riders. The sides littered with rocks that varied in sizes from pebbles to small houses.

Pausing just ahead of them, she pushed a boulder about the size of a man into the gap. It tumbled in and scraped the walls nosily.

Roars and screams emitted from the deep fissure before the rock silenced them once and for all.

She waited and listened as others called to one another from deep inside the Cat's Eye.

Judging from the sound of different voices, there were four still alive in the passage and they were nearing the exit.

Alice sprinted along the edge of the fissure, leaping across to the southern side to move down the slope to the east.

The Kyhur Circuit continued past the Cat's Eye, where it turned to the south, towards her home.

She needed to end this soon.

Twenty-Five

Baldwyn Palmer swung the wood axe and split the large chock in two. He tossed the two pieces onto a pile he had been working on for most of the morning. He wiped the sweat from his brow as he rested the axe head upon the ground, using the handle as a staff to lean on as he peered up to the mid-afternoon sun.

It was autumn, and the cool breeze was welcome, but he felt intolerably hot.

He smiled as he saw a young, dark-haired woman approaching with a canteen.

"You've been working hard, husband," she said, offering the container. "Save some of your energy for me."

"I will, my love," he replied, taking the cork from the mouth of the canteen before sculling a few mouthfuls of water.

She moved her gaze over the vast pile of timber.

"I think you have cut enough to last until next winter," she told him. "How about you come and rest?"

"Are you trying to temp me, woman?" He grinned, handing the canteen back.

"I have to *tempt* you now?" She raised her brow playfully. "Don't I appear attractive to you any more, Balwyn Palmer?"

"Ay!" He dropped the axed and wrapped his arms around her. "You are the most beautiful girl in all the world. I've sailed over the seas from Ostford to Dendadia and beyond. I've seen women in the tropics to the south that barely wear a thread of clothing. I've seen queens and princesses in the finest dresses ever made. I've fought beside the Erilian women who are both exotic and deadly. But none of them compares to you, Elka, my love."

"You can always make a woman melt with those words that you form on that tongue of yours," she said as she pressed her forehead gently against his.

"I can do more than make words with my tongue, my love," he said, and smiled.

"You dirty bugger!" She smacked his shoulder playfully.

He laughed as the distant rattling of an approaching carriage grabbed his attention.

The couple separated a little, holding hands as they moved their attention to the eastern edge of the clearing. One horse pulling a small wagon with two passengers appeared in the glade, slowly making its way towards the encampment.

Footsteps beside Baldwyn made him quickly turn to see who was approaching. Glaun, carrying a bundle of wood, walked over to the hearth slowly, keeping his eyes on the newcomers.

"Are you expecting more people from Woodmyst?" he asked as he dropped the wood onto the ground.

"No," Baldwyn answered, lifting the axe from the ground. "Go back to the hut, Elka."

She turned and followed her husband's command, retreating to the safety of Alice's cottage.

Both Glaun and Baldwyn moved to intercept the approaching wagon, placing themselves between the camp and the two riders.

Others in the camp stopped what they were doing and stood to watch as the rattling grew louder, and the vehicle neared.

Some placed their hands on the hilts of their swords, others tightened their grips around daggers and hunting knives.

"Have you got something to fight with?" Baldwyn asked the other, repositioning his feet to favour his left leg. A dull ache had formed in his thigh, a persistent reminder of his journey to Blackrock Haven many years ago.

"I left my axe back by the trees," Glaun replied.

Baldwyn reached into his belt and retrieved his hunting knife.

"Here," he said, offering the blade to the other. "I'll want that back when we're done."

The horse-drawn wagon moved slowly across the open ground. The driver waved his arm in a wide arc.

Squinting, Baldwyn tried to see who was riding upon the carriage. He recognised the forms of a woman and a man, but they were still too far for him to identify them.

"...aldwyn," the man's voice called. "Baldwyn."

Uncertain whether to wave back, Baldwyn watched suspiciously as the carriage moved towards them.

"Baldwyn!" The man waved. "It's me. Andris Hill. My wife, Sevrina."

"Andris?" The other furrowed his brow. "Come over."

"Andris?" Glaun asked the man to his side.

"He's a friend," Baldwyn told him. "You won't be needing that."

Glaun looked at the knife in his hand.

"Of course." He turned it over and handed it back to the owner hilt first. "Thank you."

"It's Andris and Sevrina," Baldwyn hollered to the others in camp.

"I'll get some tea brewing," Emily called back.

Soon, the wagon parked by the tents and the horse hobbled so it could wander on the grass. Baldwyn led the new arrivals to the hearth, where several others had already taken up positions around the flames.

"Why are you two here?" Baldwyn asked. "Are you joining us?"

"Not exactly," Andris replied.

"Hello Andris." Joanne smiled as she took Sevrina by the shoulders, steering her away to a gathering of females to one side of the campfire.

"Hello Joanne," he replied as he smiled at his wife. She smiled back and allowed the other to take her away.

"I guess I'll be over here then," she said.

"So why have you come?" Baldwyn pressed. "I don't mean to be rude, but with the climate the way it is currently, you'll need to forgive my suspicions."

"Of course," Andris replied as the men sat in a circle of sorts to the side of the hearth. Andris peered around to see most of the *Adelandria* crew men, including Ewan Cunningham, seated across from him. "I don't see Simon, Oliver or Lor. Are they safe?"

"They are currently out hunting with Rhydra, Sharek and Akasati," Jeremy replied.

"And Alice," Arthur added.

The captain nodded.

"That's a rather large hunting party," Andris said.

"With so many mouths to feed," Arthur replied, "we need as many people gathering food as we can. They're our best hunters."

Andris nodded. His eyes were still inquisitive.

"Why are you here, Andris?" Baldwyn asked, bringing the conversation back to the matter at hand.

"I've been sent to treat with you and also to bring some bad news," he replied.

"What's the bad news?" Jeremy asked.

"I think I'm better off speaking alone to the individual it affects," he said.

"Someone died?" Gustav Steinman asked jokingly.

"As a matter of fact," Andris replied.

"Aw, bugger me." The other spat, feeling terrible for his paltry attempt at humour.

"We are family here," Jeremy told the visitor. "We stick up for one another. It's the reason this camp exists. What happened?"

Andris swallowed as he looked over to the leathery face of Ewan Cunningham.

"I'm sorry, Ewan," he said. "Henry and his family were killed sometime last night."

The old man stared blankly at the other.

"They were discovered this morning after not showing up for a council meeting," Andris continued. "I dispatched a guard to collect him, but instead, he found them in their house. They were all in their beds."

"Mercy and Ronald?" Ewan asked, his chin quivering, his eyes welling over with tears.

"All of them," Andris answered. "I am so sorry."

"No..." The old man shook his head. "Not the little ones. Not my son."

Arthur stood and crossed the ground to place his hands on Ewan's shoulders.

"Let's go inside," he offered. "I'll make you some tea and we can talk."

"They are only babies," Ewan sobbed as he rose to his feet.

Arthur guided the man away, leading him to the cottage.

Takmel rose from his chair and followed them.

"I think I'll be of more use in there," the boy offered. "Please excuse me."

Jeremy nodded, following the lad with his eyes, seeing him hold his hand up as a signal to Catherine. She was halfway out of her seat, intending to follow him to the hut. Takmel shook his head subtly to her and continued after Ewan and Arthur.

"That was all the family he had," Baldwyn said, his eyes peering to the ground.

"What was the reason?" Gustav asked. "Robbery?"

"I don't know," Andris replied. "Richard went to the Cunninghams' to see for himself.

Chief Gyfford and Ruttger were attending to the situation at Chief Harling's dwelling when I left to come here."

"Chief Harling?" Gustav blurted. "What happened to him?"

"The same thing," Andris told them. "The guards said he was in his bed also and that there was a great deal of blood."

"Murdered then," one of the other men seated nearby said.

"In their sleep," Baldwyn added. "Do they have any suspects?"

"No," Andris replied. "We've discarded any possibility of it being anyone here. No one has returned to Woodmyst since you all left to come here. No one has left the city, except for me. The killer, or killers, are still there somewhere."

Jeremy breathed a deep sigh as he leant back in his chair, scratching at the stubble on his chin.

"Usually, I would feel compelled to offer our services in tracking the culprits down," the captain told them, peering towards the cottage. "Especially since one of us has been directly affected by this tragedy. But I think we are better off staying here for the time being. Let Woodmyst deal with this. We have our own issues to be concerned with."

The other men nodded, agreeing with him.

"What's the other matter, Andris?" Baldwyn asked.

"It seems rather trivial after bringing this news to you," he replied. "But I was sent to treat with you concerning the management of the quarry.

"Chief Gyfford and the council wish for the quarry to continue producing stone. We need to complete the building of the walls and we can't get this done without your help."

"Chief Gyfford booted a little girl out of his city," Gustav offered.

"I know." Andris nodded, moving his eyes over the faces of those gathered. "I don't agree with his decision concerning this, and as a member of the council, I did not offer him my support. But as commander of the guard, I know we need those walls built. To do that, we need stone.

"You are the quarry master, Baldwyn. The masons will return to work if you are there to oversee the operation. We need you and the crane drivers."

"He expects us to simply go to work for him as if nothing transpired?" the other asked.

"He's afraid of her, I think," Andris told him. "I don't know why. But he knows Woodmyst is on the brink of falling apart. I believe that if we completed some of the unfinished work, we may maintain the sense of security in our community.

"Chief Gyfford wants to trade," Andris continued. "He knows we need you more than you need us. But we are hoping we can bring stores and supplies here for you to last through the winter. In return, we get the full supply of stone needed to complete the walls."

"And what of the pavers?" Gustav asked.

"The walls are our preference over all other stone work at the moment."

"What sort of stores and supplies?" Jeremy asked.

"We know the weather is cooling," Andris said. "We will bring grain, oats, straw, timber for building, blankets, canvas, livestock, whatever you need."

"Baldwyn?" The captain moved his eyes to the man seated across the circle from him.

"It sounds fair," he replied. "And I know Woodmyst can afford to spare enough from their stores for us to last the winter through."

He turned his attention to Andris.

"We will want all that you have offered, as well as tools for farming, at least two ploughs and oxen to pull them." He gestured to Glaun and the other three men from the north. "We need to consider the new arrivals and the possibility of others who may come during the cold months ahead looking for shelter."

"We will want excess," Jeremy reiterated.

"I understand," Andris replied. "I can draw up a list with you and take it back to Woodmyst with me."

"You'll be staying the night here," Jeremy told him. "We won't take no for an answer. We can spend some time to consider what we need and have the women contribute."

"You let your women have a say?" Glaun asked.

"I've found women to be far more level-headed than most men," Jeremy said, and smiled. "Some even far wiser. Ignoring the counsel of a woman is an ill-informed practice amongst most men."

"I meant no offence," the other replied. "It's just Zael let none of us contribute. Especially the women. In his view, women were good for two things. Fucking and cleaning."

The men in the circle moved their attention upon Glaun. He felt their heavy stares boring into his flesh.

"First," Baldwyn said, "mind your language. Second, where is Zael now? Beaten by a little girl and turned to ash on a pyre. Where did his view of women get him? Killed by a woman. That's where."

Glaun nodded, his eyes fixed upon the ground, the corners of his mouth turned down.

"I apologise. I..." He looked at the other three men that had arrived in the glade with him. "*We* will abide by your rules. But please, be patient with us. We have become somewhat disconnected from people. We were an isolated settlement with a tyrant in command. Some habits are harder to break than others."

"We were sailors by trade," Jeremy told him. "We know all about how hard it can be to change. We haven't seen the ocean for years. The ocean was our home. It still is, deep inside our hearts. But we adapted. So will you, if you want to be a part of this fold."

"Thank you." Glaun bowed his head.

Andris furrowed his brow, moving his eyes from one man to another, finally landing his gaze upon Baldwyn.

"Who are these strange men?"

Twenty-Six

The rukyul stopped again, waiting for the riders to catch up to him. He sniffed the ground before spraying fluid onto a tree. Scratching at the dirt after relieving itself, the beast turned his massive head back to the six steeds climbing the embankment towards him.

"I don't know if I trust that thing," Oliver informed the others.

"Alice does," Simon told him. "And I think it's loyal to her. Besides, it hasn't killed us yet."

"A matter of time..." The other shrugged as the beast trotted up the hill from them.

"Don't say that," Akasati rebuked. "It's keeping its distance. It's done nothing to indicate that it means us any harm."

"It's a wild animal." Oliver pointed to it. "It could be taking us to meet its family. For supper, if you get my meaning."

"It's taking us back along its own trail," Rhydra said, peering over the right side of her steed to study the ground. "We've got rukyul and horse tracks leading in the other direction over here. They're spaced reasonably far apart. Looks as though they were running. He's leading us to the last place he saw Alice."

"Marking his territory along the way." Oliver gestured to the animal with his hand. Sure enough, it was urinating again.

"Even the dogs and cats in Woodmyst do that," Lor offered.

"Not like that," Oliver argued.

"Hell, I've seen you do that on the wall outside the tavern in Dweagan, Oliver," Lor stated. "Many times, during the night. Are you a rukyul too?"

195

"You were drinking?" Simon asked.

"We were in Dweagan," the other answered defensively.

"Gathering supplies," Simon interjected. "At least, that's what you were supposed to be doing. Please, don't tell me you were lying with women there as well."

"I'm a happily married man," Oliver assured him. "A night of drinking does not result in a night of infidelity."

"The last time you ever go to Dweagan without me." Simon shook his head.

"Why?" Sharek asked. "You want to partake in the ale also?"

"That's not funny," Simon scolded. "You know why we don't allow fermented drink into our community. By the same measure, we should not be giving ourselves to it when we venture into other lands. Not if we can help it."

"You're right," Rhydra replied solemnly. "We must all remember. So please, don't forget." She peered around at each of them. "Oliver, the naughty boy, must never be allowed to leave our sight ever again."

The crew chuckled. All except Oliver.

"Not funny," he said, frowning. "I'm a grown man."

"I'm a grown man," Akasati mocked in her best Oliver Weston voice.

They sniggered a little louder.

"I'll just shut up then," he grumbled.

"I'll just shut up then," she repeated.

Simon broke into a loud belly laugh that echoed through the trees.

He wiped his eyes and noticed the rukyul facing towards the south, standing rigid. His hackles were on edge and his head sat lower.

"Hold up," Simon said to the others.

The horses pulled to a stop as Simon drew nearer to the beast. It was growling, watching something in the distance.

The man peered through the trees, past the next rise to the mountainside ahead of them.

Seven dark forms raced through the trees. Horses.

"What is it?" Lor asked.

"Riders," Simon replied. "A good distance away and heading east."

"What's east of here?" Oliver asked.

"The Kyhur Circuit," Akasati replied. "She's taken them there."

***

Yuri raced his steed as fast as he could, passing the first marker post with a dragon's head on top of it. The trail left by the other horses was clear and easy to follow.

"They can't be too far ahead," he called to the others.

"What are these posts?" Gharnef asked. "Markers for the Haigok?"

"The Haigok didn't have such fine work in their valley," Yuri replied. "I think men put these in place."

"For what purpose?"

"I have never pretended to assume I know anything of men," the commander answered. "I'm not about to start now."

Following the tracks and the marker posts, the riders eventually came to the rock wall that stretched on and on in either direction to the north and south.

The seven Agrodien pulled their steeds to a halt and searched the ground. The tracks led their eyes to a thin fissure, marked by two posts and blocked by fallen debris.

Yuri searched to the south a short distance while Nola'ee drove her horse a few feet to the north.

"Only one set of tracks here," she called. "They went north and returned again."

"Same over here," Yuri turned his horse back to face the others.

"They went in there," Gharnef pointed to the narrow passage. "The rocks closed the pass behind them."

"Not of their own free will, I would suspect." Yuri frowned.

"What should we do, Commander?" one rider asked.

He considered the choices. "We obviously can't go through after them. We could go north to find a way across, or south."

"North would be hard going," Gharnef advised. "It's uphill and very steep. South is downward going. Greil was intending to head south. Perhaps we can discover a way to the east and find his tracks again."

"Agreed," Yuri said. "We shouldn't tarry. The longer we stay, the farther they get from us."

"We're ready, Commander," Nola'ee reported.

Yuri turned his steed back to the south and galloped along the foot of the tall rock face. The six other riders were quick to follow.

Ducking under low branches and leaping over shrubs and fallen logs, the Agrodien warriors searched in desperation for a way across the barrier.

It was a long ride, but they finally came upon a section where the rock face vanished beneath a slight rise in the terrain, forming a natural ramp to climb over the obstruction.

The seven riders tore over the embankment and drove their horses towards the east.

Fixated, Yuri gave his thoughts to finding Greil. His entire focus was upon finding the Kayl'sro and what he was going to do once he had his hands on the tyrant.

His mind suddenly went blank.

He couldn't think of a fitting way to dispose of the self-appointed leader. Nothing that would be justifiable. Only acts of murder.

But why shouldn't I just kill him?

Who cares how?

He killed Kayl'sro Marrok.

Yuri struggled with the thoughts. He was angry and tired.

He could challenge Greil to a duel, but it would still wouldn't be a justifiable battle.

Greil would accuse him of attempting to usurp the position. From the view of his own followers, the Kayl'sro's opinion would appear accurate.

Yuri just wanted him dead. He didn't care for the title of Kayl'sro. He just wanted his family and himself to live without the threat of Greil constantly in their thoughts.

"Commander," another warrior called.

Yuri snapped back to reality and pulled his horse up, turning to see the riders peering to the ground.

"What is it?" he asked. "What's happened?"

"Tracks," the warrior called. "Heading southeast."

"Horses?"

"No, Commander," the rider replied. "Human."

***

Breaking from the forest and back onto the circuit, Alice sprinted along the well-worn trail, making sure her prints were clearly visible. She knew the four riders on her tail were not far behind.

A glance over her shoulder told her they weren't within viewing range yet. But it wouldn't be long.

She climbed a sloping rise and stopped at the top, standing in the middle of the trail as she peered to the section below her.

The trail ran straight, and continued to do so, except for a deep ravine at the bottom of the gully before her. Two large well-weathered poles with dragon's heads glared back at her from the chasm's edge. Iron clasps along the sides of the posts were the only sign that a rope bridge once stretched across the expanse. Mirroring the two giant poles were two more on the other side of the ravine, facing away to the south.

With another look behind her, she tightened the straps of her sheaths and belt. She twisted this way and that, working her arms of her clothing so they were comfortable. She needed to move freely, especially for what was to come.

Her eyes moved back to the stretch of the Kyhur Circuit before her.

She had only ever achieved this once.

She had barely made it then.

Now she needed to.

The sound of approaching horses brought her head around again.

Four reptilians appeared in view, hurtling towards her at great speed.

She waited for them to draw nearer, just close enough for them to see where she was.

The female opened her mouth and pointed to her.

That was enough.

Alice turned and ran as fast as she could.

She drew her breaths in deep, long inhales as her legs pumped and her arms swung close to her frame. Her body leaned forward as far as she could as dust and leaf litter flew into the air behind her.

She was halfway down the embankment when the reptilians reached the crest behind her.

Alice paid them no attention.

Her mind was on the deep, wide gap ahead.

The horses continued to tear up the ground, chasing, chasing.

The girl drew nearer to the ravine.

She had to time it just right.

Her feet needed to be in the correct position for this to work.

Closer.

Closer.

The leader roared as he dug his claws into his steed's sides, drawing blood from the horse in his frustration.

The beast screamed as it tried to comply with the rider's wishes, increasing its speed a little more.

Alice ran and ran.

Her legs burned and her breath increased with each inhale and exhale.

Faster.

Faster.

Closer.

Closer.

Closer to the ravine.

She leapt, pushing as hard as she could with her legs.

Her form arced through the air as she continued moving her legs and arms, hoping the motion might help her across to the other side.

She kept her eyes fixed upon the trail ahead, preparing to catch the ledge if she needed to.

Her body landed with a thud before she skidded across the gravel and rocks.

She had cleared the Rakmha Trench for the second time in her life.

Alice pushed herself from the ground, seeing a few streaks of blood on her hands.

Minor scratches from the landing.

A strange, warm sensation moved along the right side of her face. She raised a hand to the edge of her forehead and winced.

In the corner of her eye, she saw the leader of the reptilians reach the other side of the trench. He lifted his feet onto the back of the steed as he rode, crouching as the horse bounded off the edge.

When the beast was at its highest point of the jump, the reptilian pushed with his legs and leapt into the air. The iron claws around his neck glinted in the sun.

Alice reached for her swords and pulled them free of the sheaths.

The horse disappeared, beginning a terrible tumble to the bottom far below.

The reptilian landed on the trail, tumbling over with his blade in his hand, scraping his face against the stony trail and opening a wound just below his left eye.

He rose to his feet quickly, licking the blood dripping away from beneath his eye with his long, forked tongue.

With a hiss, he lunged for the girl, swinging his blade down.

Alice ducked beneath the sword and slid one of her own across the reptilian's chest, sending a sizable portion of the bearskin he wore fell to the dirt.

He roared ferociously, stepping back and away from the girl. His hand went instinctively to the wound.

Dark blood flowed over his fingers.

She had cut him deeply.

Alice peered over to the other side of the trench to see three riders glaring at her from the other side.

There was a way over to her if they cared to look carefully enough; a trail down to the ravine's floor sat just to their right. Once there, they would find another leading up to where she stood on the other side.

For now, they were oblivious to the trail.

She was fine with that.

Turning her attention back to the leader, she readied for another attack.

He was hissing heavily and glaring at her.

"Come on," she taunted, rolling her blades over in her hands.

The reptilian crouched, tore the bearskin from his shoulders and tossed it on the ground. He bellowed a tremendous roar and coiled his tail behind him.

Alice dug her heels in.

She prepared herself.

He leapt into the air, his blade pointing to her chest.

She gripped her swords tighter as he drew nearer, nearer.

His blade came closer, closer.

Twenty-Seven

Yuri and his six followers rode through the wooded area and onto a trail. He was still looking to the ground, following the human tracks, when he noticed other prints covering them over.

Horses.

He pulled to a stop to look at them a little more closely, dropping from his steed to crouch on the ground.

"What is it?" Gharnef asked.

"They passed here," he answered. "Heading south. They gave chase to the human, I think."

"Wait." Nola'ee cocked her head.

"Wait for what?" Yuri asked, rising to his full height.

"Quiet," she said.

He looked at her quizzically before turning to Gharnef.

"That is no way to speak to your commander, young one," the other older Agrodien rebuked her.

"It's all right." Yuri held a hand up to him as he watched the female. She was listening to something his hearing, possibly due to age, couldn't pick up.

"There," she said, pointing along the trail. "Blades clashing."

Yuri followed her finger and saw a rise along the road, but no sign of swordplay.

"Good ears," he complimented her as he climbed back onto his steed. He pulled his sword from its sheath. "Let's get them."

The others drew their weapons and charged after Yuri towards the rise.

***

Alice blocked with her swords and dived under the reptilian's swinging blade again and again, barely keeping from being struck. Considering his enormous frame, he was faster than she expected.

She kicked towards him, mostly out of frustration, also to give herself some room.

Her boot connected with his chest, striking the wound she had given him, sending him sprawling across the ground.

He growled, scrambling to get back onto his feet.

She readied herself, lunging forwards to strike.

He was up, blocking her blade to the left effortlessly.

She counteracted by jabbing with her right, but he saw it coming and swiftly kicked out with his left leg, hitting her hard in the stomach. Alice flew through the air and smacked into a tree on the side of the trail.

She tumbled to the ground. Pain shot through her spine and her lungs emptied of air.

He was stronger than her.

With great difficulty, Alice sucked in as much air as she could.

Gasping.

Gasping.

She realised her hands were empty as her senses came back. Glancing to the left and right, she couldn't see her blades anywhere.

The reptilian snarled as he raced towards her, sword held high, ready to strike.

She reached for the knife strapped to her thigh, the only weapon she had left.

Preparing for the worst, she allowed her mind to venture back to her home. There, she saw the faces of her mother and sister, her aunt Joanne and Lucy, her half-siblings Antony and Holly. Last of all, the face that stayed the longest in her thoughts was Arthur's.

How will he survive in the glade without me?

She frowned as her lungs continued to fill with air.

A tear welled in her eye as the large attacker drew closer.

She wasn't ready to die.

Not yet.

But she wasn't ready to fight.

And her time was about to run out.

A sudden call from across the trench brought the reptilian to a halt.

Words she didn't understand were being called across the gap.

The reptilian looked to the girl for a moment before turning his attention to the others, moving away to speak to them.

"What is it?" Greil barked

"Horses approach from the north, Kayl'sro." Zeveera pointed over her shoulder.

"Then deal with them," he growled. "I'm a little preoccupied."

As he spoke, seven riders appeared on the crest in the trail behind his three remaining loyalists, racing towards them in haste.

Greil turned to see Alice rising to her feet, pushing with her arm against the tree as she lifted herself upright. She was looking around the sides of the trunk for something on the ground.

It was then he realised her two swords were missing. Instead, she had a hunting knife in her grasp.

He sniggered, walking towards her slowly, confidently. The battle would soon be over.

Yuri charged down the hill. He saw three riders racing towards him.

"Attack," the commander called, pointing his sword.

After closing the distance, Yuri leapt from his steed and knocked one loyalist to the ground, tumbling through leaf litter and dust.

He could not move his arms enough to swing his blade. Instead, he used his sword arm to keep the warrior close to him while he hit into the ribs of his foe with his fist and kneed his privates.

The loyalist fought back, digging his claws into Yuri's flanks, drawing blood.

The commander cried out, releasing the warrior from his grasp.

Yuri buckled in pain as the loyalist curled in a ball, groaning from the commander's attack.

Turning, the Agrodien saw a horse charging directly for him. His hands were pressing against the wounds inflicted by the loyalist on the ground behind him. He could not raise his sword in defence before the steed would reach him.

"When I'm done with you," Zeveera called from the charger's back, raising her blade to attack, "I'll return to eat the flesh of your wife and children."

Yuri prepared for death, closing his eyes to think about his family.

Another horse crashed into the side of the attacker's, sending her and steed tumbling across the ground.

The piercing squeals of two horses made Yuri open his eyes.

Nola'ee was sprinting towards Zeveera, her sword already swinging towards the fallen female.

Zeveera saw the approaching attack, bringing her own blade up to block the younger warrior's blow.

"Let me guess," the female loyalist hissed. "You're Yuri's new plaything."

"I serve him," Nola'ee replied. "He is the rightful Kayl'sro."

"Traitor bitch," Zeveera growled. "Your Kayl'sro is over there."

With that, she swung her blade over her head, thrusting it in a downward arc directed at Nola'ee's head.

The young female ducked and weaved through the assault, blocking and parrying the other's blade. The sound of iron against iron rang in her ears.

Yuri turned his attention back upon the fallen loyalist. He was already up, facing the commander. His hand was clutching at his trousers, rubbing his privates and wincing slightly after the barrage the older Agrodien had given him.

Placing both hands upon the hilt of his sword, Yuri let the blood streak slowly from his wounds. They weren't deep. Just painful.

"Yuri," Gharnef called, leaping from his steed. "I'll finish this one. You need to get across to the other side of the gorge. Greil is over there. You must be his vanquisher if you are to be our Kayl'sro."

"Make it quick, then," the commander instructed his friend.

As Gharnef moved in for the attack, Yuri ran for the edge of the trench. Four of his warriors awaited him, watching the skirmish between the human girl and the self-appointed Kayl'sro.

Yuri turned back to see Nola'ee and Gharnef engaged in battle. The third loyalist lay dead to the side of the trail, his belly sliced open from side to side. He turned his attention to the four warriors nearby.

"You," he said to one. "Go help Gharnef. You go help Nola'ee. You two help me."

Yuri looked to the left and right for a way across as the two warriors raced off to help their comrades.

"There, Commander." One of the Agrodien pointed. "The trail continues down."

"Should we get the horses?" the other asked.

Yuri quickly evaluated the state of the path before them.

"It would be quicker to go on foot," he replied. "We'll fetch the horses later."

He and the two warriors sprinted down the long, narrow ramp that would take him to the trench's floor.

Alice rolled across the ground as the reptilian's blade struck the stones where she was standing.

Like a flash, she sliced to the side with her knife and cut deep into the tendon near above the attacker's left heel.

He roared in agony, shaking the air with his thunderous cry.

Crouching low to the ground, Alice held her blade at the ready as the reptilian crashed to the dirt.

He stretched his sword towards her, chopping the blade onto the leaf litter and pebbles.

Alice rolled backwards, out of his reach, as he rolled onto his belly. He used his right leg to push himself off the ground before starting towards her.

His left foot brushed the ground with the slightest touch. Still, he roared in pain.

Dark blood spilled from the wound, leaving a stain on the ground behind the reptilian as he hobbled slowly towards his intended prey.

Alice touched her brow.

The wound she'd sustained earlier was still bleeding.

She peered up at the approaching creature, who was glaring back at her, edging closer with each step.

Seeing an opportunity, Alice ran forwards.

The reptilian wasn't ready for her.

She leapt and hit him in the face with her knee, plunging her knife between his shoulder blades. Completing a somersault, she landed on her feet and rolled across the ground, turning in time to watch her foe fall upon his back.

He turned his head to look at her, hissing loudly as he tried to roll back onto his belly.

She waited for the right moment. When he was on his side, she sprinted.

Distracted with trying to get to his feet, he didn't see her as she tumbled forwards, over his body before digging her knife into his flanks just below the ribcage.

He roared again as she turned, keeping low to the ground.

With a lash of his tail, he struck her in the neck, sending her sprawling on her side.

As he pushed himself to his feet, she put a hand against the fresh wound. There was a deep sting, no blood. She knew it would bruise badly.

Rolling her head from side to side, she stretched the muscles in her neck. There was no time to be concerned with her injuries now. Her attacker was back on his feet, sword in hand, and hobbling towards her again.

Nola'ee slashed her blade across Zeveera's back. The female loyalist was too busy watching the other three Agrodien surrounding her.

"Bitch," she spat, bringing her gaze back to the young warrior, dropping to her knees.

"You should just surrender," Gharnef offered as the four Agrodien surrounded the female loyalist. "All of your fellow supporters are dead."

"Traitors," she barked. "All of you."

"Yes," Gharnef replied. "We all are. We betrayed Kayl'sro Marrok. We betrayed the Agrodien way. And we intend to make amends for our betrayal by seeking the mercy of Q'sharh."

"Q'sharh will strike you all down," Zeveera sneered. "Your wives. Your children. They will all die by the wrath of Q'sharh."

"Perhaps," Gharnef agreed. "But you will go before us."

He plunged his sword deep into her chest.

The surrounding Agrodien warriors followed suit, burying their blades into her flesh.

With four swords in her torso, she shrieked a piercing cry before breathing her last breath.

The four Agrodien retrieved their blades and let the remains of Zeveera crumple to the ground.

Greil roared furiously as his eyes fell upon the fallen form of his lover. He dropped to his knees and bellowed another cry into the air, losing control of himself.

Alice seized the moment and darted forwards.

She leapt over the kneeling reptilian and booted him hard in the back of the head.

He fell forward onto his face, his arms sprawled to his sides as his sword bounced noisily across the ground and out of his reach.

Kneeling on his scaly back, Alice reached into his mouth with her fingers, wrapping them over the top row of his teeth. She pulled back with all her strength, lifting his face off the dirt.

He made a strange sound as his throat stretched, trying to call but emitting a harsh crackling noise.

CRUNCH!

Alice felt his jaw snap beneath the pressure.

She jabbed her blade into the top of his neck and plunged it deep into the tough flesh.

Sawing.

Sawing.

The reptilian tried to reach her with his arms.

His tail twitched and thumped on the ground, not quite reaching the girl on his back.

She made a deep incision that followed the base of his head, ran to the notch where the jaw met the skull.

Three more reptilians appeared on the edge of the trench, swords in their hands. She glared at them, moving her eyes to the others on the other side of the ravine and then to the sword her prey had dropped.

She could reach it before they made it to her.

Heaving with all her might, she tore the upper portion of the reptilian's head free from the body, leaving the jaw and tongue behind.

Her foe's arms dropped lifelessly onto the ground. His tail stopped moving.

Alice lifted herself upright, moving to the discarded sword as she dropped the head of the reptilian into the dust.

Bending, keeping her eyes on the three newcomers, she lifted the heavy sword and prepared to battle again.

One of them unbuckled his belt, removing his sword and sheath from his waist. He handed it to another nearby.

Slowly, he stepped forward with his arms stretched out to his sides, his open palms in plain sight.

Alice believed the gesture to be one of peace, but she wasn't ready to put her trust in signs and signals. Especially from strangers.

She watched him warily as he approached.

"Alice," a voice called from the north.

She glanced to see six riders and the rukyul charging down the embankment towards the four reptilians on the other side of the gap.

The one closest to her called out something to the others, and they immediately dropped their swords on the ground and held their arms out just as he did.

The rukyul was faster than the riders, closing the distance between itself and the reptilians rapidly. Its teeth bared.

"No," Alice called to it. "Stop."

The beast pulled to a stop and looked at her. She held up her hand to it.

"No," she repeated.

It snorted disapprovingly and sat on its haunches.

"Alice," Simon called. "What's going on here?"

"Just wait," she commanded them. "Do nothing yet."

"These are Agrodien," Lor told her. The word seemed to draw the attention of the one near to her. "They attacked Woodmyst with the White Witch."

"Agrodien," Alice murmured. She looked at the one closest to her, confused.

The reptilian moved his eyes back upon her. He tapped his chest with his hand and nodded.

"Agrodien," he replied. "Yuri."

He gestured to her.

"Alice," she offered.

"Alice," he hissed. He turned to the others behind him and repeated her name a little more loudly. "Alice."

They stared back at her; their attention fixed upon her.

Yuri gestured to the body of the fallen Agrodien near her feet, wanting to approach.

She nodded reluctantly, gripping the sword and preparing to defend herself.

"Alice," Simon called again. "You watch that bastard."

She did.

Yuri reached to the fallen Agrodien's neck and removed the iron claws from the body. Holding his hands out to her, offering the necklace, he kneeled with his head bowed.

"Kayl'sro Alice," he breathed.

The other Agrodien bowed where they stood, lowering their heads in respect.

"Kayl'sro Alice," they repeated.

The riders looked to the kneeling reptilians and over to Alice, who appeared as confused as they were.

"Kayl'sro Alice," they repeated over and over.

"What is happening here?" Akasati asked.

"I think she has just become their leader," Sharek replied.

"Collect their weapons," Simon told them. "We'll bind them to their horses and take them back with us."

"And then what?" Lor asked.

"We'll let Alice decide their fate," he replied.

Twenty-Eight

Standing upon the wall, staring across the southern valley, David breathed deeply as the afternoon sun sank towards the woods to his right. The sound of shuffling feet moving upon the walkway made him turn his head.

Richard approached him slowly, peering over the farmlands, focusing particularly upon a series of large windmills some distance away near the foot of the mountains to the southeast.

"It still boggles my thoughts how those things work," he said, and smiled.

"How did you get up here without injuring yourself?" the chief asked.

"With great difficulty," he answered, resting against the stonework when he pulled alongside the other. "Did you know; I was standing on the southern wall during the last night of the Night Demons' assault?"

"You have told me this," David replied as he returned his gaze to the plantations. "Yes."

"I was more or less over there." Richard pointed to the western corner. "Well, more like back there." He turned and gestured to a place to the north, closer to the river. "The wall didn't stretch this far to the south back in those days. Woodmyst was a lot smaller."

"You think the Night Demons have returned?"

"No," the old man replied. "I don't think that they will ever return, as long as they are left to themselves. I don't know who or what murdered our fellow councilmen. What I do know is that it was murder."

"For what purpose?" Chief Gyfford asked. "Theft? Vengeance?"

"Not theft," Richard scratched at his beard. "There was a valuable tea set in the Cunninghams' possession, sitting in plain view on the mantel above the fire. It's decorated with gold. A thief would have taken it without a second thought.

"As far as vengeance is concerned," he continued. "What have the Cunninghams done to anyone? For that matter, what has Seamus Harling done? Apart from being members of the council, they don't really hold positions of influence or wealth anymore. What is there to gain from their deaths?"

"An attack on the council, perhaps?" David frowned.

"But why?" Richard shifted his legs. "My knees aren't what they used to be. These were terrible acts of violence. I cannot even begin to comprehend how they were killed. I've seen the bodies. My own eyes have looked upon the carnage. But how did the killer, or killers, actually do that?"

Richard moved his arm to adjust his weight.

"We should get you back down so you can find somewhere to sit," David offered.

"We should disband the council and hold elections after we hold pyre," the old man told him.

"Give up our seats on the council?"

"There is no council, David," Richard argued. "Four members do not make a council. We would have better debates in the marketplace than we would between the four of us. You're the chief. I'm one of the original men of Woodmyst, from a time before you were even born. I was a soldier during the Realm War. Andris is our Commander of the Guard. Ruttger was Commander of the Western Forces. It would appear we are a little military persuaded. At least, it would appear so to the people of our city.

"We need people. Everyday people to represent other everyday people on the council. To do this successfully, we need to hold elections."

"It would take time to organise," the chief replied. "I'm not disagreeing with you. But we need to organise this. Until then, we will continue to hold council as we do. We should discuss this more when Andris returns."

"Fine," Richard conceded.

"Good." David smiled, but his eyes appeared deeply sad to the old men. "Now, let's get you down and into a chair before your wife kills me for keeping you up here too long."

"I just arrived," Richard objected.

"Try telling her that."

***

As the six riders tethered their reptilian prisoners, using leather cords from canteen strapping, saddlebags and wherever they could find them, Alice searched for her two swords. Near the tree where the leader had kicked her earlier, she found the blades half buried in leaf litter a short distance from the trail.

She wiped the blades clean on her sleeve and replaced them in the sheaths upon her back. Her hands, she noticed for the first time, were smeared in the dark blood of the leader. Alice cleaned them off as best as she could by rubbing them on her trousers.

The iron claws dangling from her neck weighed uncomfortably upon her. She wore them out of respect for her prisoners. They had offered them to her, and she believed it would offend if she removed them.

She hoped to make peace, not discord.

Binding the Agrodien wasn't her preference, but her uncle and the Erilian women advised her to show caution. The Agrodien didn't seem too bothered by this, freely offering their hands to the others, willing to be tethered.

Alice, however, commanded the others to tie their hands in front, not behind their backs, allowing the Agrodien to hold the manes of their steeds. The captors held the reins as they led the prisoners and the other horses back to the glade.

"They don't look like the Agrodien described in the books of history," Alice mentioned. "Arthur will be disappointed. No big spikes over their backs or teeth the size of daggers."

"Who wrote the books of history?" Simon shrugged. "It's all a matter of one's point of view, really."

Alice nodded, contemplating his words.

"Are we ready?" she asked them all.

"When you are," Simon replied as Alice leapt upon one of the spare steeds being held by her uncle. "Which way? I'm not too familiar with these parts."

"We'll follow the Kyhur Circuit south," she replied, reaching to Akasati for the reins of Yuri's horse. "It runs to the stream before turning back to the west. From there, we follow the stream all the way home."

"Are there any more obstacles like this?" he asked.

"No more," Akasati informed him. "It's a clear run."

"Lead on then." Simon smiled. A deep sense of pride overwhelmed him as he watched the girl take command.

"Come," she called to the rukyul.

The monstrous beast jogged along the trail to her side, growling at the Agrodien prisoner on the horse to her side.

"Kayl'sro," Yuri said, his voice emitting fear at the sight of the creature.

"He won't bite," she replied, not expecting the reptilian to understand. "Not unless I want him to."

The party set off along the trail as the shadows of the trees stretched over their path.

The day had been long, and the night was fast approaching.

***

Arthur assisted Jeremy with fitting the doe to a spit over the hearth. This wasn't an unusual part of the process for him, having usually received his cut of the meat from Alice or his father to prepare for cooking.

Today, however, even though he didn't make the kill, he felt a small sense of achievement after cleaning the carcass with his own hands.

Jeremy ran his knife over the flesh, scoring it in several places.

"And that's it," the captain said happily, turning to the old man sitting in a seat nearby.

"Looks good, lads." Ewan smiled. His eyes were still glistening with moisture.

"You all right, my old friend?" Jeremy asked.

"No," he replied honestly. "Some bastard killed my family."

"I am deeply sorry," the captain said, placing a hand on the other's shoulder.

The old man stared into the flames. "It doesn't help."

"I know," Jeremy agreed. He looked over to Karlena, who was near the cottage, helping Emily and Joanne with peeling spuds. "When I lost Meaghan, I thought I could never replace her. Between you and me, I never did. I can't remember what she looked like anymore, but I still remember her as though she's a part of me. It's a pain that never left. I expect this one will be with you for always, too."

Ewan let the tears fall again.

"If you need to talk," Jeremy told him, "you know where to find me. Anytime."

"Thank you, Captain," the old man replied.

"Someone approaches," a call resounded across the camp.

Jeremy and Arthur turned their faces to the northern edge of the glade. They saw the husband of one of the Seven pointing to the woodland.

Movement beneath the trees drew their attention as their stomachs tightened, and Jeremy wished he had his sword in his hand.

"All is well," a familiar voice bellowed from beneath the cover.

"Simon?" Jeremy hollered. "Is that you?"

"It is," the voice replied.

The captain watched as the dark form of the rukyul appeared on the edge of the clearing. The knot in his belly eased a little, but the smile didn't form on his face until he saw Alice riding closely behind it, leading another horse by the reins.

"Thank the gods," he gasped. He turned to share his relief with the boy, but it was too late. Arthur was already sprinting through the camp to meet her.

She saw him and quickly tethered the cords in her hand to the horn on her saddle. She dropped to the ground, ran into his arms, and embraced him tightly.

"I've returned," she told him.

"I was worried," he admitted. "I missed you."

She kissed him, holding him tightly.

Emily watched from the porch, Joanne standing by her side.

"If they haven't already," Karlena stated, "they will become husband and wife tonight. Surely."

Emily closed her eyes to consider her friend's words.

"I don't want to think about that," she admitted. "She's only twelve."

"I was younger my first time," the Erilian shared.

"I thought Captain Tarkin waited until...?" Joanne questioned.

"Oh, he did," she replied with a smile. "But he was not my first."

Continuing to watch the two embrace each other, Emily nodded, accepting the facts placed before her. The two were in love and trying to hinder the natural progress of their relationship would be like trying to stop the sea.

She stepped off the porch and started across the camp to hug her daughter.

"Are you going to try to talk them out of it?" Lucy asked from the doorway.

"Have you ever known a time when you could talk Alice out of anything?" Emily replied.

***

Small children ran around the tents and through the camp, laughing and playing as the others continued to prepare for the night's meal. Alice and the riding party, her family and the Seven, sat around the hearth where the girl debriefed the party about her adventure.

Yuri watched them closely, moving his gaze from the children to the people gathered about the hearth. He and his warriors still bound, placed in a circle, some distance to the western side of the camp.

"What are we doing, Yuri?" Gharnef asked. "We should tell the Kayl'sro that we have families heading to the south, before other men or the Haigok find them."

"Or worse," Nola'ee contributed, peering to the rukyul who rested beside the girl, glaring at the Agrodien with hungry, dark eyes.

"I know," he admitted. "But it is difficult to communicate with someone who doesn't speak our words."

"Does she deserve the right to be Kayl'sro?" a warrior asked. "As you have said. She doesn't know our words."

"She defeated Greil," he replied. "It is our way. She is now the Kayl'sro. She wears the Iron Claws of Agrodia."

"Perhaps you should call her," Gharnef suggested.

"I think she's reporting to the others," Yuri speculated.

"She is not leader here?" the other older Agrodien asked.

"I think that red woman is her mother," he replied. "She cleaned the wounds on her head and hands as she was speaking. That boy is her husband. I don't know which man her father is. They all dote on her as if she is their own."

"Perhaps all of them?" a young warrior suggested.

"You fool," the female Agrodien hissed. "It doesn't work like that. Don't you know anything?"

Gharnef chuckled.

***

"Dragons!" Oliver shook his head. "So, the Night Demons have returned."

"I don't think so," Alice replied before turning her attention to Glaun. "They killed the four men that you arrived with. The ones I went after. They removed their skins and stretched their insides out and wrapped around the branches of the trees. They put them on display, as if they wanted to frighten someone."

"That sounds like the Night Demons," Simon said. "They used that same tactic before attacking Woodmyst. They put a body on the hill, where Joanne and Lucy kept bees. Some men, including your grandfather, retrieved it and brought it into the town. It too, had been skinned."

"Perhaps it's another warning of what's to come," Lor suggested. "Perhaps they intend to attack us again."

"The bodies were facing towards the north." Alice shook her head. "I think they were left for the Agrodien to see. I just stumbled upon them by sheer coincidence. They just happened to be where those men ran to. The Night Demons reacted and used it to their purpose."

"So, they murdered four men they had never seen before," Andris put in. "Makes me wonder if they didn't pay a visit to the city during the night."

Ewan Cunningham shifted in his seat slightly as he thought of his son, daughter-by-law, and grandchildren.

"How did you escape the dragons?" Takmel asked.

"I made their fire dance," she answered.

"You made fire dance?" Joanne questioned. She recalled the time when the Seven destroyed the plantations during an attack on Woodmyst, sweeping the land with flames in order to destroy an invading army of straw men. But it took all seven of them with their combined energy to accomplish the task. "On your own?"

Alice nodded.

"How?" Tricia Bell, Simon's wife and one of the Seven, asked the girl.

"I don't know," she replied. "I just did it."

The Seven exchanged quick glances with one another. Joanne looked over to Catherine, who was gripping Takmel's hand tightly.

"It doesn't matter how," Linet Verney, Lor's wife, offered. She rose from her seat and moved behind Alice, placing her arms around her neck and kissing the top of her head. "She's safe and back home. That's all that matters."

Alice placed a hand on her aunt's forearm.

"Kayl'sro Alice," a voice called. "Kayl'sro Alice."

All heads turned to see one of the Agrodien prisoners standing to gain attention. He beckoned to her with his bound hands.

"We should give them something to eat," she said. "I'm sure they're hungry."

"You would have them eat our food?" Catherine quizzed.

"These are my lands, sister," Alice said, rising from her seat. "These are my prisoners. I would have them treated with the same respect that I expect to be treated with. They need food and water."

"I'll get them something," Arthur announced, rising from his seat and moving towards the cottage.

Alice started towards the reptilians.

"And where are you going?" her sister called after her.

"I'm the Kayl'sro." She jangled the iron claws around her neck. "I'm going to speak with him."

The rukyul followed the girl across the grass to the circle of Agrodien. They cowered slightly at the sight of the creature approaching.

The reptilian standing lowered himself onto his knees, bowing his head respectfully.

"Kayl'sro Alice," he greeted her.

"Yuri?" she asked, uncertain of his name.

"Yuri," he repeated, thumping his chest, letting her know his name again.

"What do you need, Yuri?"

He looked at her, confusedly. The others offered no help as he turned to each of them, speaking in a language that was foreign to her.

"Do you want food?" she asked, gesturing with her hands, pretending to eat.

Yuri pointed to the children playing near the tents and wagons.

Alice, after seeing where he was signalling, placed her hand on the hilt of her sword above her right shoulder.

Yuri shook his head.

He pointed to them, thumped his own chest and pointed to the woodlands to the west.

Alice furrowed her brow.

He repeated the movements; pointing to the children, thumping his chest and gesturing to the woods again.

"Your children are out there?" she asked.

Yuri cocked his head, not understanding.

Alice pointed to the little boys and girls playing.

"Children," she said.

"Cheel-d," he grunted.

"Children," she repeated, pointing to the younglings.

"Cheeldrin," he managed. He pointed over his shoulder at the forest. "Cheeldrin. Yuri cheeldrin. Agrodien cheeldrin."

Her eyes moved to the woods and to the sun sinking behind the mountain peaks.

She pointed to the people around the hearth, who were watching intently.

"Family," Alice told him. She tapped her chest and pointed to the adults and then to the little ones by the tents. "Family."

He nodded, breathing heavily as tears welled in his eyes.

"Cheeldrin," he said again. "Kayl'sro Alice. Agrodien cheeldrin."

She understood.

She raced back to the hearth.

"What is it?" Simon asked.

"Keep something aside for me," she told them.

"You just got back," Emily stood, glaring at her daughter, wide-eyed.

"That one there," she said, pointing to Yuri, "and I are going out there right now."

"Why?" Her mother shook her head, placing her hands on the girl's shoulders.

"His children," she explained. "His family is out there. Their families are out there."

"It could wait until morning," Simon insisted.

"No, it can't," Takmel interjected. "I informed David of an approaching force of Agrodien invaders."

"He's right," Andris added. "We informed the guards before I came here. If they find themselves near Woodmyst, the soldiers on the wall will wipe them out."

"It begs the question of where the rest of their forces are, Alice," Oliver advised. "It could be a trap. I'm coming with you this time."

"As am I," Akasati said.

The girl nodded to them both.

"I should come too." Simon got to his feet.

"No," Alice told him, pointing to the prisoners. "I need some of you to stay back here to watch them. What if it is a trap? If there is no one here to defend the camp, we could lose everything."

He nodded.

"I could use your company if you're up for it," she said to Sharek and Rhydra.

"I was already coming," Rhydra replied.

"And you?"

"I've nothing better to do." Sharek smiled. "I guess it'll pass the time."

"Good." Alice started towards the cabin. "You'd better get the horses ready. Get one prepared for him as well." She pointed to Yuri, who was still kneeling by the others.

Alice stepped onto the porch.

"Where are you going now?" Catherine asked.

"I need to say a proper goodbye this time," she said, entering the dwelling and closing the door gently behind her.

Twenty-Nine

"I assumed responsibility for the placement of our forces tonight," Ruttger announced, moving through the aisle of the assembly hall. "Two guards on each tower. One patrolling the wall in each sector. Three sentries on each gate and a small concentration of troops on the unfinished sections of the walls."

"Thank you," David replied. He was sitting in his chair at the council table, nursing a mug of steaming brew, staring at the empty seats around him.

Ruttger sat down in a seat near to the other. "Why are you here alone, David?"

"If I was in my house, I would still be alone, Ruttger," the chief replied.

"That's not what I meant," the old soldier told him. "My invitation to sup with Courtney and me is still open. Come with me."

"None of this happened until I exiled her," David said, pointing to the empty chairs with his chin.

"So, this is her fault too?"

David looked to the other and dropped his gaze to the table.

"No," he replied. "Henry, his family and Seamus. I think someone would have killed even them if she was still here. It is probably for the better that she wasn't, otherwise I may have blamed her.

"This is my fault," the chief confessed. "I was so blinded by my anger that I wasn't able to see this coming."

"No one saw this coming, David," Ruttger reached across the table and touched the man's arm. "Come back with me. Courtney always prepares way too much for one meal. I swear she's trying to fatten me up and slow me down. Please help me prevent that from occurring?"

David smiled, nodding, silently accepting the invitation.

"Good." He stood up. "I've appointed guards for each of us, just in case this is an attack on the council. Two men stand outside each of our houses and we each have one assigned to each member of our households. I hope you don't mind."

David moved around the table, following the other to the doors of the hall. "Not at all. I think we need to use precautions."

"Has there been any word of the Agrodien threat?" the old man asked.

"I was about to ask you the same," the chief replied. "Perhaps the Gomatha was wrong."

"It seems odd that it would report anything at all," Ruttger put in. "I heard they were simply observers by nature, not spies."

"Vonavo favours the boy, I think," David replied. "He was his carer almost since he was born."

"Slave, don't you mean?"

"Prisoner of the White Witch, yes," the chief said. "But I only have the word of Takmel to base my understanding of his relationship with the Gomatha."

"And we only have his word regarding the impending threat from the Agrodien," Ruttger offered.

David stopped walking, pausing by the great doors of the hall, turning to face the other.

"What do you mean?" The chief furrowed his brow. "Do you think he lies?"

"It's not my place to make such accusations, David," the old soldier replied. "All I'm saying is that I heard the prophecy about the boy. I'm not saying that I believe it. I've seen with my own eyes what sort of man he is turning out to be. He appears trustworthy and true to his word. He's a likeable lad.

"But I trust my own instincts more than the words of any man. I'm a sceptic by nature and I need to see things with my own eyes before I pass judgement. I trust you unquestioningly, but if you told me that an army marches upon our walls and we need to prepare, I would still be tempted to send a scout or two."

"And we haven't done that," David admitted.

"No, we have not," Ruttger agreed.

"We should do so immediately." The chief turned for the door and stepped into the cool air of the evening.

"It's dark." Ruttger looked to the sky, seeing flecks of pink and purple on the edges of distant clouds hovering over the mountains to the south. "It can wait until morning. The guards on the walls will notify us if someone approaches. Besides, you agreed to a meal with my wife and me. She's been preparing all afternoon and I'll be a dead man if I don't return to her soon."

David smiled again. "It can wait until morning, then."

"Good." The old man clasped his hand around the other's shoulders as they started along the street together. "Just make sure you tell Courtney how wonderful the meal is, please. She's a terrible cook, but she tries so hard."

***

"Stay close," Alice called over her shoulder to the other four riders. Darkness shrouded the land, making the way difficult to see. She followed the rukyul closely as it led them along the route taken by the riders earlier in the day.

"I can't see a bloody thing," Oliver admitted. "I hope that creature of yours doesn't lead me into a low branch or something, Alice."

"Keep low then," the girl replied.

"Keep low then, she says," he grumbled. "You know; you could have asked Baldwyn to come along. Or Stephen, or John, or one of the other men sitting with their wives back in the glade."

"You offered to come," Alice pointed out.

"And I'm glad to be here," he said. "But another man on the ride might have been nice."

"You don't like us, Oliver?" Rhydra asked. "Don't we offer stimulating conversation?"

"He's lonely," Sharek teased. "He misses his friends."

"Hilarious," he grunted. "Let's all pick on the only male in the group."

"You're not the only male, Oliver," Alice started. "The rukyul and my stallion are both male. I think Akasati's horse is a male."

"It's a gelding," she corrected.

"Close enough." Alice smiled. "And there's Yuri."

"Kayl'sro Alice?" the reptilian quizzed, not understanding what the conversation between the riders was all about.

Alice held her hand up to him.

"Sorry Yuri," she assured him. "All is fine."

"There's the level of deep conversation any of us can have with him for now," Oliver remarked. "I'm not happy about you untying his hands, either."

"He's unarmed," Alice commented. "There are five of us and a rukyul. What chance does he have?"

"How much farther?" Sharek asked.

"The bodies of the men I searched for are just over there." She pointed to her right. "Keep in file behind me. There's a ledge to the left."

"What's that stench?" Rhydra complained.

A powerful scent wafted their way, carried on the wind.

"Death," Sharek stated.

"I left the bodies of the men where they lay," Alice informed them. "There are also Night Demons on the ground nearby."

They passed by one of the slain, cloaked figures sprawled upon the ground.

"Haigok," Yuri said.

"Haigok?" Alice repeated, looking over her shoulder to the Agrodien.

The reptilian pointed to the slain Night Demon.

"Yuri says they're Haigok," Alice told the others.

The rukyul lowered his head, sniffing at the ground, turning slightly to descend to the left.

The riders continued to travel for some time.

A thin, bright sliver breached the peaks behind them. The moon was rising above the mountains.

A silver haze swept over the leaf litter beneath their steeds and illuminated the forest before them. The rukyul stopped a few feet from Alice and turned to face her.

"I think we've reached a fork in the road," she called over her shoulder.

"Cheeldrin." Yuri pointed to the left.

Alice pointed in the other direction.

"What's that way?"

Yuri shook his head.

"Haigok." He pointed to the left again. "Agrodien cheeldrin."

She nodded, understanding his intended message.

"We go this way," she said to the other riders.

"Have you been this way before, Alice?" Akasati asked.

"Not very often," she answered. "And not during the night. I know we can come back to the quarry eventually or ride all the way to Lunkhul Forest."

"Which will take the Agrodien all the way to the western road," Oliver pointed out. "Then on to Woodmyst."

"Go," she commanded the rukyul, pointing to the left.

The beast sniffed the ground, taking a few steps, finding the trail again before trotting off. Alice urged the stallion forward, keeping in pace with the dark creature leading her on.

"If they make it to the quarry," she told the riders following her, "they will still ride on the Woodmyst. All roads that they find lead back there."

"They've been at it for hours, Alice," Oliver put in. "I don't like our chances of finding them before the men on the wall see them."

"Neither do I," she admitted.

***

Arthur sat on the porch, staring towards the mountains to the west. He knew she was there, somewhere, but he wished for her to be here with him.

Most of the camp slept, all except for a small few. Agnes Weston sat inside the cabin with Joanne, sipping tea and fretting over her husband. Their sons Tomas and Ivo were both sleeping on Alice's bed.

My bed too now, I guess, Arthur thought, frowning up to the moon that hung high in the sky.

Karlena and Jeremy sat side by side near the hearth, worried for the Erilian women. There weren't many times when any of them had separated from one another, except for only one that Arthur recalled. That was the week after the captain's wedding night, when Karlena closed the door to their hut so she could have her husband all to herself.

Catherine and Takmel had retreated to their tent. Arthur couldn't be certain if they were awake or asleep. He assumed they would be wide-eyed and worried, just as he was. At least, he hoped they would be.

Emily sat down beside him, handing him a hot mug.

"She'll be fine," the auburn woman assured him.

"I know," he replied. "But I can't help worrying."

"Me either," she said, spreading a blanket she had draped over her shoulder so that it covered the boy as well. She looked up at the moon and drew him against her. "You two were in there for a long time before she left."

Arthur peered to her, his eyes exposing a hint of fear.

"Did you two...?" she began. "You know."

He nodded sheepishly, trembling a little beneath her arm.

"I will admit that I believe you both to be too young," she told him. "But I also knew that I wouldn't be able to prevent her. I'm not angry, Arthur. By the traditions, you are her husband now.

"She won't adhere to domesticity like many others' wives do. She's not much of a cook and her cleaning skills are lacking. She's a hunter. A warrior. She has more of her father in her than I'd like to admit. He was a good man, but he wasn't one for roofs and chairs, or porches, for that matter. You understand?"

"I don't want to tie her down," he replied. "I love her because she is who she is. By all measures, we shouldn't even like each other the way we do. I read books. She can shoot a bow. We are opposites. Complete opposites. But I love her."

Emily tightened her hold on him.

"I know you do," she said, smiling. "And I know she loves you."

"You're not upset?" He gave the woman a puzzled look. "We are still young."

"Very young. But you're part of the family now," Emily told him before kissing his forehead.

***

Lying on the ground by a small fire, she held her youngest son to her chest, peering up to the moon with thoughts of her husband in her head.

"I want to go home, Mama," a youngling whispered to her side.

"You should be sleeping, Corandra," she replied. "We have far to go when the sun rises."

"I can't sleep," the other whimpered. "I miss Papa."

"Me too," she admitted.

"We should all be sleeping," another adult whispered.

"Sorry, Evalad." The other frowned. "Did we wake you?"

"No," she replied. "While you fret for your Yuri, I fret for my Gharnef. How can I sleep without him by my side?"

"I hope they're safe," Galonia offered.

"Q'sharh goes with them," a female near another small fire told them.

"My apologies," Galonia said. "We woke you."

"No," the other replied. "I don't think many of us are sleeping well. I know I haven't since we left the canyons. I weep every night for my husband, who didn't return from Mohaa. So many dead for a handful of horses." She wiped her eyes. "We should never have left our homeland."

"I am so sorry for your loss," Evalad offered, rising from the ground, clutching her infant son in her arms and moving over to the other.

"You both have lovely children," the female said. "You must be proud."

"May I sit with you?" Evalad asked.

"Of course," the other replied.

"My name is Evalad, wife of Gharnef," she said, introducing herself. "That one there is Galonia, wife of Yuri."

"I am Aalre, wife of Khdue," the other replied. She looked at two younglings sleeping soundly beside her. "These two are Kazule, my son, and Neenu, my daughter."

"This one is Kh'shekh, my younger one." Evalad stroked the baby's head. "My daughter over there, sleeping, Unonia."

"Corandra, my daughter," Galonia whispered.

"Hello," the young female offered.

"Hello, little one." Aalre smiled.

"My son, Koryn." Galonia pointed to her second-born sleeping beside her, before putting her hand back upon the infant against her chest. "And this one is Donhran."

"They all look strong and healthy," Aalre said. "Like their fathers."

"You know my father?" Corandra asked excitedly.

"All Agrodien camped here know your father," the female replied. "They pray to the great Q'sharh for his safety. They pray he overpowers Kayl'sro Greil and takes the Iron Claws of Agrodia for himself."

"Then we can go home," the youngling added.

Aalre looked to Galonia and Evalad for the right words.

"We can't go home, daughter," Galonia said. "We have no home now."

"We must make a new home for ourselves," Aalre added.

"Then we are going to take the lands of men?" Corandra asked.

"No, my daughter," a voice said from behind her.

The group turned to see a giant, dark creature moving into the firelight, baring its teeth menacingly. Behind it, a group of riders approached through the trees.

They were all human, except for one,

"Papa!" Corandra was on her feet and racing towards her father before the others had time to process what was happening. Her tiny form darted past the rukyul, ignoring the beast.

Yuri quickly jumped down from his steed and moved to intercept her, lifting her from the ground and wrapping her in his arms.

"I think it's time to go home," he said.

Thirty

It wasn't long before every Agrodien gathered together to hear Yuri speak. They hung on every word that he told them as he described the violent exchange between warrior and warrior on both sides of the ravine where Greil's loyalists met their end. Eventually, his tale moved to Alice's involvement.

Yuri pointed to her as she sat by the fire with the rukyul lying by her side with his head resting on her lap. Her hand rubbed the creature behind the ear, to which he responded with soft, gratified moans. She looked up to see all eyes upon her as he spoke and gestured with his body and mimed movements made during the battle.

The Erilian women and Oliver watched with interest, not understanding the Agrodien's words, but knowing the tale he told. Oliver, sitting by Alice's side, grinned and thumped her gently on the arm.

"He's taking about you," he said. "At least, I think he is. Excellent talker, this one."

Alice almost laughed out loud, pursing her lips to contain the sound.

"Kayl'sro Greil, shakarh se tarhn." Yuri made a motion as if he had something wrapped in his left arm and he was peeling the top of it off with his right hand. He pretended to drop the invisible object onto the ground while holding the invisible item up for all to see, or imagine that they could see. "Kayl'sro Greil puol ke se tarhn."

He pointed to Alice with his left hand.

Her stomach tightened as he faced the crowd of one-hundred-and eighty strong.

"Du jhun se ti, Kayl'sro Alice," he turned and bent his knee to her. "Kayl'sro Alice."

The adults reacted immediately, kneeling towards the girl. The older among the younglings followed suit. The younger toddlers stared in awe.

Alice moved, disturbing the rukyul who complained with a grumble. She rose to her feet, the iron claws glinting in the firelight.

"You're their leader now," Akasati told her. "They will look to you for hope."

"What do I do?" the girl asked.

"I'm not quick to trust anyone." Oliver stood by her side. "But I believe these creatures to be an honourable race."

"Then why did they side with the White Witch and attack Woodmyst?"

"False promises?" The man shrugged. "Who knows? Maybe they were a different group to these. What I can see is that they have only a handful of warriors. Not enough to take on Woodmyst. They need help, Alice. And I think you're the one to give it to them."

Alice walked around the hearth and touched Yuri on the shoulder. He looked up at her.

"Kayl'sro?"

"Tell them," she began by gesturing to her mouth and then to the crowd, "to gather their belongings." She moved her hands down and pretended to scoop up something and hold it to her chest. "We need to go home." She waved her hand towards the Agrodien and pointed in the glade's direction.

Yuri nodded, saying something as he pointed to the horses, then to the east.

"Agrodien cheeldrin!" He pointed to the multitude, and moved his hand to the girl, "Kayl'sro Alice cheeldrin." He then gestured to the east again, "Kayl'sro Alice fahmlee."

She swallowed hard and nodded.

"Yes, Yuri," she said as she placed her arm under his and guided him to his feet. She pointed to the Agrodien massed nearby. "Kayl'sro Alice's children. And now we go home."

He nodded, turning to the crowd. His voice was loud as he relayed the message. At least, Alice hoped he did.

It wasn't long before they packed the horses and prepared to move.

"Which way should we go?" Sharek asked. "It's a long way back to where you fought the Haigok and the western road will take us too close to Woodmyst."

"We climb the next ridge and move to the east," Alice replied, peering up at the moon that was already sinking in the western sky. "We'll pass by the quarry pretty close, but there won't be anyone there. We should be safe.

"By the time we get back to the glade, the sun will be up," she continued, turning to Akasati and Rhydra. "Could I ask you both to ride ahead and inform Arthur that I'm safe?"

"Your husband, you mean?" Akasati smiled.

"No!" Oliver gasped. "No. Alice, no. You didn't."

"I'm not a little girl anymore, Oliver," she said, and shrugged.

"You are to me."

"And Arthur isn't a little boy either." She smiled.

"By the gods," the man huffed. "I don't want to know. Please."

The Erilian women giggled as they mounted their steeds.

"You want us to go now?" Rhydra asked.

"No," Alice answered. "I think once we reach the quarry. It's not that far. Perhaps an hour or two."

"Kayl'sro Alice," Yuri called.

The girl turned to see all fires extinguished, and Agrodien mounted for the journey.

"Let's go," she said, lifting herself onto her stallion.

***

It was slow going, much slower than Alice expected. The young-lings were tired and expressed their discomfort with persistent crying and complaining. Even with the barrier of understanding their words, she could hear the tone of their voices, which were not that dissimilar to a human toddler whinging to their mothers when something wasn't going their way.

The climb to the top of the ridge was the worst part. It was long and constant. Always upwards. Always ascending. Some places steep. Some places less so. But always, always up.

Alice urged Oliver to take the lead when they reached the summit so she could wait for the last of the riders to reach her. The Erilian women took to the rear of the pack, helping the stragglers along. When she saw them, receiving a signal from them that all was clear, with a wave of Sharek's hand, Alice turned her stallion around to return to the front of the line.

This exchange repeated several times during the journey, and would have moved along much more quickly if every Agrodien didn't slow down to bow to her, acknowledging her by name.

"Kayl'sro Alice," they would say. The words rebounded around and around in her head. She knew that when the time came to put her head down to rest, she would hear these words again and not be able to sleep.

As the moon sank into the forest behind them, a purple glow appeared on the eastern horizon. Alice pulled her cloak about her tightly, feeling the cool against her skin. She sidled up to Oliver, who was looking over the land ahead of them.

"I think I know where we are," he said. "The quarry is just to the right, beyond that ridge."

She nodded and pointed directly ahead.

"We're going to follow the rise to the left. After that, we'll come back upon our own trail and then we're home."

"You should send Rhydra and Akasati on ahead," Oliver suggested. "They might help prepare food and water for this lot."

Alice nodded as they continued plodding along.

"That's a lot of food," she surmised.

"You might need to consider some more items to add to the list that Andris intends to take back to Woodmyst," the other advised.

"Good idea," she acknowledged. "I could use your help with that."

"You needn't ask," he told her, slapping her on the thigh.

The rukyul growled.

"It's all right. I know her," Oliver said to the creature.

It continued to watch the man warily as Alice snickered.

"I'll go back and tell Rhydra and Akasati it's time to go," she said, pulling the stallion around again before galloping towards the back of the mob.

"Kayl'sro?" Yuri called softly.

"It's all right, friend." Oliver held his hand up and smiled, assuring the Agrodien she was fine. "We're almost home."

"Home?"

"Ah," Oliver thought of words that the other might understand. He then pointed to himself and then to the ridge ahead. "Family. Children."

The Agrodien nodded slowly, seeming to comprehend.

"Home," he repeated. "Fahmlee. Cheeldrin. Home."

***

The few cattle and sheep brought from Woodmyst gathered at the far eastern end of the glade. The sun was slowly making its appearance above the distant peaks, sending a golden veil of light over the camp.

Arthur, who had not slept a wink all night, busied himself with collecting water from the stream. He was already on his fifth trip, carrying two full pails back to the cabin so he could top up the barrel in the kitchen.

He passed through the group of horses, treading carefully, avoiding the clumps of manure left by the steeds. He considered collecting it to fertilise a garden he planned to start near the hut.

Emily was kneading dough on a table inside. She had opened a second small sack of flour and used it all, making several smaller loaves.

Arthur saw a few steaming cakes of bread sitting on the bench near the stove. Inside, a few more were baking.

"We'll have enough bread for a week," he said, lifting the pails onto the bench next to the barrel.

"I don't think so," she replied. "I have a strange feeling I will need to make even more yet."

He removed the lid of the barrel, eyeing her questioningly as he lifted the first pail of water and poured it in.

"What is it?" Arthur quizzed.

"We'll need food and water," she told him, squeezing the mix between her fingers. "Lots of it. There are people coming."

"How do you know?" He lowered the empty pail to the ground and picked up the second one.

Emily shook her head and frowned. "Just a feeling."

"She does that too," he said. "Did you know?"

"Alice?" she asked, turning to him.

He nodded.

"I've seen her use her intuition," Emily replied as she returned to the dough.

"No." He shook his head, lowering the empty pail to the floor. "It's something else. As if she can see without understanding what she can see."

He placed the lid back on the barrel.

"She once told me of fire sweeping through Woodmyst," he said. "It was a while ago, not that long after Tomas passed."

"She was probably having dreams of the catapults or what the Seven did on the night of the straw men."

"I don't think so," he replied. "She talked about the walls standing strong, but the great oak turning to ash. The oak in the ruins wasn't all that big at the time.

"When she spoke the other night about making the dragon fire dance, it reminded me of it. And now, seeing you making all this bread because of a feeling you have, makes me wonder if she wasn't seeing something yet to come."

Emily had stopped kneading, absorbing Arthur's words.

Both stood motionless, blankly staring at nothing in particular, until the boy snapped out of his trance and lifted the pails again. Emily seemed to snap back to reality and continued rolling the dough.

"Did you tell your father of this?"

"No," the boy replied. "I wasn't certain what she was talking about. I'm still not. What would I tell him?"

She nodded, considering what Alice could have meant by her words.

"I should fetch some more water," Arthur said, moving to the open door.

He stepped off the porch and peered across the glade to the six Agrodien gathered by the fire. Simon was offering them tea, and they were gladly taking it, bowing their heads respectfully.

His eyes focused on the tree-line to the west.

Two figures were moving beneath the cover, too far for his eyes to distinguish.

"Someone approaches," he called to Emily, dropping the pails and rushing to the hearth. Simon looked over to him as he drew nearer. Arthur gestured to the western end of the glade.

The man turned to see two horses appear on the open ground, trotting towards them. He recognised the riders immediately.

Emily rushed to his side, smiling as she watched them approach. She moved her attention over to the trees behind the two riders, waiting, hoping to see her daughter.

Her smile slowly faded as the Erilian women neared the camp.

"They're on their way," Rhydra announced.

"Where is she?" Arthur asked them.

"She's safe." Akasati smiled. "Mister Alice."

Rhydra giggled.

"What?" Simon furrowed his brow. "Mister Alice, what?"

He looked at the boy, who was blushing. His eyes moved to Emily, who was trying not to smile, then to the two women on horseback who were continuing to giggle.

"No!" He shook his head. "No bloody way. Did you let this happen?"

Emily stared at him with wide eyes, placing her dough-covered hand on her chest.

"By the gods, Arthur," Simon fumed. "Couldn't you keep it in your pants for just a year or two more?"

"It's not entirely his fault, Simon," Emily pointed out. "Alice has a mind of her own and can be a little forceful too."

"She sure can," Arthur said, smiling.

The Erilian women guffawed at the comment.

"Unbelievable!" The man shook his head. "What's your father going to say when he finds out? Oh, bugger me. Bugger me now."

"While Simon comes to grips with his desire to be buggered," Akasati started, "we need to prepare for almost two hundred Agrodien."

Arthur looked at Emily's stained hands, realising this was probably what she was sensing.

"We should remove the bindings from these ones," the Erilian continued. "They're not a threat. Alice has become their leader. Their queen, I think. They call her Kalsrow."

"Kayl'sro?" one of the Agrodien said, offering a curious glare.

"Kayl'sro," Akasati repeated.

"Kayl'sro Alice?" He stood up, looking into the woods.

"She's coming," Rhydra assured him. "They're all coming."

"This one is Gharnef," Simon told them.

"Gharnef," the Agrodien repeated, thumping his chest softly. "Simon," he said, gesturing to the man.

"That's right," he replied, approaching the Agrodien to undo his bindings. "I'm Simon. I've been learning their names. Bloody hard, if you ask me." He moved to the female and helped her off the ground, pointing to another reptilian sitting nearby. "That one is Nakrah. That's Mralnar, then there's Bein. I think his name is the easiest to say. I like him the most. The one next to him is Vaktor and this lovely lass is Nola'ee."

He dropped her bindings on the ground and moved to the next.

"How do you tell them apart?" Akasati asked, moving her eyes from one to the other.

"Well," Simon said, frowning. "The female has tits, for a start."

"You idiot," the Erilian breathed.

Simon chuckled.

"They have got distinguishing features," he pointed out. "Just like us. Bone structure, colours and patterns on their scales. I don't expect it to be easy, but with time you'll be able to tell them apart."

"We'll have two hundred of them here soon," she told him. "Do you plan on learning all of their names?"

"I'll try." He smiled. "Maybe, I'll try to learn their words too."

"You?" Arthur raised his brow. "Learn?"

"Don't you start." Simon pointed a finger at him. "Mister Alice."

Thirty-One

"We don't have enough tents for them," Alice said to Oliver as they entered the glade. "We'll need to get everyone working to clear the entrances to the caverns along the southern edge of the glade."

"That's a lot of work," he replied. "I don't think we have enough hands to get it done in one day."

She thought about that for a moment.

"We'll clear the big one first," she told him. "The one to the east. Where you were all taken as children by the Night Demons. The Haigok."

"Haigok?" Yuri tuned in, recognising the word.

Alice shook her head. "No Haigok. Not here."

"We can house them all in there until we clear the other caves," Oliver agreed. "It might be cramped."

"I don't think they will care," she replied. "We just can't have them sleeping on open ground."

She looked back to the exodus of reptilians behind her.

"They will need blankets," Alice observed, seeing a few coverings draped over the shoulders of the younglings. "We'll need to scrounge what we can until we send our list to the council for supplies."

"Do you think David will give over so much if he knows we were aiding the Agrodien?" Sharek asked.

"We'll send a message on the list," Alice replied. "We'll tell the council we are all well. We'll inform them that the Agrodien has had a recent change in leadership and has sought refuge with us in the glade.

We'll say that the new Kayl'sro wishes to treat with Woodmyst and awaits invitation for peaceful negotiation."

"A leader of a people for less than a day," Oliver said, "and already speaking like a politician."

***

Arthur had arranged for makeshift tables to be set up near the cabin. Some wide planks of timber, hoisted upon stumps, ran parallel to the porch. The camp busied themselves, placing as many plates and bowls they could find on one table, stacking them together at one end. Twenty large loaves of Emily's bread were placed near to two large pots of venison stew, made from the leftover meat from the spit they enjoyed the night before. Seeing the multitude approaching through the trees, Arthur hoped there would be enough for all of them. He looked at the food again and had his doubts.

"We'll need more," he said to the others. "We don't have enough."

"Let them eat first," Lucy said, and smiled. "We ate last night. My guess is that they probably did not. They'll appreciate whatever we can spare. You've done well to organise all of this in such a short time. Don't fret."

He nodded, trying to push his worries aside.

Alice guided the stallion to the end of the porch, where she tethered the beast before turning her attention to her new husband.

As she moved towards him, the rukyul sniffed at the contents of the tables.

"Get out of it," Arthur rebuked.

It growled grumpily.

"Move," Alice commanded, pushing past the creature. It lowered its head and sauntered a few steps away before settling itself on the ground.

She wrapped her arms around her husband, planting a long kiss on his lips. The Agrodien migrants watched in awe as their Kayl'sro exchanged a moment of affection with the other. Some muttered to each other, smiling. The younglings giggled or asked their mothers questions as they observed the two.

"Why do they press faces, Papa?" Corandra asked her father.

"They are in love," Yuri answered, watching Gharnef reuniting with his family with embraces and kisses. He directed his daughter's attention to his friend. "They are just like us, see."

"I don't think I've ever seen you and Mama press faces like that," she said, squinting.

"There are a lot of things that you haven't seen your mama and me do," the Agrodien smiled.

"Yuri," Galonia chided with a smile. "She's not old enough to know."

He kissed his daughter's head, returning his gaze to the human girl.

"Something tells me her elders don't believe she is old enough either," he perceived.

"What do you think?" his wife asked, cradling their infant son as she moved to his side. "Will she make a good Kayl'sro?"

"It doesn't matter," he replied. "She *is* the Kayl'sro. I pledge myself to her. I will say this; she differs from the rest of them. They are weaker than her. Softer."

"That is easy to see," Koryn, his son, said. "Look at their skin. It's smooth and fair. And why does the fur only grow on the females' heads and not on the faces also like the males?"

"I'm uncertain." Yuri shook his head. "They are a strange creature, these men."

***

By mid-morning, they made a list and terms for the Kayl'sro to meet with the leaders of Woodmyst before Andris left with his wife Sevrina to deliver them.

With the previous night's meal completely devoured, and knowing they would all be famished by supper time, Alice prepared to butcher a heifer and set the women to baking bread and preparing potatoes for the next meal. She also ordered the men to clear the larger cavern.

Yuri, upon seeing this, instructed his twelve warriors to assist the humans in the clean-up. Using axes and bare hands, the crew cut shrubbery away and moved fallen trees to allow for uninhibited access.

By midday, the cavern's entrance was clear, bread was baking and a cow's carcase hung from a tree on the northern edge of the glade. Alice gave the innards and offcuts to the rukyul as the hounds looked on jealously, unwilling to challenge the massive creature to the claim.

Many of the Agrodien females rested and their younglings slept soundlessly upon the grasses of the glade. They were exhausted, worn out from the travelling and sleepless nights, fearing what lurked in the darkness.

"How do you want to do this?" Arthur asked Alice, standing nearby with his eyes on the carcase. "Spit or stew?"

"We'll portion it out," she replied. "Let them decide how they want to prepare it. I'm claiming these ribs for us." Alice ran her knife around the large section of beams on the cow's right torso. "There's plenty of meat there."

"More than enough," the boy nodded, peering at the flesh wrapped around the long stems of bone.

"Can I put my bid in?" Jeremy asked, standing by Arthur. Grit and dirt covered the two of them from head to toe, after contributing to the clean-up at the cavern's entrance.

"Of course," she replied.

"I'll take the other ribcage," he said. "I plan to stew it and make it go as far as I can for the crew."

"We'll give the rest to the Agrodien," Alice said. "It should be enough with bread and potatoes."

"Then we need to concern ourselves with tomorrow's meals." Jeremy sighed.

"We'll hunt and fish tomorrow," Alice replied. "And again, the next day and the next. We can start drying some meat, build a smokehouse, and set up a store in the cavern behind my hut. With the supplies from Woodmyst, we'll last this winter."

"As long as David upholds his end of the bargain," the captain said.

"We have the quarry," she pointed out, sliding her blade beneath the shoulder of the carcase. "He wants a wall."

***

David read through the list. Andris watched quietly as the man ran his eyes over the contents twice. The chief placed the parchment on the table and slid it across to Richard, who read the message and the demands.

"Kayl'sro?" the old man muttered. "I'm assuming this is the leader of their kind."

"It is." Andris nodded, keeping the finer details to himself.

"Is this their title or name?" Richard queried.

"It's the title," the commander of the guard answered.

"And do they have a name to accompany the title?"

Andris thought hard and carefully, trying to choose his words.

"Their names are difficult to say, my lords," Sevrina said from the front row of seats. "Kayl'sro is the preferred title."

Richard muttered and nodded as he returned his attention to the list.

"Seems reasonable," he offered, sliding the parchment back to David. "Are you willing to accept their terms?"

"What's your take on this Kayl'sro and the Agrodien?" David asked the commander.

"I trust them," Andris replied. "I think we should meet with the Kayl'sro to discuss terms. We should send an envoy to invite them here. They are willing to come. In the meantime, we should gather supplies and send them with the envoy in good faith. Most of the items on that list benefit our people, not just the Agrodien."

"Agreed," Richard stated.

"As do I," Ruttger nodded. "Besides, it's not often we get to treat with another species. I'd like to meet this Kayl'sro."

David looked at the list and read it through again.

"Even if I thought otherwise," he started, "the majority has the vote. We will send an envoy and everything on the list on the morrow.

If these Agrodien seek a peaceful coexistence with us, we should be willing to assist them.

"Send blankets, timber, iron and tools. They should try to build shelters before the snows come. Their children should be warm and in beds of their own, if they sleep in beds.

"Inform the Kayl'sro that it would please us to receive their presence at their leisure," David continued, directing his attention to Andris. "We'll meet here to discuss terms. Emphasize that the day after to-morrow might be preferable. But don't make it sound like a demand. The sooner we can start working together, the better."

***

Alice sat in a deep cushioned chair inside her cabin, sleeping soundly as her family cleaned up after their meal of ribs and taters. Even with all the ruckus of plates scraping and cutlery falling, she didn't stir one bit.

"How is she able to sleep like that?" Catherine questioned, watching the girl in awe.

"She's exhausted," Joanne replied. "The sooner we get this cleaned up, the sooner we can leave her in peace."

"I don't think you could wake her if you tried," Arthur replied. Dark rings had formed under his eyes from the sleepless nights of worry.

"Then we'll be quick so we can leave you in peace," Emily told him, placing an arm around his shoulders.

From outside, loud crunching and cracking resonated. Lucy stood at the open door, holding Holly's and Antony's hands.

"He's eating the bones," the little boy laughed, pointing to the rukyul lying on the grass just beyond the porch. Arthur peeked through the gap between the boy and the door frame.

Sure enough, the great creature crushed the discarded ribs in his teeth, happily groaning with each munch. A few of the dogs that had followed some of the residents from Woodmyst sat a few feet from the beast, watching and hoping for a share. The rukyul eyed them warily, growling if one ventured a little too close for comfort.

"Promise you'll keep the children away from him," Arthur said to Lucy.

"I've got them," she assured him. "Besides, they're not game enough to go any closer to him than I am."

Soon after, they cleaned and stacked the plates, polished and put away the cutlery. Takmel and Catherine said their goodbyes and retired to their tent for the night.

Emily, Joanne and Lucy prepared to leave, but Arthur, in a half-sleepy stupor, asked them to stay for tea.

"Usually, I would say yes, Arthur," Emily replied. "But tonight, I am going to refuse."

"Same for me," Lucy said, lifting Holly into her arms.

"And me," Joanne told him, taking Antony's hand. "You need to sleep, Arthur. Blow out the candles when we leave and put your wife and yourself to bed."

Arthur was secretly thankful. He really wanted to go to bed.

"Perhaps another time," he offered politely.

"Another time." Lucy kissed his cheek.

After they bade him farewell, he followed them to the porch and watched them as they returned to their tents for the night. The rukyul continued crunching the ribs, seemingly oblivious to what was occurring around him. Arthur looked over at it as he reached for the doorknob.

"Goodnight, ugly," he said, smiling, shutting the night outside.

He moved to Alice and lifted her by the arms. She awoke, moaning groggily as he raised her.

"I can walk," she protested.

"I've got you," he said, carrying her through the sitting room and into their bedroom to the rear of the cottage.

Arthur lowered her gently into the bed, where she instantly fell back into a deep sleep. He removed her boots and trousers, leaving her in her undergarments before lifting the covers over her.

Returning to the sitting room, he moved her sheathed swords from the floor where she had placed them earlier in the day to a hook upon the back of the door. Checking the latch, he made sure the door was secure before moving around the cabin to extinguish the lanterns, two in the sitting room posted on opposite walls, and one in the kitchen dangling from a length of chain above the table.

Carefully, he navigated his way around the furniture, feeling his way in the dark, back to the bedroom. Finding the bed, he sat on the edge and removed his own boots and trousers, leaving only his breeches on.

Sliding under the covers, he shivered slightly as he tried to find his comfort zone. Before he could, Alice stretched an arm and leg over him, nestling her face against his neck.

He was trapped.

Arthur hoped he was tired enough to fall asleep, no matter how uncomfortable he felt.

Sure enough, his eyes grew heavy as his body relaxed.

The sound of the rukyul crunching bone grew fainter and fainter as a sensation of total ease swept over him like a gentle wave.

Before long, he was sound asleep.

Thirty-Two

Arthur woke with a start.

There was noise outside the cabin. The sounds of people taking and moving about were faint, but clear. He looked over to his side to see Alice still sound asleep, half covering him with her body.

He didn't want to get up. He was happy here. He had found his comfort zone. Arthur was content to lie there forever.

Then she stirred.

"Good morning," she whispered.

"Good morning to you," he replied. "Did you sleep well?"

"Mm'hmm." She stretched her arms to the side. "What time of the day is it?"

"I don't know," he answered. "We might have slept through an entire year for all I care."

"We should get up," she told him, resting her head on his chest.

"I don't want to," he replied, running his fingers through her hair. "Let's just stay here."

She smiled and kissed him.

"I would like so very much to do that," she said, sitting up. "But we have much to do."

She was right, but he still didn't want to leave the cot.

"I'm your husband, woman," he said, as sternly as his playful attitude would allow him. And I say we will stay in bed all day long."

She giggled, looking at him lying on the mattress as he held his arm out to her.

Alice took his hand and hoisted him towards her, flinging him up and into her arms.

"We'll stay in bed all day when it's more convenient," he told her, trying to maintain his demanding voice.

"We will," she promised. "But not today."

He nodded, swinging his legs over the side of the bed.

***

"Sleeping late?" Emily asked the couple as they approached the fire together.

"Mama!" Alice exclaimed, comprehending the hidden message in her mother's question. "We were sleeping. That's all."

The sun was sitting just above the mountain peaks, far to the east. It wasn't as late in the day as Arthur had thought it to be. Most of the dwellers in the glade were finishing breakfast while others like Oliver, Sharek and most of the Agrodien were just waking up to start the day.

"Looks like another wonderful day ahead," Arthur announced, looking up to the clear sky.

"Looks like visitors." Alice nudged him, peering across the glade to the eastern tree-line.

Several wagons appeared on the open ground, one by one. Some pulled by horses while others dragged by bullocks.

Behind them, herdsmen upon steeds guided horses, sheep and cattle into the grassland, using whistles and calls as dogs raced around the animals, keeping them in a tight group.

"Looks as if your requests have been met," Simon commented to the girl before turning to Baldwyn. "I guess that means you'll be back at work soon."

"I guess so," the other replied, seated next to his wife, Elka, holding her hand. "I should probably head out there today with a few others and get things in order."

"I'd offer my help," Jeremy told him. "But we need to get some fishing done."

"And hunting," Simon put in, notifying everyone of what he was intending to do.

"It's all right," Baldwyn assured them. "Gustav and I, maybe five or six others, will be enough to check the equipment. We'll be home well before dark."

A rider in leather armour raced across the glade, overtaking the wagons and galloping towards the camp. A few Agrodien, gathered by a fire at the entrance to the large cavern, watched him ride by.

"I have a message from the council," the soldier called as he pulled his steed to a halt. He held a rolled parchment in his hand. "It's intended for the mediator to the Kayl'sro of the Agrodien."

"I'll take it." Arthur held his hand out to the rider.

"I'm to give it directly to the Kayl'sro or his mediator," the soldier informed them. "My orders were specific."

"The boy is the mediator for the Kayl'sro," Lor replied. "Give him the parchment and he'll make sure to relay the message."

"My apologies, my lord." The soldier handed the message to Arthur. "I was also instructed to inform you that all the requests specified have been fulfilled. In good faith, Woodmyst extends her hand and welcomes the good people of Agrodia and wishes for our two people to—"

"Yes, yes, yes," Simon interrupted the warrior. "Tell David, thank you very much. Now, would you like some tea or water? Something to help you relax before you return home?"

"No, my lord," he replied. "I'm to return as soon as the Kayl'sro gives his response to the message on the parchment."

Arthur was already reaching the end of the letter.

"Alice," he quietly called his wife and started walking towards the eastern edge of camp. Alice was quick to reach his side.

"What is it?"

"Let's go down to the Agrodien camp," he told her softly. "This one thinks the Kayl'sro is a *he*. I don't think he needs to know right now that it is not."

The rukyul watched them moving by and got up to follow.

"No." Alice held her hand up, signalling the creature to stay. It plonked itself back down and lowered its head to the ground.

Yuri saw them approaching, rising to meet them a short distance from the hearth.

"Kayl'sro," he gestured to the campfire, offering the girl and boy a place by it.

"Thank you," Alice replied before sitting down. Arthur sat between her and Yuri, turning to see Simon talking to the soldier, who was looking at both him and Alice warily.

"The rider is watching," Arthur informed her. He turned to Yuri and pointed to the parchment. "This is for the Kayl'sro."

"Kayl'sro Alice." Yuri pointed to the message.

Galonia sat beside Yuri, trying to listen to the conversation.

"Yes," Arthur replied. "But the rider is watching Kayl'sro Alice." The boy pointed subtly over his shoulder, to his eyes, and then to his wife.

Yuri turned to look at the rider talking to the other men. He could see the soldier's face peering towards them.

"I need you to pretend to be the Kayl'sro," Arthur explained, pointing to Yuri.

Yuri seemed offended.

"Bhak'sha Kayl'sro," he thumped his chest, shaking his head. "Du jhun se ti, Kayl'sro Alice."

"Yes, yes," Arthur nodded. "She *is* Kayl'sro Alice. But I need you to be Kayl'sro just for now."

"Bhak'sha Kayl'sro Yuri." He appeared to be angry.

Galonia thumped him on the arm and said something in their words. There was a moment of exchange between the two.

Something about it was amusing to one youngling seated by the fire. He started clapping his hands and laughing before pointing to Yuri.

"Du jhun se ti, Kayl'sro Yuri," the little one hooted.

"Koryn," Yuri reprimanded. The youngling tried to contain himself, snickering quietly to himself. "Kayl'sro Yuri."

Galonia thumped Yuri again and gestured to the parchment, whispering something softly to her husband as she looked over at the rider still upon his horse.

Yuri nodded to the boy.

"Good," he said, smiling. He turned his attention to Alice. "They've requested a meeting with the Kayl'sro. We're to ride to the assembly hall in Woodmyst to treat with the council members.

"They've left it up to us when we should have this meeting, but have stressed that they would prefer sooner rather than later. It's a fair request, considering that they have sent us all these supplies and winter is approaching."

Alice looked over to the wagons moving across the glade, loaded with sacks of flour, bundles of clothes and blankets, canvas, rope, and so much more.

She nodded slowly, looking at Yuri.

"Kayl'sro will meet with the council tomorrow morning, at an hour after sunrise," she said.

Arthur stood up and started towards the rider. Still looking at Yuri, Alice tilted her head subtly towards her husband, a signal for the Agrodien to accompany the boy.

Yuri flashed a questionable look at Arthur and back to Alice. Galonia thumped him on the arm again and hissed something to him, which set the youngling off in a laughing fit again.

Quickly, Yuri jumped to his feet and walked alongside the boy.

Galonia peered at Alice and shook her head with a smile.

The girl nodded, lifted herself from the ground and put a comforting hand on the female's shoulder before following the two others back towards the cabin.

"The Kayl'sro has agreed to meet with the council," Arthur informed the rider.

The soldier looked to the Agrodien and was clearly astounded by the sheer size of the being. Yuri's eyes darted from Arthur to Alice and then to the soldier apprehensively.

"We will arrive an hour after sunrise to treat," the boy finished. "Please pass our intentions onto the Chief of Woodmyst and his councilmen."

"Kayl'sro come," Yuri grunted.

"Yes, my lord," the rider replied, bowing slightly and nervously to Yuri as he pulled his horse around to leave. "Kayl'sro."

With that, the soldier jogged his horse out of the camp before setting off at a high speed out of the glade.

Alice put her hand on the back of the reptilian and smiled. "You did well, Yuri."

The Agrodien inhaled a deep breath and let out a sigh of relief.

"No Kayl'sro Yuri," he grunted. "Du jhun se ti, Kayl'sro Alice. Se ti, Kayl'sro." He pointed to the iron claws around her neck.

"Never again," she said, understanding what he was trying to tell her. "No more Kayl'sro Yuri."

He nodded and was about to turn, until Alice wrapped her arms around his waist, silently thanking him for doing something that he was obviously not comfortable doing.

He placed his large, leathery hand on her back.

Emily smiled as he watched the exchange between the two new friends.

Arthur suddenly felt the Agrodien's arm on his shoulders, drawing him into the embrace as well.

Simon chortled out loud at the strange sight.

"All right, Yuri," Alice said, wanting to be released from his grasp, patting him on the back. "You can let go now."

He held her a little longer.

"Yuri," she repeated. "You can let go. Please."

Thirty-Three

While Baldwyn, Gustav, and a few of the crewmen from the *Adelandria* paid a visit to the stone quarry, the rest of the camp spent the day hunting, fishing and sorting supplies. They cleared several of the caverns nearer to the encampment to store the goods received from Woodmyst.

Alice oversaw the operation in one cave, instructing the men where they should keep the timber planks and boards, placing them in stacks according to their sizes and lengths. Ewan Cunningham managed another cave, guiding the men under his charge, with neatly piling sheets of varying materials in different locations throughout the cavern. To the rear, he placed the canvas sheeting to make tents. Closer to the front, he started a heap for blankets, as they would be required more readily.

Emily busied herself with the dried goods, persuading the Seven and the women from the north to help her start a store behind Alice's cottage, inside the cavern. They brought sacks of flour, wheat, and oats through the front door, through the kitchen and out the back door into the dark expanse of the cave.

Lanterns were lit and taken into the hollow. The women spent a good portion of their day sorting out the area as Lucy and a few of the other wives watched the children outside.

As the reptilian males joined the hunting party, many of the Agrodien women had set themselves to duties as well. Some took up axes from the fresh supplies and gathered wood for the many fires needed in their community. Others chopped timber in the forest and carved crude stakes. A few used shovels, setting the freshly made posts into the ground to mark out a fence line to house the livestock, while some of the older children made a temporary enclosure near the eastern edge of the glade using ropes brought on the wagons.

It was a busy day for all, and when the time came to rest, they were thankful for the two pails of mullet, twelve rabbits and three deer the hunting party brought back with them.

After the meal, some of them gathered around the hearth near the cabin, Agrodien and man side by side.

Simon set to telling the tale of the journey to Blackrock Haven.

"This was the time when the greatest warriors of Woodmyst ventured into the winter wilderness to rescue seven little ladies from an evil sorceress," he explained, standing up and making wild gestures with his arms as he spoke.

The Agrodien seated by the fire, children and adults alike, held captivated by the man, hanging on every word, even though they couldn't understand any part of it.

Simon eventually reached the part where they met the crew of the *Adelandria*. The mention of Captain Dakmel Tarkin resulted in an eruption of cheers from the old crewmen.

The reptilians looked at one another in confusion, but caught on quickly. Every time Simon mentioned a hero of the tale, a cheer resounded. Before long, they joined in.

The night wore on and the story continued. Simon reached a part the crew remembered all too well.

"Then the White Witch slayed poor Ivo after having her way with him," he said. "Captain Tarkin confronted her, calling her by her real name, *Sumaiyya*. She embraced him and called him *Papa* before she slit him open and left him to die.

"She escaped into the night, leaving the good men of the *Adelandria* and of Woodmyst to build a pyre for their friends. And we still weep today when we remember Ivo Hamond of Woodmyst and Captain Dakmel Tarkin of the *Adelandria*."

"Hear! Hear!" Jeremy held his mug up to toast the men.

"I'm going to stop there," Simon announced, sitting beside Tricia and taking her hand in his.

"But you were getting to the best part," Alan, Lor and Linet's son, whined. "You know. Where you storm Blackrock Haven and free the prisoners. And when the Seven use their magic and make the Sovereign go *splosh* all over the throne room." He motioned his hands as if he was exploding.

As others laughed, Oliver and Simon exchanged quick glances.

"Someone else tell a story," Joanne pleaded, looking to the Agrodien. "Maybe one of our new friends."

Corandra urged her father, pushing his arm and hissing words to him. Yuri shook his head, saying something back. The other reptilian children also pressed him to tell a story.

He looked to his Kayl'sro for rescue.

Alice smiled and nodded to him, gesturing to the ground by the fire.

He shook his head and smiled, rising to his feet.

His leathery hand rubbed his chin as he considered what tale to tell. Then he turned to the children and started.

The words were harsh-sounding and strange to their ears. Only the wide eyes of the reptilian younglings told Alice that the story was an exciting one.

Yuri made a motion with his fingers, like someone running. His hand swooped in a slow, downward motion before returning to the running gesture again.

Placing a finger to his lips, his voice lowered and his body bent a little as he pretended to creep across the ground.

He then mimed riding a horse, raising his volume to an exciting level. His hand motioned an upward slope before returning to the invisible reins of the horse he was riding.

"BWOAR," he called. "BWOAR." The Agrodien younglings widened their eyes and stared excitedly at Yuri.

Suddenly, his hands flew out to his side, flapping up and down like bird's wings. His voice was still full of excitement. The Agrodien children were hanging on his every word.

Alice watched as her half-brother and sister leaned forward, soaking in the tale, watching Yuri intensely as he roared.

His hands moved to his face, his fingers wriggled and writhed at the sides of his mouth.

He stretched his arms out again and pretended to fly.

Dragons, she thought. *He's telling them of dragons.*

Yuri returned to riding his invisible steed and finished his tale.

The Agrodien children clapped, signalling the others to join in.

"Yuri," Alice called to him. He turned to face her as he resumed his place by his wife. "Haigok?"

He nodded.

"Haigok." He pointed to the horses.

Alice nodded, understanding.

"What is it?" Arthur asked.

"They stole the horses from the Night Demons," she told him. "That's why they were up on the ridge. They were waiting for the Agrodien to arrive."

"You defeated them," Simon reminded her. "So, it's over."

"Why did the Night Demons attack Woodmyst?" she asked.

"Because of something done during the days of the Realm War," he replied.

"That's right," she said. "They remember."

Simon absorbed her words and slowly realised what she was saying.

"Oh, shit." He frowned.

"We need to return their horses, and then some more in good faith," she told them.

"You killed quite a few of their people," Oliver reminded her. "I don't know if returning property to them will be enough of a compensation for the deaths of their kin."

"I have a feeling that they are a little more honourable when it comes to death in battle," Lor offered. "Otherwise, they would have killed Richard a hundred times over."

"No." Simon shook his head. "I disagree. They killed everyone except for us. They left Richard alive because he protected two of their own. Everyone else died. Men, women, elderly. But only the council members were responsible for what happened to the Night Demons during the Realm War. They don't think like us."

"I don't think you should go," Emily told Alice. "I know that's what you're thinking of doing. I'm begging you not to."

"They'll come for retribution," Alice told them. "Could be in a week. Could be a year from now. It could be when your children are your age now. They will come. They remember."

***

Arthur tidied in the kitchen while Alice used her whetstone on her swords on the porch. She peered to her right, towards the Agrodien campfire, where she could see Yuri and twelve other reptilians cleaning their own blades and preparing their garb for the meeting with the council.

Simon and Oliver remained by the hearth, bidding each person a goodnight as they thinned out one by one, retiring to their tents. Eventually the two men were left alone, watching the young Kayl'sro dotingly.

"It can't be her," Oliver told him. "She wasn't even there. Hell, she wasn't even here. She was off battling Night Demons and lizard men."

"I know," Simon replied. "I know it wasn't her. But do you remember what Tomas told us? Do you remember his account of what happened in the palace at Blackrock Haven?"

"I do," nodded the other. "He said she was ripped apart."

"By the Seven," Simon reminded him as he ran his fingers through his beard.

"You think the Seven are responsible?"

Simon peered at the fire, shaking his head slowly.

"Tricia is your wife, Simon," Oliver said, leaning towards his friend. He continued to watch Alice sharpen her blades. "Do you really think she is capable of murder? I mean, we're not just talking about two men here. They killed children too. Are any of them capable of that?"

"I will say no," Simon replied. "Besides, they were here. How could they have?"

"But you have your doubts." Oliver leant back in his chair.

"Ever since little Alan brought it up tonight," he replied," I can't help but think of the Mirikin. Sumaiyya, Tarkin's daughter, was twisted and manipulated into becoming what she was."

"They all were," Oliver said.

"But they could have all decided not to be that way," Simon argued. "Think about Amicia Elynbrigge. She was the Fuchsia Mistress. She chose to ally herself with us."

"Not until after she destroyed Oakbeach," the other reminded him. "We had friends in Oakbeach."

"I remember." The other scratched at his beard again, thinking back to his younger years. "Now we have friends in Newholt and Dweagan. My point is, Amicia made a choice. Sumaiyya made a choice. The others of the Mirikin made a choice."

"And whoever killed Seamus Harling and Henry Cunningham's family," said Oliver, peering back to him, "they made a choice too."

"Exactly," Simon replied. "I think, as much as it could have been the Seven, there may be a possibility that another witch lives in Woodmyst."

***

Alice stood up, rubbed the rukyul behind the ear, repeated the gesture on her hobbled stallion, chewing on the grass nearby, and returned into the cabin. She placed her swords into the sheaths hung upon the hook on the back of the door and crossed the room to Arthur, kissing him on the back of the neck as he stacked plates on the bench.

He turned to watch her lift a lantern from the sitting room wall before moving to the back door. Opening it, she stepped into the cavern and glanced around at the piles of supplies stacked against the rock walls.

"We should build shelving in here," she told him. "Find some way to keep these sacks off the ground."

"I was thinking about that," he told her as he stepped through the door. He wrapped his arms around her waist. "We'll put racks on both sides and mount lanterns next to each one. I had a quick look today. I think we can build six big shelves on the left, four on the right, and perhaps one long rack against the back wall.

"When we get settled and build dwellings for everyone, we can consider doing something similar in some of the other caves. Maybe the big one can be converted into a stable of sorts," he continued.

"I'm scared," she said suddenly, leaning into him.

He took the lantern from her hand and placed it on the cave floor so that he could wrap his arms around her tightly. She turned towards him and buried her head against his chest.

"I'll be with you tomorrow," he assured her. "I won't leave your side."

"I know," she replied. "But they don't want me. My people don't want me."

"You're the Kayl'sro," he reminded her. "Your people will follow you tomorrow. Your husband will be by your side and they will tremble in your presence."

She smiled, moving her eyes to his.

"I am so glad to be yours," she said, before pressing her lips to his.

Thirty-Four

Dressed in her cloak, hood over her head and swords strapped to her back, Alice saddled a mare, a black steed that was brought to the glade by the Agrodien. Her stallion watched her, snorting and neighing loudly to gain her attention.

"You're staying here," she told him before turning her attention to the rukyul. "You too."

The beast grumbled as he plonked himself on a place by the porch that he had seemed to claim for himself.

The sky was still dark, the first hint of light just breaching the horizon. The sun wouldn't be far from touching the peaks in the distance.

"Kayl'sro Alice," a voice called to her.

She turned to see Galonia and Evalad approaching. Galonia carried a bundle in her arms. She unravelled it before Alice, holding it up for her to see.

It was a dark, earthy-coloured leather cape with a fixed cowl. The inner lining was fine, black silk that ran the entire length of the garment, except for the inch-wide hem where the leather had doubled over. The stitching was so fine that it was barely visible.

Galonia offered it to the girl. "Kayl'sro."

Alice removed her straps.

"No," Evalad told her.

"But I should remove this one," the girl said, holding one flap of her cloak up.

"No," Evalad repeated, gesturing with her hands for Alice to stop.

Galonia draped the cape over the girl's shoulders, concealing the swords upon her back and changing her form, appearing like a hunch-back. It trailed on the ground behind her a few inches and touched the ground near her toes.

The Agrodien females appeared pleased with themselves as Alice ran her hands over the soft leather. It had some weight to it, but she didn't find it at all restricting.

"What animal is this made from?" she asked them.

They responded with curious glances.

Alice ran her hand over the leather. "What type of animal does this skin belong to?"

Galonia seemed to understand, pointing to the cattle grazing in the glade.

"Ou'aong," the Agrodien replied, the word reminiscent of the sound a cow made.

Alice smiled, admiring the attire. She then wrapped her arms around Galonia, before moving to Evalad to do the same.

"Thank you," said the girl, wrapping the cape around her.

"Looks good," Simon told her as he approached. "I had to look twice to see if it was you under there."

"I think that's the idea," Alice replied as the two Agrodien females fussed over her, brushing the shoulders of the cape with their hands.

"How are you feeling?" Simon questioned. "Are you nervous?"

"Yes," she admitted.

"And so you should be," he told her, placing his hands on her shoulders. "You're performing a mission of diplomacy. So, being nervous is perfectly normal."

"How does everyone else appear?" she asked.

"Knots in stomachs," he replied. "Arthur, I think, might shit in his pants. But all in all, we're fine."

Alice smiled.

"We're ready to ride when you are," Simon told her. "Counting my-self, Oliver, and your uncle, you have got eight men of Woodmyst, one captain of a sunken ship, four Erilian ladies, seven witches, two of the northern men, fourteen Agrodien warriors and one husband riding by your side.

"Am I missing anyone?"

"I don't think so." She shook her head, her smile widening. "I don't think I asked any of them, or you, to attend with me. Except Arthur."

"Arthur asked," he admitted. "He did the rounds yesterday after the rider left. Everyone in camp would have come. Women and children too. There's not a chance in hell that I'm going to let you go without me. You, your sister, your mother... I think of you all as my family. Joanne and Lucy. Those two little snot bags too."

She fell into him and wrapped her arms around his large, barrel chest.

"Thank you, Simon." She wept.

"It's all right, little one," he replied, giving her a soft squeeze.

***

Simon led the party of thirty-eight riders out of the glade. Beside him rode Arthur, Lor and Oliver, followed by Joanne and the other six women of the coven. Five other men, the husbands of some sorceresses, surrounded the group, forming a barrier around the Agrodien representatives.

Alice sat upon the black mare, her leather hood pulled low over her face, allowing her a view of the ground and the hind legs of the horses walking in front of hers. With Yuri on her right and Gharnef on her left, steering the beast was practically unnecessary. Their proximity to her directed the steed along the trail with little effort from her.

"Kayl'sro Alice," Yuri said in a low voice. "Good?"

He was learning her language quickly. She hadn't learnt one word of his apart from the meaning of *Kayl'sro* and a few of their names.

"I am good," she replied. "Thank you, Yuri."

He said something in his language, to which Gharnef replied. He then spoke to the warriors riding to her back.

"We keep eyes for you, Kayl'sro Alice," he said.

"You watch for me?"

"Watch," he replied. "Yes. We *watch* for you. You no scare."

She nodded, trying her best to not be afraid.

But she was.

The burden of responsibility felt heavy on her shoulders.

As the sun climbed higher, her nervousness grew more intense.

They were climbing a rise that would put them in view of the city. Sensing that they were getting closer, Alice cried.

Yuri noticed, saying something to the others around him.

"Kayl'sro stop," he said, pulling his horse to a halt beside hers. She yanked gently on the reins and whimpered.

"Arthur," Gharnef called. His voice sounded almost like a roar.

It wasn't long before her husband reached her side.

"Alice?" he said, pulling up to her right. He placed his hand on her thigh. "Are you all right?"

"I don't think I can do this, Arthur," she wept.

"We can turn back if you want."

She shook her head.

"I'm scared," she told him.

"Me too," admitted Arthur.

"I just need a moment." She wiped her eyes with the balls of her hands.

He reached into his pocket and fetched a square piece of material.

"It's the cleanest one that I could find in the cottage," he said, handing it to his wife.

"You didn't clean your nose with it, I hope?" she asked, dabbing her tears away.

"Once or twice," he said, smiling. She slapped his arm playfully and snickered.

"Ow," he whispered.

He took her hand in his as she moved her head to peer from underneath the hood to him.

"When we get back home," he said, "you are going to sit on your arse and let me do everything for one week. You will deserve a break after today."

"I can't," she replied. "We need to return the horses to the Haigok."

He sighed.

"All right," he agreed. "Then I will come with you and wait on you hand and foot the entire way there and back."

"I'm so glad to be yours," she smiled.

"And I'm so glad you are mine," he replied, kissing the back of her hand.

***

A small procession of twelve guards on horseback met the approaching representatives from the glade at the eastern gate into the city. The Agrodien scanned the giant wall in awe, remarking to one another as they moved through the entrance into Woodmyst.

The reptilians tightened their circle around their Kayl'sro. Alice kept her head low and covered well as people lining the streets gathered to watch the strangers moving through their streets.

The sound of hoof falls upon the stone streets was almost an outlandish noise to her. She hadn't heard it for what seemed an extraordinarily long time. It rebounded off the walls and along the alleys that the riders slowly passed as they continued to move into the township.

Alice felt eyes upon her, drilling into her skin, into her mind. She felt vulnerable, naked, and pulled the cape over her exposed hands, hiding as much of her identity as she could.

"Kayl'sro," Yuri grunted, signalling to her it was time to stop.

She pulled the mare to and waited for her two guards, Yuri and Gharnef, to dismount. When they did, she carefully slid from her steed, keeping herself concealed from prying eyes.

Facing the black horse, she wrapped the cape over her, hiding her hands beneath the leather garment.

Arthur moved to her side as five of the men travelling with them led the steeds by hand, a little farther along the road. There, they would wait with the horses until the meeting was over.

"I'll walk before you," Arthur informed his wife. "Follow my feet and mind the stairs."

Alice heard the doors to the assembly hall open with a loud creak.

The procession started up the steps to move into the hall.

As soon as Arthur started forward, Alice stepped in line behind him, Yuri and Gharnef at her flanks.

She took the stairs carefully, not because they were difficult to navigate, but because her nerves were flaring up again. Her stomach tied itself into knots and her breathing became shallow.

Stepping inside the hall made her feel worse as she realised all the rows of seats had filled with observers. She felt as if she was on display as more gasps and whispers filled her ears. Alice knew it was a reaction to the sight of her reptilian companions, but she didn't feel any less comfortable about it.

They were there to see the Kayl'sro.

How disappointed they could be when they see what lies beneath this cover, she thought.

"Chief Gyfford," Simon announced as he approached the platform, "Council members.

May I introduce the Kayl'sro, leader of the Agrodien nation."

The procession stopped in the aisle, not too far from the steps leading up to the stage.

"Arthur?" David called excitedly from his seat. "You came back."

"I'm here as mediator to the Kayl'sro," he replied.

"Oh," his father breathed, letting his smile fade. "I see."

"Did you receive everything on the list, Simon?" Richard asked.

"Yes, we did," the other answered. "Thank you very much. We may require more building materials. Our population in the glade has increased somewhat with the arrival of northern settlers and the Agrodien population seeking refuge."

"It was reported to us that the Agrodien were coming with hostile intentions towards Woodmyst," Ruttger stated. "Is there any truth to this?"

Arthur moved to Alice.

"What do you want me to say?" he whispered softly.

"Tell him the truth," she replied, keeping her voice to a breath.

He turned to face the four councilmen seated at the table on the platform.

"The Kayl'sro has asked me to tell you that this was true," Arthur began. Murmurings built within the hall as people turned to one another so that they could express their opinions. "But the previous leader made that decision, Kayl'sro Greil. The current Kayl'sro wishes to treat and make peace with the good people of Woodmyst, to allow our two peoples to live in harmony and work together so that our communities may thrive."

"Just how did this Kayl'sro get their position?" Andris asked.

Arthur turned to his wife again.

"Tell the truth," she whispered.

"Kayl'sro Greil was killed in conflict by the current Kayl'sro," Arthur replied, turning to face the council again. "According to their traditions, the one who vanquishes a Kayl'sro becomes Kayl'sro."

"So," Ruttger furrowed his brow, staring at the hooded figure suspiciously. "To become the leader, they kill their leader. They kill their own. Sounds barbaric."

"Not all peoples in this world are as civilised as yourself, Councilman Harrow," Simon put in. "And not all leaders have been great at their duties. It wasn't that long ago when you would tell me such truths. Remember the Mirikin?"

"This is a little different," Ruttger replied.

"Ay," the other agreed. "The Mirikin wanted to burn us all. These people want to treat with you and have peace. I would say that was a little different."

"You've told us of Kayl'sro Greil," Richard said. Oliver shot Lor and Simon a quick look of concern. "But we haven't been formally introduced to the new Kayl'sro."

Alice heard people shuffling in their seats as all eyes moved to her.

Arthur turned to Alice again.

"What do I do?" he asked softly.

"Introduce me," she replied.

His chin quivered as the corners of his mouth drooped.

"I love you, Alice," he whispered.

She smiled as one tear streaked down her cheek.

"Chief Gyfford," Arthur called loudly, "Councilmen and citizens of Woodmyst. Let me *formally* introduce you to my wife, Kayl'sro Alice Gyfford."

Alice threw the cape from her shoulders and onto the floor.

Silence fell across the room as she lowered the hood of her grey cloak.

The jaws of the four councilmen dropped open as she stepped forward, moving to her husband's side.

"I am Kayl'sro of the Agrodien," she told them.

"No." David shook his head.

"These people are under my protection," she continued.

"No," the chief said again, louder.

"David," Ruttger said softly. "Control yourself."

"I banished you from this city," the other yelled angrily, thumping his fist on the table as he stood to his feet.

"You banished Alice Warde," she replied. The fourteen Agrodien moved their hands to the hilts of their swords. "You invited here the Kayl'sro. Here am I to treat for my people. Here am I to make peace."

"Treat?" David barked as he moved around the table.

"David, what are you doing?" Ruttger stood up.

"Peace?" The chief stepped down from the platform. "You killed my wives and my baby daughter. Why would I want to treat with you?"

"What?" Alice's expression changed to one of confusion. "I didn't..."

David pulled his sword free.

"Papa," Arthur yelled. "Put that away."

Simon freed his blade and moved to intercept the angry giant. The sound of swords being pulled from sheathes rang through the room. Agrodien prepared to defend their Kayl'sro. Lor and Oliver readied themselves to protect the girl. Guards posted around the room equipped themselves for battle.

"You killed my family," David hollered, gripping his sword so tightly that his knuckles turned white, tears streaming down his face. "Why did you do that?"

Thirty-Five

"David," Simon bellowed. "You will have to fight your way through all of us to get to her."

"Guards," Ruttger called from the platform. Men lining the room stepped forwards. The Agrodien prepared to fight.

The odds were against them all.

"Sheath your swords," Ruttger commanded.

The guards about the hall looked questionable at the men on the platform. Andris moved to the edge of the stage.

"You heard the councilman," the commander called. "Put your weapons away."

A chorus of clacks resounded around the room as the soldiers slid their blades back into their sheaths and stepped back into their positions.

"Yuri." Alice touched the Agrodien on the arm. He glanced at her before returning his eyes to the guards lining the wall, unsure of what was happening.

"Kayl'sro?"

"Put the sword away," she instructed.

He peered at her again, tilting his head slightly. She pointed to his blade, then to his sheath.

"Put it away," she repeated.

He looked to the guards, to the angry man at the front of the room, and then to her. His expression told her he wasn't happy to follow her command, but he complied reluctantly.

"Kayl'sro?" he hissed.

"It will be fine," she said, smiling, tears streaming down her face. She gestured to the Agrodien warriors, still holding their swords. "Tell them."

He relayed the command, to which he received curious stares. He had to repeat the order once more before they slid their blades back into their coverings.

"Simon, Uncle Lor, Oliver," she said calmly. "Sheath your swords and step aside."

"Alice," Lor began, "this is what this bastard wants. I'm not about to let him hurt you."

"And I'm not about to let my people be hurt because of this either," she replied, gesturing to the reptilians who were still on edge. "Sheath your swords and step aside."

David's eyes flicked around the room to each man before him before landing on the girl standing in the middle of the room.

"We should leave," Joanne, standing behind the Agrodien warriors, leaned towards her. "We can back out of here and just go home."

"This is your home," she replied. "I was the only one exiled. Not you. Not the Seven. Not the crew of the *Adelandria*. Simon, my mother, my husband. They banished none of you along with me."

She turned to face David, who was red in the face, clutching his sword tightly.

"If you defeat me," she began.

"No, Alice," Arthur protested, stepping towards her. He felt as if he had just been punched hard in the stomach. "Don't do this."

"I have to," she replied.

"You pit my own son against me," David growled.

"You did that yourself," Oliver replied, putting his sword away. "What happened to you?"

"We can just go." Arthur placed his hands on her shoulders. "Let's just go."

"My people need a home, Arthur," she said. "They won't have one if David remains the chief and I'm still breathing. I'm the Kayl'sro. He won't grant them peace if I lead them."

"I'm your people," he sobbed. "Me. We can find another land far away."

"This is our home," she cried.

Arthur turned and pointed an angry finger at his father.

"You do not know what she did," he shouted, stepping towards the hulking man. "You weren't even there."

"I was standing on the road," the chief replied. "I saw what she did. I saw her face. I saw her eyes. She made those horses run. She made them cross the bridge."

"I watched as the bridge broke," he continued. "I watched as your mother, Martha and your little sister fell into the water."

"You have it wrong." Arthur shook his head. "You have it so wrong. You're blinded by your hatred. You falsely blame my wife for something she didn't do."

"I've seen her control beasts," David roared. "I've heard about the rukyul in the glade.

Don't tell me she didn't call those horses with her witchery."

"She was trying to stop them, Papa!" the boy shouted. He took a step forward and lowered his voice. "She was trying to stop them."

David's eyes moved to meet those of his son.

"I told you this once before," Arthur said. "But you didn't listen to me then, just as you are not listening now."

As Alice pulled her blades free, the sound rang out through the room.

David tensed as he moved his glare back at the girl.

"Papa," the boy pleaded.

Taking a deep breath, Alice lowered her swords and placed them on the stone floor. She took her hunting knife out and put it next to the long blades before standing to full height again.

"Kayl'sro?" Yuri looked at her questioningly.

With tears still streaming from her eyes, she smiled to the Agrodien and stepped towards her husband.

"Step aside, Arthur," she told him.

"No," he replied, keeping his eyes on his father.

Alice kneeled on the floor behind him, holding her arms out to her sides to show that she was unarmed.

"If my end is what will give him peace," she said as she lowered her head, "then he should strike me down."

"Then, he will need to kill me also." Arthur stood defiantly between his father and his wife.

"David," Joanne cried from the back of the room. "Please don't do this."

"You are making enemies today, Chief Gyfford," Simon said, frowning. "You think you're suffering with pain now? You think losing your wives and daughter justifies this action? If you touch that boy and girl, I swear I won't stop until I end you. I swear it by the gods, David."

"She was trying to stop them, Papa," Arthur said, attempting one more try at negotiating peacefully.

"I move that Chief Gyfford be stripped of his position as leader of this community and member of this council," Richard quickly said, taking the only action he could in such limited time. "Do I have a second?"

"Ay," Ruttger replied.

"Ay," Andris repeated.

"It's unanimous," the old man decreed. "David Gyfford, you are no longer chief of Woodmyst or a member of this council. With such a limited number on the council, I feel that representation is not reflective of Woodmyst's needs and move that this council be disbanded until a time when reformation of its members can be established. Do I have a second?"

"Ay," the two other members chorused.

"It's unanimous." Richard frowned. "Council is adjourned."

The hulking man continued to glare at Alice. His sword hand shook slightly as beads of sweat formed on his brow.

Not seeing a chance that this would end well, Alice reached out and put her hand on Arthur's heel.

"I'm so glad to be yours," she sobbed.

"And I'm so glad you are mine," he replied, standing his ground.

David's chin quivered as he pursed his lips. His hand went to his face as his emotions seemed to explode.

His sword clanged loudly on the stone floor as he dropped to his knees, bawling uncontrollably.

"I'm sorry," he blubbered. "I'm so sorry."

"Guards!" Andris signalled to two men by the edge of the platform to move over to the kneeling man.

Arthur wanted to comfort his father, but felt a stronger need to be by his wife as the two soldiers approached.

"Take former Chief Gyfford to the barrack's cells," the commander instructed. "Make sure he is comfortable and that his needs are seen to."

The two men reached under David's arms and hoisted him to his feet.

"I'm sorry, Alice," he sobbed as they moved him into the aisle. Alice stood and moved to the side to allow them to pass. "I'm sorry," he continued to say as the guards escorted him out the door.

The crowd murmured.

"I apologise to the Kayl'sro," Richard announced, calling the assembly back into focus. "This unforeseen event has changed the regular proceedings somewhat. I believe I speak for all of Woodmyst and her citizens when I say that we hope to have peace with the Agrodien nation.

"Although unofficial, I extend my hand in a gesture for peaceful relations between our people, hoping together we can not only live side by side, but unite as one community from this day forward."

Richard leant upon his chair with his left hand, holding his right arm out to Alice.

She looked to Arthur, who nodded to her.

"Go on," he whispered.

Alice wiped her tears away and started up the steps to the platform. A lump formed in her throat and a knot tightened in her stomach.

Reaching out, she took Richard's hand.

"Welcome home, Alice," he whispered, smiling proudly. Before she replied, he pulled her in to him and wrapped his arms around her. "Welcome home."

Applause resonated through the room as people rose to their feet.

"And they say politics is boring," Oliver quipped.

Simon replied with a soft jab to the other's ribs, continuing to applaud as Richard released Alice so she could shake the hands of the other former councilmen.

***

The breeze was cool, swimming through the leaves of the great oak. Alice listened to the rustle of the foliage and gentle creaking of the limbs as she stood a short distance from the tree, watching the Seven who gathered by the trunk.

The women were kneeling in a circle, holding hands in silence. The girl was unsure of what passed between them when they met like this, but it seemed that it was a requirement for them.

"Strange that the Mirikin didn't need to gather like that, don't you think?" Arthur asked, seeming to know what she was thinking as he moved to her side. "Yet, their power was rather potent."

"How did the meeting go?" she asked.

"Simon told them he wanted negotiations to go ahead for the sake of the people in the glade," Arthur said. "He said, with winter approaching, there was an element of desperation to consider. To which Andris and Ruttger agreed, but they feel that there needs to be some leadership put in place and they would prefer that sooner rather than later. They'll call another assembly tonight to put a provisional council in place until they can hold elections.

"You should attend," he told her, peering to the fourteen reptilians sitting on the lawn nearby. "An Agrodien representative would be a benefit for them. Someone who understands the language of the council would benefit more."

"Yuri is learning rather quickly," Alice replied.

"I was thinking of you," he specified.

She shook her head.

"My place is at the caverns," she said, putting her arms around his shoulders. "I've never truly felt at home here. You're the only piece of it that makes sense to me."

"Then we'll stay at the caverns," he said, and smiled.

"And you're fine with that?"

"All I want to do is to be with you, Alice."

She kissed him, holding him against her.

"We should leave them here," he said, tilting his head towards the Seven. "I've asked for some bedding to be moved into your mother's house."

"I thought we would go back today."

"They made a request for the Seven to attend the meeting," he said. "I thought we could stay at your mother's house for the night and return tomorrow with your aunt."

"And the Agrodien?" She looked over at the warriors on the grass. "Where will they stay?"

"There's room," he replied. "Remember, most of those who travelled with us have dwellings here. They can stay in their own homes for the night, and the Agrodien will stay with us."

She nodded.

"We leave first thing in the morning," she insisted.

"Of course," he said, and smiled.

"And we must send word to the caverns so that the others are aware of where we are," she ordered.

"Already done," he answered. "Glaun and Kygra have ridden back to the caverns to tell the others. They weren't too comfortable staying in a big city after being in the wild for so long."

"All right," she said, nodding.

"I have a feeling, though, that your aunt may not be returning with us," Arthur surmised.

"Why do you say this?"

"The Seven have favour with a vast majority of the people here," he replied. "There's already talk that they may be chosen to sit on the council."

"With who else?" Alice asked, hoping that Richard offered to represent the people once again.

"No one." He frowned, shrugging. "Just the Seven. They're fair and kind. All of them married to good men, except your aunt. But the people still see her as the wife of Tomas Warde and they still regard him as one of the best men that Woodmyst ever had. It looks very promising."

Alice's mind swam suddenly, replaying the words her husband said to her only moments ago;

Strange that the Mirikin didn't need to gather like that, don't you think?

Alice moved her eyes to Joanne as she considered the deaths of Chief Harling and the Cunninghams.

Yet, their power was rather potent.

The girl's mind raced back to the night around the campfire, when Simon was telling them all the tale of the White Witch. In particular, she remembered her cousin, Alan Verney, expressing his disappointment when the story was cut short.

But you were getting to the best part, he had said. *You know. Where you storm Blackrock Haven and free the prisoners. And when the Seven use their magic and make the Sovereign go splash all over the throne room.*

Joanne slowly opened her eyes and fixed her gaze upon her niece.

Arthur took Alice's hand, turning to lead her away from the ruins.

"Come on," he said. "Becka and a few of the other ladies are putting together a feast for lunch. We're all invited."

Alice kept her eyes on her aunt.

Her stomach tightened, and a chill moved along her spine as she pieced it all together.

Smiling, Joanne perceived her niece's thoughts, pressing a finger to her lips.

Thirty-Six

Joanne slid the little chest out from under the bed and opened it, peering at the contents inside. Carefully, she lifted the black dress and draped it carefully upon her bed, straightening the folds as best as she could. She then took the long cloak out of the box and spread it beside the other garment.

Black stockings and knee-high leather boots were next to be lifted from the container. She stared at the clothing for what seemed a long time, listening to the clatter emitting from the other rooms in the house.

Arthur fussed about in the kitchen, occasionally looking to the eight Agrodien warriors setting places to sleep on the floor around the sitting room. The only one of them to take a separate room was Nola'ee, who took Emily's bedroom for the night.

Yuri and Gharnef found a place in Lucy's room. Three other reptilians found suitable places to rest in Takmel and Catherine's room.

Alice had closed the door to her and Arthur's room. Something had upset her, but he did not know what it could be.

He had asked her, but she clearly didn't want to talk about it. So, he left her to herself, occupying himself with roasting some meat, boiling some vegetables and baking some bread for supper. He hoped that, with time, she would talk.

The sound of a door opening made him turn to look past the Agrodien gathered in the sitting room. A dark figure moved past the doorway to the corridor that led to the rest of the house. It seemed to glide from right to left, from Joanne's room to the doors leading to the other sleeping quarters.

He recognised the dark form as Joanne, but he felt a sense of unease when he noticed her dressed the way she was.

The sound of another door opening and closing informed him she was entering Alice's room. Something turned in the pit of his stomach.

Something wasn't right.

***

"I'll be heading to the assembly hall soon," she told her niece. "It would be good if you were there."

"I think I'll be fine staying here, thank you," Alice replied as her aunt sat down on the bed beside her. She felt nervous. Afraid. Anxious.

"I love you, Alice," Joanne told her, placing her arm around the girl and kissing her on the forehead. "I would never hurt you. Everything I have done and will ever do is for our family."

"You're wearing the black again," Alice said, not making eye contact with her aunt, choosing to stare at the floor and keep her arms by her sides.

"We have decided that it is time for the colours once again," she replied. "There are good times ahead. If they placed us as auxiliary council, it could open doors for us. Our entire family could be together again right here."

"I'm returning to the caverns tomorrow," the girl replied. "I won't be remaining in Woodmyst."

"Why not?" Joanne appeared confused. "*This* is your home. Your father is *here*. You belong *here*."

"My people need me," she answered. "I am Kayl'sro."

"I can't allow this." Joanne stood to face the girl. "If you stay out there, my sister will remain with you. I need her with me, Alice. I need my family here."

"Or else what?" the girl stood, locking eyes with her aunt. "You'll gather your witches and show me what happened to Henry Cunningham and his wife and children?"

"You don't know what you're saying," Joanne said softly. "You think you know what occurred, but you can see only one tiny piece of the picture, my dear. You really have no idea."

"And if I decide to tell the council?"

"There is no council," Joanne replied, placing her hand on Alice's shoulder, close to her neck. "Besides, there is no proof. The Seven were at the caverns. So were the Erilian warriors and your mother. Everyone known to have potential power was accounted for. Except for one."

Alice's heart seemed to stand still.

She was the one that her aunt referred to.

Although she was sleeping on a rock face, overlooking Greil and his crew during the night when the two councilmen and their families were slaughtered in their beds, there were no witnesses to support her story. Not even the Agrodien, setting up bedding in the house, saw her during that night.

Alice knew there was every possibility for the distrust that David had to be used against her at a whim.

She was cornered.

"Who are you going to tell, Alice?" Joanne placed her other hand on her niece's shoulder. If she were to adjust them, she would have her fingers around the girl's throat. "I told you I would never hurt you. *I.*" She lowered her hands and moved to the door slowly. "But as I also said, you can only see one little piece of the picture. *I* won't hurt you. You should ponder that for a moment.

"Besides," she said, smiling, "this can only be a good thing. Negotiations between Woodmyst and the Agrodien will surely be favourable. Supplies and protection will be given. Everything you need and more will be handed over to you. Everybody wins."

Alice heard the words echo in her mind. *Everybody wins.*

Her thoughts, however, pictured the bodies of Chief Seamus and the Cunninghams, torn apart from the inside and left strewn around their bedrooms.

"Now," the woman said as she opened the door, "straighten yourself and join your husband, your *people* and me for supper."

***

"I like your chances," Arthur said from the head of the table, the closest seat to the kitchen. Alice sat to his right with Yuri by her side.

"Thank you, Arthur," Joanne said from his left, directly across from the girl. "And may I say, you outdid yourself tonight. This was delightful."

"I have tea brewing, if you like," he offered, pointing over his shoulder with his thumb.

"No," she replied. "I think I should leave soon. The meeting won't wait for me. Will I see you there?"

He looked to Alice, who had remained silent during the meal. Even the Agrodien appeared a little concerned, looking to her now and then, sensing something was wrong.

"I think I should stay here tonight," he replied politely. "I apologise, but it would appear Alice isn't well and I wouldn't be a good husband if I left her tonight."

"I understand." Joanne smiled, meeting her niece's eyes.

"Well," Arthur said, standing as he lifted his plate and cutlery. "I should get this cleared."

"Yuri help Arthur," the Agrodien offered, as he moved his eyes from Joanne to the boy at the end of the table.

"Thank you, Yuri," he replied, turning towards the kitchen.

"Are you sure you won't come?" Joanne asked Alice.

The girl nodded.

"All right, then." The woman in black got to her feet. "I'll talk to you later."

Joanne started for the door. She made it outside and onto the porch before Alice jumped to her feet and raced after her.

Closing the door behind her, Alice stepped to her aunt's side. She looked to the sky to see a thick, black veil covering the stars and shielding the moon from sight.

"Tell me one thing," she said in a low voice. "Did you kill David's wives?"

"The horses did that," she replied. "Their combined weight was simply too much for the bridge."

"But did you?" Alice persisted. "Did the Seven have anything to do with that?"

Joanne placed her hands on Alice's arms and looked her directly in the eyes.

"As I said before, you can see only one little piece of this picture," she replied. "But I can honestly say, the Seven did not have a hand in that."

"Then who?"

Joanne turned and walked away. "We'll talk later, Alice."

With that, the woman vanished into the night, appearing again as she passed under the orange glow of lantern lights that lined the street.

"Everything all right?" Arthur asked as the girl entered the house, closing the door behind her. She leant on the panel and frowned.

Her entire world had turned upside down and there wasn't a single person she could report it to who could do anything about it.

"We need to leave," she said, moving into the sitting room. "Tidy up. Take what we came with. We are leaving now."

"It's dark out," Arthur argued. "And your aunt has only just left."

"She's not who she appears to be," Alice told him. "She never was."

"Alice..." The boy offered a confused look. "This is your home. You've finally been welcome back into Woodmyst."

"Yuri," Alice called to the reptilian as Arthur continued.

"Kayl'sro?"

"Pack our gear," she ordered. "We're going home."

"Home," he agreed, leaving the kitchen duties and moving to the sitting room to collect equipment.

"My father has been imprisoned, and the council disbanded," Arthur continued. "All of this has happened today. It couldn't have worked more in your favour if it had been orchestrated."

"Exactly," Alice replied. "And it was."

Yuri relayed the order to the other Agrodien warriors, who immediately rose to their feet and left the table to gather their belongings.

"What?" Arthur stared at her.

"It was orchestrated," she replied. "Everything. The deaths of your father's wives and your sister. My expulsion. The division in the community. The death of the Cunninghams and Chief Harling. The termination of council. And now, the ascension of the Seven."

He shook his head, not fully comprehending her words.

"All of it is connected, Arthur," she tried to make him understand. "The only thing they didn't count on was the Agrodien. But they used it to their advantage."

"The Seven killed my mother?"

"No." Alice shook her head. "My aunt told me they were not involved in that. But she wouldn't say who was."

"We need to tell someone." The boy was shaking.

"We can't," she replied.

"Why not?"

"Because we don't know who else is involved." She held his arms. "We need to pretend we know nothing for now."

He looked around the room and saw the Agrodien standing and listening to them.

"Bad here?" Yuri asked.

"Yes," Alice answered. "Very bad."

"I can't leave my father in prison," Arthur said. "He's in danger here."

"We're all in danger wherever we go," she replied. "But we'll break him out tonight after we fetch the horses."

***

As the Kayl'sro moved into the stable house with her warriors, the assembly hall's seats filled. Richard took to the podium to make an announcement, holding his hands up to signal for silence.

"Fair Woodmystians," he began, winking at his wife in the front row. "After careful deliberation, a decision has been made. It is clear there really was no other suitable option for placing an auxiliary council.

"So, with no further ado, I will announce the names of the council members in no particular order. Christina Brocas," Richard gestured to a chair set in front of the long table, facing the auditorium.

The woman in a gold cloak kissed her husband seated beside her and rose to her feet. The assembly applauded as she walked up the steps to take her place on the line.

***

Alice saddled the black mare and draped the cape given to her by the Agrodien women over the neck of the horse.

The reptilian riders mounted their steeds and prepared to follow their Kayl'sro.

"What's your plan?" Arthur asked, sitting on his steed and holding the reins of another saddled horse.

"We go to the barracks," she replied. "We ask nicely. If they don't respond, we fight our way in and back out again."

She urged her steed forwards, moving out of the stable house and onto the road.

Suddenly, she pulled to a stop as a lone figure blocked her path.

***

"Gilda Smythe," Richard announced.

The Jade woman moved up the steps, shook the old man's hand with a smile and sat beside the other council member.

***

"Where are you going?" Lor asked, standing in the middle of the road.

"We're going to get David," Alice replied. "And then we're going home."

"While your aunt is engaged in a ceremony?" he queried. "What's going on?"

"I could waste time telling you," she replied. "Or you could get your horse ready and meet us at the gate."

"They won't let you out this late," her uncle told her. She looked at him for a seemingly long time. "You'll need to pass beneath the scaffolding to the northeast, where the wall isn't built yet. I'll meet you there."

"Uncle Lor," she said as he started past her. "We can't tell anyone."

"I gathered that when I saw you were willing to leave me behind," he answered. "Which is something we will talk about once we get home."

***

"Isabel Barnes," the old man called.

The applause continued as the lady in white moved across the floor towards the platform.

***

It wasn't a long ride to the barracks, just a quick gallop down the road. Two soldiers stood at the entrance to the structure, eyeing the party as they approached.

"We need to see Chief Gyfford," Alice told them. "It's important diplomatic business."

"Listen to this one," a soldier remarked. "Important diplomatic business."

"It's late and there is a meeting in the assembly hall," the other told her. "We have orders to not let anyone pass by."

"Didn't I beat you two in skirmish training?" Alice laughed.

"Yes," the second guard replied. "Unarmed combat. You had twelve of us down in less than two minutes."

"That's right," she grinned. "So, now I'm armed and I want David Gyfford released. What chance do you think you have against me and fourteen Agrodien warriors at my command?"

"We need to inform the lieutenant," the first guard told her.

"Didn't I beat him, too?"

***

"Tricia Bell," Richard called.

"The most beautiful of all," Simon hollered as his wife, dressed in scarlet, stood up to take her place on the stage.

***

"How do I explain this?" the lieutenant, a young man not much older than a boy, asked her as he brought David through the entrance.

"Make something up," Alice told them. "Say that I used my powers."

"Powers?" the first guard quizzed as he stepped back from the hulking man.

David looked at Alice sheepishly.

"Don't send anyone after us," she warned. "You do not want to confront me out there, in the dark."

With that, the three humans and fourteen Agrodien raced away along the road. The guards watched as they vanished into the night.

"What are we going to say?" the first guard asked.

"Nothing," the lieutenant ordered him. "They sneaked in under our noses. We didn't notice the prisoner gone until it was too late. Got it?"

***

"Sarah Fitzwillyam."

The lilac woman stood up and started towards the steps, waving to the clapping people as she walked by.

***

Lor waited in the shadow of the north-eastern tower, keeping as quiet as he could as the others approached.

"There are two up top," he whispered. "If we head north through the scaffold and straight on, we will come to the quarry road."

"We go through the quarry?" Arthur whispered.

"No," Alice put in, turning to her uncle. "We take the road but go past, onto the ridge. It's quicker. We'll come back into the glade from the west. Just like we did the other morning."

"Are you up for it?" Lor asked David.

"I think so," he replied. "Yes."

"Too much talk," Alice said, moving forwards, ducking her head as she steered the mare through the tangle of timber beams.

***

"Claire Staunton!" Richard smiled.

Dressed in olive garments, Claire beamed as she approached the podium with all manner of grace.

***

Peering over their shoulders, moving the horses at a slow trot, the riders moved to the north across open grassland.

It surprised Alice that they hadn't been detected, even with the thick clouds covering the moon.

It wasn't long before they heard gravel beneath hoofs, signalling that they had reached the quarry road. Arthur turned to see they had made some distance from the towers.

"I think it's safe now," he announced.

"Then we need to increase our pace," Alice instructed them, digging her heels into the mare's sides.

Within moments, the party was galloping along the road and away from Woodmyst.

**

"Last, please congratulate Joanne Warde." The old man gestured to the only seat left, one that the others had strategically left empty for their prime. The one in the centre of the set.

Joanne rose from her place to the sound of thunderous applause. She made her way up the steps to the platform slowly, deliberately, before shaking hands with Richard.

"I'm so proud of you," he told her.

"Thank you, Richard," she replied, barely audible over the clapping and cheering.

She moved to her place and took her seat between Tricia and Isabel. The seven women smiled and waved as the auditorium stood to their feet.

"Ladies and gentlemen," Richard announced, waving his hand to silence the room. It was no use. The crowd ignored him and continued to cheer. He gave up and gestured to the Seven.

"Your council," he announced, turning to applaud them himself.

Thirty-Seven

Emily stared into the hearth as the morning sun climbed over the mountains' peaks. She had been sitting there, silently watching the flames dance, since Alice shared with her what she knew of her aunt.

Seated around the mother and daughter were a trusted few. David and Arthur, Lor and Linet, Jeremy and Karlena, all bit their nails or twiddled their fingers as they tried to come to grips with Alice's tale.

"We can't tell anyone else," David warned them. "We don't know who could be involved. It would appear this has been something in the making since before the death of my wives and daughter. And I don't believe we have seen the end of this yet. We must use caution."

"Should we at least tell Lucy?" Emily asked.

"No," Alice was quick to reply. "David is right."

"We left Oliver behind." Arthur shook his head, disappointed with himself.

"He was at the meeting," Lor told him. "Seated at the front of the room by Simon."

"Why did you come back for us?" Alice asked.

"I was waiting by the door for you," he replied. "When you didn't appear, I worried."

"Worry?" She creased her brow.

"Your aunt was about to be named an auxiliary council member," he clarified. "I thought you would want to be there."

She nodded.

"I'm sorry for not coming to get you," she told him. "But I needed to get away from there. I needed to come home."

"No apology is necessary." He smiled. "I know I would have done the same thing if I were in your shoes."

"She will come here," Emily said, turning to her daughter. "She will come for you."

"I know." Alice nodded, scratching behind the ear of the rukyul lying by her side. "She'll come today. Her boy is still here and I know she wants to be reunited with her family."

"It won't just be her," David leaned towards her. "She'll bring the other six with her. She may bring her guards as well. Remember, Andris was her personal servant in the house of Yasmeen Svoboda. Now he's commanding the armed guard of Woodmyst and he follows her orders again."

"My own sister!" Emily wept. "Was this who she was the whole time?"

"Perhaps the influence of the Sovereign still lurks inside the Seven," Linet offered. "Perhaps she twisted their minds just enough to damage them for good."

"Which would mean that the Seven were playing us all since we brought them back from Blackrock Haven," Jeremy put in.

"But for what purpose?" Lor shook his head. "To sit on the bloody council for a city in the middle of nowhere?"

"Woodmyst is no city in the middle of nowhere," Karlena corrected him. "Its location is a stronghold. Surrounded by mountains that make it hard for an army to advance upon. We saw that when the White Witch tried to take it. And that was without the walls it has now."

"Also," she continued, "there are only two other fully functioning cities that lie nearby, other than Woodmyst. Dweagan and Newholt. We can't be certain who else is out there. Let's say someone lays siege to either of the two coastal cities. Woodmyst would be the only haven within reasonable travelling distance.

"No matter how you look at it, there is a possibility for power to present itself. Strategically, Woodmyst is an ideal location."

"Besides..." Alice spoke up. "It's as David said. We haven't seen the end of this yet. Someone, or something else, is orchestrating all of this."

"I'm so sorry for accusing you of the death of my wives and child, Alice." David shed a tear as he looked at the girl. "I'm so sorry for calling you dangerous."

"You were right about that part," she told him. "I am dangerous. I made fire dance on the northern slopes overlooking the western plains. I've killed Haigok and Agrodien, tearing the head from the Kayl'sro before taking his title. Soldiers fear me so much that all I had to do was speak words to get you released from prison.

"You were wrong to accuse me of murdering your wives," she continued. "And yes, I know they were murdered. I just don't know by whom. But you were right about me being dangerous, David. And if the Seven, or whoever is behind all of this, tries to hurt my family, my friends or my people," she gestured to the Agrodien and the settlers moving about the glade, "we're going to find out how dangerous I can be."

***

It was close to noon when the first rider from Woodmyst, dressed in leather armour, appeared at the edge of the glade. One by one, more appeared, forming a line upon the grassland to the east.

The rukyul, lying by Alice on the porch, raised his head and snorted. His eyes moved to the visitors, watching them warily as they approached. He emitted a tiny growl as their numbers increased.

Six, eight, ten riders, armed and wearing full regalia. Alice rose from the bench that lined the outer wall of her cabin and moved towards the door.

"Shhh," she hissed to the creature, stroking its head before moving to the door. "They're coming."

Arthur moved from the kitchen towards the doorway, wiping his hands on a towel and tossing it on the table. The cleaning would need to wait.

He reached behind the door and lifted the sheaths and swords from the hook, and brought them to his wife. She took them, strapping them to her back as she watched the Seven, adorned in their colours and hoods over their heads, ride into the glade. Behind them, far to the back, rode one lone man, Oliver Weston.

Emily and the Erilian women rose from their seats beside the hearth and walked over to the cabin, their blades strapped to their hips.

"I haven't done this for a while," Emily confessed, pulling the belt of her sheath around to a more comfortable position.

"She's not going to attack," Alice told her, stepping onto the grass, the rukyul walking slowly at her side.

Lor, David, and Jeremy gathered behind the women as the Agrodien warriors positioned themselves between the camp and the approaching procession.

"We should move to the Agrodien," David suggested. "There are children here. If something were to happen…"

"You're right," Alice nodded, moving towards Yuri and the others, waiting a little further to the east of them.

Jeremy gave a whistle and pointed towards the riders moving across the glade.

Baldwyn was first to move, kissing his wife Elka as he tightened his belt. He walked around his tent and started forward, joining the others as they formed a line.

Gustav was next to unite with them, followed by Ewan Cunningham and twelve others, including the four settlers from the north. A line of thirty-six armed individuals and one angry rukyul came to a stop on the glade, waiting for the approaching party.

"Are you sure you want to be here, old man?" the captain asked the old dock master.

"Just try to peel me away," Ewan dared him.

"Not I." Jeremy smiled.

***

"What's going on, Arthur?" Lucy asked the boy standing by the cabin, seeing the potential of a confrontation unfolding. Agnes, Oliver's wife, and several young children gathered behind her.

"Negotiations," Arthur replied.

"Something bad has happened." She looked at him. "Hasn't it?"

"Yes," he replied truthfully. "But that's all I can say about it."

The women looked to him for answers.

"What do you mean, that's all you can say about it?" Agnes queried. "Is my husband involved in something he shouldn't be?"

"I honestly don't know," he told her. "I really don't. What I know is that my wife is down there and I'm scared for her and I don't know what to do about it."

Catherine and Takmel came racing over, their eyes fixed upon the two groups about to meet in the glade.

"What's happening?" Takmel asked.

"Why is my mother wearing her sword?" Catherine enquired.

"Arthur says they're negotiating," Lucy replied.

"Is that Aunt Joanne?" The girl looked puzzled. "What are they doing, Arthur?"

"I'm not at liberty to say," he replied.

"Arthur?" Takmel called, frustrated. "Tell us something, please."

"I can't," he answered. "I simply can't."

***

The Seven rode past the guards and stopped their steeds a few paces from the line of men and reptilians standing before them. Joanne looked down from her horse to her niece, measuring her with her eyes for the first time as a potential foe.

Or so it would seem, Alice thought.

The woman in black moved her gaze along the line slowly.

"Are you all right, Oliver?" Lor called out.

"Fine," the other replied. "I don't quite understand what's happening though."

"You outnumber us," Joanne said. "I brought only ten guards. We are no threat to you and yours. I came to treat with you peacefully. My plan is to uphold the agreement and perhaps discuss more benefits for our two communities."

Alice considered her aunt's words.

"You little bitch," Emily growled.

"So, you told her," Joanne surmised, speaking to Alice.

"Of course, I did," the girl replied. "She's my mother."

"And my sister," the other added. "I guess there won't be any convincing you. It will all be for the better. Everyone will benefit from this."

"Unless your name is Isabel," David replied. "And Martha. And Katerina. You remember them? What about Seamus or Henry?"

"And Laila," Ewan put in. "And Ronald and Mercy."

Joanne looked down at the ground and shook her head.

"You don't understand," she told them. "There is something far bigger at play here. We could stay out here and name people all day long and get nowhere. Or we can negotiate."

"You killed my family, you bitches," the old man yelled, tears streaming down his face.

"What proof do you have?" Joanne countered. "We were here. Right here in this glade, when it happened. She was the only one that can't be accounted for."

The woman in black pointed to Alice.

"She can make fire dance," she continued. "Something that we can do only when we unite our strength. She did it on her own. Who's to say it wasn't her that murdered your family? She has far more power in her than any of us on our own."

"And that frightens you," Emily said. "It always has. I see it now."

"It doesn't matter." Joanne shook her head. "We have an army in Woodmyst. You have this ragtag bunch. You can either negotiate with us, or we simply run our cavalry through here to clear our land of vagrants."

"You can't threaten us like—" David began.

"Quiet," Joanne commanded. "These are not your lands, remember? They were given to her."

Alice gritted her teeth.

"What say you, Alice?" the woman asked.

The girl sighed. She knew she was cornered, and she didn't like it.

"Your demands." Alice frowned. The eyes of the others on the line with her turned to her. Some wore confused expressions while others understood her decision to treat.

"We want the quarry opened and back in business by tomorrow morning," Joanne said. "We want to gather the belongings of the council members to be transported back to Woodmyst, and I want my family to come and live with me. Including the Kayl'sro, but not her subjects. The Agrodien and these settlers from the north can remain here."

"You'll have the quarry opened in time," Alice replied, looking to the ground. "You can hitch your carts and take your property back to Woodmyst today. Anyone wishing to return with you to the city can do so of their own free will. Any wishing to remain here will be granted allowance, regardless of who they are.

"The quarry will be included as part of the territory belonging to the owner of these grounds. We also want another two hundred horses, preferably colts, brought to the glade by dusk. An ample supply of timber and building materials and enough grain, oats and flour to get us and the livestock here through the winter and a little beyond."

"Us?" Joanne queried.

"What?"

"You said us," she explained. "Why would you say us when I already said that I want you to return with me?"

"Oh, I'm not going back with you," Alice clarified, her voice expressing some confidence. "I am choosing to stay here. See, I called this negotiating. You put your demands forward, I do the same."

"And if I refuse all of your terms and command you to follow my instructions?" the woman in black questioned.

"Then I'll command my rukyul to eat your steed while I cut you into a thousand pieces," the girl answered.

Joanne stared at the girl, fury building on her face. Behind the façade, Alice saw something else lurking behind her aunt's eyes.

"Peace?" Alice took a step forward, the large, dark creature to her side moving with her. "Or death?"

The line of people behind her pulled their blades free.

"You have an army," Alice acknowledged, glancing at the soldiers behind Joanne. "But it is you I will kill first. You. After that, it won't matter. Will it?"

Joanne saw the girl had the upper hand.

"All right," she agreed. "We will meet your terms."

"I have your word?" Alice asked. "You won't return to Woodmyst and send your army?"

"You have my word," the woman replied.

"And the word of the council?"

"I can vouch for them."

"I want to hear it from their lips," Alice gestured to the other six.

Joanne turned to the others and nodded.

Each of the six women agreed one by one.

Alice waited until they had all said their piece before giving one last demand.

"If I see any of you," the girl stated, "or any armed guards near the caverns or the quarry, I will deem this treaty broken. Test me in this, and I will come for you."

"Understood," the woman replied.

"Two hundred horses by dusk," Alice reminded her. "You may pass to gather your things. But I want you gone in one hour."

"Agreed," Joanne answered as the girl signalled for her supporters to allow the procession through. The woman in black started forwards, moving towards the encampment by the cabin.

"Alice," she called, pulling her steed to a stop.

"Mmm?" The girl looked at her aunt. Her emotions were still fiery.

"I would never hurt you," she replied. "I wouldn't let any other harm you, either. I love you, even if you don't believe me."

"Stop talking to my daughter." Emily was shaking with fury. "Take your belongings and leave us."

Joanne looked to her sister as if Emily had just stabbed her in the heart. A tear streaked down her cheek before she nodded compliantly, moving away with the rest of her group in tow.

Thirty-Eight

Riders, horses and wagons snaked away across the clearing, entering the eastern tree-line. Antony and Holly waved from the back of a cart, driven by Lucy.

Alice resumed her place on the porch, sitting on the bench as Emily argued with

Catherine, who was packing another wagon to leave the glade.

"Your sister is here," the auburn woman wept. "I'm here. Why won't you reconsider?"

"I don't belong here, Mama," the girl replied. "Just like how Alice says that she doesn't belong in Woodmyst, I don't belong here. This is not my home."

"We could make it home," Emily pleaded. "Stay."

Catherine stopped packing the wagon to face her mother.

"I can't," she wept.

"Won't you say something to her?" Emily turned to Alice.

"I gave my word," she replied. "She can stay or she can go. It's her decision."

"Where will you stay?" Emily returned her attention to her eldest daughter.

"In our house," the girl replied.

"With your Aunt Joanne?"

"And Lucy, Holly and Antony," Catherine answered. "It's our home."

"But your Aunt Joanne..."

"Won't hurt us," she interjected.

"Alice?" Emily turned to the younger girl.

"She won't," came the reply. "She still loves us. I believed her when she said that."

"Don't let her whisper things into your ears," Emily warned, looking at Takmel as well. "Both of you. Do you hear me?"

"I understand," the boy replied, tying down a canvas tarp that covered the contents of the wagon. "We can think for ourselves."

"And there's the evidence of that." Alice gestured to the wagon as she rose to her feet, walking towards the hearth where Arthur and several others had gathered.

"You're not even going to see us off?" Catherine asked, tears welling in her eyes.

"No, I'm not," the younger girl answered, slapping her thigh to summon the rukyul.

"Why not?" the other called after her. "I would if it were you leaving."

"I'm not leaving," Alice replied smugly. "I'm not the one making a tragic mistake. That would be you. However, when you realise what an error you have made, you will be welcome back with open arms, dear sister. Until then, farewell."

***

"It's all a bit of a fucking mess, isn't it?" Glaun blurted as he stretched his hands towards the flames. He suddenly looked about him, realising what he had just said. "Sorry. Filthy habit."

"Don't concern yourself with it," Alice told him, peering to the sun sinking low in the western sky. "You're right in what you said."

"Almost dusk." David poked at the embers with a stick. "Still no two hundred horses."

"What will you do if they don't show up?" Emily asked.

"Not supplying the steeds will be a breach in the treaty," the girl replied. "I told her what I would do to her."

"You would kill your own aunt?" Oliver asked.

"That woman is no longer my family," Alice said coldly, peering into the flames.

A thick silence fell upon the group.

Soft crackles emitted from the hearth as orange and yellow flames lapped the stumps and timber cuttings placed within the circle of stones.

"Kayl'sro," one of the Agrodien warriors called from the entrance of the large cavern. His voice reverberated around the glade as the men and women gathered by the fire stood up to see what the matter was.

The reptilian pointed to the far end of the clearing where horses spilled from the tree-line and onto the grassland.

"She kept her word," Arthur stated. "That's got to be worth something."

"Tell that to my grandchildren," Ewan told him.

"I'm so sorry," Alice said to him, sitting back down.

The others lowered themselves to their chairs, keeping warm by the fire.

"You're not going to see to the horses?" Lor asked.

"Yuri and Gharnef will see to them," she replied.

"I don't blame you," Ewan eventually said, looking at the girl with sad eyes. "They forced your hand, Alice. You had to make a deal with those witches for all our sakes. I do want revenge. I really do. But that was not the right time."

"When the right time presents itself," Alice told him, "I'll hold all seven of the bitches down for you."

"I think we should send a message to Newholt," Arthur suggested. "Queen Elynbrigge should be apprised to what has occurred here."

"We should send a party," David agreed with his son. "We could establish new relations with them, bypassing any agreement in place with Woodmyst."

"We have little to offer," Alice informed them. "The quarry is under our control, but the best way to transport it to the coast is by the Twisted Road to the south. All we have between here and there is rough terrain and mountains.

"But, I agree," she continued. "We should send an envoy to at least let them know the situation. I will need some to go with me to treat with the Haigok. I already have arranged for Nola'ee, Nakrah and Bein to accompany me."

"I'll be coming with you too," Arthur reminded her. "I'm not leaving you alone this time."

She took her hand in his.

"Then I'll be coming along to watch you both," David insisted. "I have a lot to make up for. I can start with this."

"Yuri and Gharnef won't be attending?" Agnes asked from Oliver's side, peering over to the Agrodien.

"They both have families here," Alice told her. "I'm only taking those who have no ties to anyone."

"You have ties here." Linet gestured to Emily, Arthur, David and herself.

"I'm the Kayl'sro," Alice said. "I must go as a representative of my people and take full responsibility for their actions."

"I'll go," Gustav announced.

"Thank you, Gustav. But I probably have enough people going with me."

"No," he replied. "Not to the Haigok. I'll go to Newholt."

All eyes moved to the man as he picked up a few tiny shards of timber from the ground and tossed them into the flames.

"You can't go on your own," Akasati told him. "I'll join you."

"As will I," Sharek proclaimed.

"Well..." Rhydra pursed her lips and shook her head. "Now I need to volunteer. None of you would survive without me. And Gustav can't strap his own boots on without someone telling him how to."

"Hey," the man remarked.

"Are you happy with that arrangement?" Jeremy asked.

"Three beautiful women on a long journey with one man." He smiled, slowly putting his hands behind his head. "I've had pleasurable dreams about such things."

Laughter erupted around the fire.

Alice believed it was the first pleasant moment they had all experienced for the entire day.

"It's settled then," Alice said, rising to her feet. "Two parties will leave on the morrow. I suggest we all get some rest. We'll need everyone at their best."

Epilogue

Joanne sat by the fireplace, dressed in her black garb and holding Antony against her chest. He stuck his thumb in his mouth as he slept soundly with his ear to her heart.

Beside her, Takmel read through a book reciting the history of the Realm War as Catherine busied herself with making tea for the household. Lucy sat in another chair, half asleep, with Holly curled on her knee.

It had been a long day for them all.

"It's not the same without them," Joanne reflected as she peered into the flames.

"You miss them?" the boy asked.

"Don't you?" she replied. "They are your family too."

He placed a piece of thin cloth in the book and closed it, giving his full attention to the woman in black.

"She was noisy," he said, smiling. "Both of them were. It didn't matter what part of this house you hid in; you could always hear them both when they were here. More so when they were together."

Catherine brought them a mug each, setting them onto a little table positioned between their two seats.

"I miss them too," she admitted, touching her aunt on the shoulder.

"I just wish she didn't know about what we had to do," Joanne confessed. Tears welled in her eyes. "Now my sister hates me."

"She may still come around, yet," Lucy tried to console her. "Maybe you need some time apart."

"She doesn't hate you," Takmel interjected. "She couldn't hate you. She crossed an entire land to save you, remember?"

"That was a long, long time ago."

"She still loves you as much now as she did then," he assured her. He lifted his mug and sipped at the steaming contents; his eyes still fixed upon her.

"Still," Joanne said, wiping her eyes, "I wish Alice hadn't pieced it together. This could have gone much more smoothly without her having this knowledge."

"It was inevitable," Lucy said sleepily. "Secrets can stay secrets for only so long."

"We need to find out that yours stays hidden for as long as we can," Catherine said, moving to a chair beside her husband, nursing a mug of her own. "Only at the time of ascension can we reveal who you truly are, Maji."

Takmel sipped his tea and peered into the fire.

He had waited this long.

He could wait a little longer.

About The Author

Robert E Kreig was born in Newcastle, Australia and grew up in its outer suburbs.

He has always had a love for books, particularly well-told stories involving action, adventure and fear.

Some of Robert's favourite authors as a young reader included J. R. R. Tolkien, Stephen King, Orson Scott Card, Ray Bradbury and Frank Herbert. As he grew into adulthood, the list continued to lengthen, adding more influential writers such as George R. R. Martin, Matthew Reilly, Nathan M. Farrugia, Dan Brown, James Patterson, Michael Connelly and Lee Child just to name a few.

Inspired by movies like Star Wars, King Kong, Jaws, Jason and the Argonauts and other great adventure pieces, Robert listened to the voices in his head and entertained the strange visions dancing through his mind to assist him with writing his fantasy series The Woodmyst Chronicles.

Robert has penned ten books for the series which follow the lives of many characters, particularly focussing upon a family who must face many trials before the epic conclusion. Clashing swords, strange creatures, flying dragons and sorcery inhabit the world surrounding Woodmyst.

Robert has also written a standalone book, Long Valley.

Robert currently lives in Canberra, Australia where he hopes to one day become a full-time writer.

Other Books By This Author

THE WOODMYST CHRONICLES

From a faraway land...
...comes a new adventure.
The Woodmyst Chronicles is the story of a small community that faces the hardest of trials in a world filled with darkness, violence and magic.

Books In This Series...
THE WALLS OF WOODMYST
THE SONS OF WOODMYST
THE HEIR OF WOODMYST
THE WARLORDS OF WOODMYST
THE HUNTRESS OF WOODMYST
THE SHADOW OF WOODMYST
THE BRIDES OF WOODMYST
THE GODS OF WOODMYST
THE WEAPONS OF WOODMYST
A FAREWELL TO WOODMYST

LONG VALLEY

In the small community of Long Valley, nestled comfortably beneath snow-capped mountains, people quietly go about their business. Everybody knows everybody and there are no worries to give mind to.

But something has awakened.

A tragic accident near the valley's army base sparks a number of terrifying events, placing the local civilians in mortal danger.

A contagion is subsequently released into Long Valley, infecting pets, livestock, wildlife and people.

It's up to the local law enforcement and a small band of citizens to try to keep the town safe.

In the end, it becomes a struggle for survival as the people of Long Valley are overcome by the urge to feed.

THE CALM VOICE

No one in the remote town of Edwards Hill could have known that she was capable of such carnage.
Least of all her parents, the first to die.
Driven by the gentle words of The Calm Voice, she inflicts a barrage of carnage and death, leaving a trail of blood in her wake.
Her goal is to bring death to all who have hurt her.
All she needs to do is listen to The Calm Voice.
All she needs to do is just focus...
Just focus...

Focus...

The Calm Voice is a dark psychological novel surrounding the actions of one girl on a fateful morning in April, 2017. Kristin Matthews is fed up with her life, her oppressive parents, and her bullying schoolmates. She is compelled by a soothing voice thrumming in her head to seek revenge on those who have wronged her. At the top of her list is a trio of girls who have taunted her to breaking point. After careful planning, she embarks on a deadly rampage through Edwards Hill State High School, bent on destroying all her pain one final time. What follows is a haunting description of the day's events, culminating in an ending no one will expect.

www.robertekreig.com

www.whitekeepbooks.com

www.ingramcontent.com/pod-product-compliance
Lightning Source LLC
Chambersburg PA
CBHW020328120726
47904CB00002B/319